CONTENTS

PART ONE: INTRODUCING *OTHELLO*

PART TWO: STUDYING *OTHELLO*

PART THREE: CHARACTERS AND THEMES

PART FOUR: STRUCTURE, FORM AND LANGUAGE

PART FIVE: CONTEXTS AND CRITICAL DEBATES

PART SIX: GRADE BOOSTER

ESSENTIAL STUDY TOOLS

PART ONE: INTRODUCING *OTHELLO*

HOW TO STUDY *OTHELLO*

These Notes can be used in a range of ways to help you read, study and (where relevant) revise for your exam or assessment.

READING THE PLAY

Read the play once, fairly quickly, for pleasure. This will give you a sense of the over-arching shape of the plot, and a good feel for the highs and lows of the action, the pace and style, and the sequence in which information is withheld or revealed. You could ask yourself:

- How do individual characters change or develop? How do my own responses to them change?
- How does Shakespeare allow the audience to see into the minds and motives of the characters? Does he use **asides**, **soliloquies** or other dramatic devices, for example?
- What sort of language do different characters use? Does Shakespeare use **imagery**, or recurring motifs or symbols?
- Are the events presented chronologically, or is the time scheme altered in some way?
- What impression do the locations and settings, such as Venice, make on my reading and response to the play?
- How could the play be presented on the stage in different ways? How could different types of performance affect the audience's interpretation of the play?

On your second reading, make detailed notes around the key areas highlighted above and in the Assessment Objectives, such as form, language, structure (AO2), links and connections to other texts (AO3) and the context/background for the play (AO4). These may seem quite demanding, but these Notes will suggest particular elements to explore or jot down.

> **CONTEXT** **AO4**
>
> *Othello* (1603) was written during Shakespeare's great tragic period; *Hamlet* preceded *Othello* in 1600, and *King Lear* and *Macbeth* were first performed in 1604–6.

INTERPRETING OR CRITIQUING THE PLAY

Although it's not helpful to think in terms of the play being 'good' or 'bad', you should consider the different ways the play can be read. How have critics responded to it? Do their views match yours – or do you take a different viewpoint? Are there different ways you can interpret specific events, characters or settings? This is a key aspect in AO3, and it can be helpful to keep a log of your responses and the various perspectives which are expressed both by established critics, but also by classmates, your teacher, or other readers.

REFERENCES AND SOURCES

You will be expected to draw on critics' or reviewers' comments, and refer to relevant literary or historical sources that might have influenced Shakespeare or his contemporaries. Make sure you make accurate, clear notes of writers or sources you have used, for example noting down titles of works, authors' names, website addresses, dates, etc. You may not have to reference all these things when you respond to a text, but knowing the source of your information will allow you to go back to it, if need be – and to check its accuracy and relevance.

REVISING FOR AND RESPONDING TO AN ASSESSED TASK OR EXAM QUESTION

The structure and the contents of these Notes are designed to help to give you the relevant information or ideas you need to answer tasks you have been set. First, work out the key words or ideas from the task (for example, 'form', 'Act I', 'Iago', etc.), then read the relevant parts of the Notes that relate to these terms or words, selecting what is useful for revision or written response. Then, turn to **Part Six: Grade Booster** for help in formulating your actual response.

OTHELLO IN CONTEXT

SHAKESPEARE'S LIFE AND TIMES

1564 William Shakespeare born into a well-to-do family in Stratford upon Avon, the eldest son and third child of eight

1565 Giambattisa Cinzio Giraldi writes the *Hecatommithi*, Shakespeare's source for *Othello*

1577 Sir Francis Drake sets out on sea voyage around the world

1582 Shakespeare marries Anne Hathaway when he is 18 and she is 26. They have three children: Susanna (b. 1583), and twins Judith and Hamnet (b. 1585; Hamnet d. 1596)

early 1590s Shakespeare moves to London and establishes himself as an actor and playwright

1599 Shakespeare buys share in the Globe Theatre

1600–6 Shakespeare writes his great tragedies, including *Othello*, written 1602–4

1603 Queen Elizabeth I dies; James I succeeds her

1603 The Lord Chamberlain's Men gain royal patronage from James I, becoming the King's Men

1604 *Othello* is first performed

1605 Guy Fawkes plot to blow up the Houses of Parliament discovered

1616 Shakespeare dies at the age of 52 after retiring to Stratford in 1611

SHAKESPEARE'S DRAMATIC CAREER

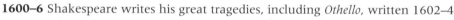

Shakespeare wrote thirty-seven plays between the late 1580s and 1613, as well as contributing to plays by other dramatists. Two actors from Shakespeare's company collected together thirty-six of Shakespeare's plays, including *Othello*, for publication in the first collected edition of Shakespeare's plays, known as the First Folio, in 1623. Shakespeare's career was highly successful. He made enough money to buy land around Stratford, as well as a large house in the town.

Shakespeare's early plays were comedies and histories. He wrote his first **revenge tragedy**, *Titus Andronicus*, *c.* 1592. This play included a Moorish villain, Aaron. Before he wrote *Othello*, Shakespeare used Venice as a setting for *The Merchant of Venice* (*c.* 1600) in which a Jewish moneylender Shylock plots against the Christian merchant Antonio, who has abused him.

Othello was the second of Shakespeare's great tragedies, which were all written in the first decade of the seventeenth century. They followed on from *Romeo and Juliet* (*c.* 1595). *Hamlet* was first (*c.* 1601), then *Othello* (*c.* 1603), followed by *King Lear* (*c.* 1605), *Macbeth* (*c.* 1606) and *Antony and Cleopatra* (*c.* 1601). In all of these works the tragic hero suffers mental torment and dies, often as a result of a catastrophe brought about by a fatal error of judgement. All of Shakespeare's tragedies end with the restoration of order, although the deaths of the **protagonists** leave audiences with a deep sense of loss.

CONTEXT **A04**

The first Moorish protagonists on the English stage appeared in George Peele's *The Battle of Alcazar* (*c.* 1591). Muly Mahamet, a dark-skinned Moor, is a scheming usurper, while his uncle, the rightful king Abdelmelec, is a fair-skinned Moor who is portrayed sympathetically. Peele's play was anti-Spanish and pro-Moroccan because of its historical context. The Spanish Armada was defeated in 1588, and Elizabeth I attempted to form an alliance with Moroccan Sultan Ahmad al-Mansur in the 1590s.

CONTEXT **A04**

One of the most negative critics of *Othello* remarked on its success as a stage play in the late seventeenth century. Thomas Rymer commented: 'From all the Tragedies acted on our English stage, *Othello* is said to bear the Bell away'. *Othello* has been performed regularly ever since it was written.

SHAKESPEARE AND THE WRITING OF *OTHELLO*

The primary source Shakespeare used when writing *Othello* was the *Hecatommithi*, a collection of tales by the Italian writer Giambattisa Cinzio Giraldi. In Cinzio's story the Moor and his wife (Disdemona) live happily together in Venice for some time before the Ensign (who falls in love with the Moor's wife) persuades him that Disdemona has been unfaithful with Cassio, a captain. Together the Moor and his Ensign plan to kill Disdemona. The Ensign commits the murder, bludgeoning Disdemona to death with a stocking filled with sand. The ceiling is then collapsed on the body to make the death look like an accident. The Moor denies his part in the murder and is sent into exile, where he is killed by Disdemona's kinsmen. The Ensign continues his life of crime, eventually dying as a result of the torture inflicted on him in prison.

Shakespeare stuck to Cinzio's tale closely, although there are significant differences between this story and *Othello*. Shakespeare compresses the timescale to heighten the emotional impact of events and makes use of two contrasting locations. He introduces the characters of Roderigo and Brabantio (Desdemona's father) and the war between the Turks and Venetians. The lust of the Ensign in Cinzio's tale is replaced by the personal and professional jealousy of Iago, providing thematic continuity. Interestingly, Shakespeare makes Emilia an unwitting aid to her husband. In Cinzio's story the Ensign's wife is fully aware of her husband's villainy but is too frightened to speak out.

SHAKESPEARE'S THEATRE

The theatre for which Shakespeare's plays were written was one of the most remarkable innovations of the Renaissance. There had been no theatres or acting companies during the medieval period. Performed on carts and in open spaces at Christian festivals, plays had been almost exclusively religious. Actors wandered the country putting on entertainments. They did not perform full-length plays, but mimes, juggling and comedy acts. Actors were regarded as little better than vagabonds.

Just before Shakespeare went to London things began to change. A number of young men who had been to the universities of Oxford and Cambridge came to London in the 1580s and began to write plays in Latin, influenced by the classical drama of Ancient Greece and Rome. Dramatists began to write full-length plays on secular subjects, taking their plots from history and legend, and the theatre became professional.

Thus, when Shakespeare arrived in London, there were flourishing theatres and companies of actors waiting for him. His company performed at James Burbage's Theatre in Shoreditch, the first permanent theatre in England, until 1596, and used the Swan and Curtain until it moved into its own new theatre, the Globe, in 1599.

Attending the theatre in Shakespeare's day was very different from modern theatregoing. Performances took place during the daytime and in the open air, so that the audience and the actors were always aware of each other. Shakespeare's theatre was a communal experience, enjoyed by a range of social classes. Wealthier spectators sat in covered galleries, but 'groundlings' could stand and watch for a penny. Audiences were less polite than they are today. People came in late, interrupted, joined in and sometimes even got on to the stage.

Theatrical conventions were very different. All female roles were played by boys. Plays were preceded and followed by jigs and clowning, and the pace of the drama was much faster than we are used to. There were no intervals between acts, and very little in the way of props or scenery which needed changing. It is thought that Shakespeare's plays were performed in around two hours.

GRADE BOOSTER **A03**

In Cinzio's tale the Moor is taken back to Venice, where he is tortured and refuses to confess to his crimes. In *Othello* it is Iago who refuses to speak at the end of the play, while Othello commits suicide to atone for his sins. Try thinking about the dramatic significance of the changes Shakespeare made to his source.

CONTEXT **A04**

Athenian tragedy is the oldest surviving form of tragedy. It was an important part of the culture of Athens, and the most famous plays to survive are by Sophocles, Aeschylus and Euripides. Athenian tragedy was performed as part of the annual state religious festival in honour of Dionysos, god of the grape harvest.

CONTEXT **A04**

In Shakespeare's London there were between five and eight theatres open at any one time. Audience figures were very large, with 18,000 to 24,000 people visiting the theatre each week.

CHECK THE BOOK **A03**

The most authoritative book about the theatre of Shakespeare's time is Andrew Gurr's *The Shakespearean Stage* (1992).

SETTING

Othello is set in Venice and Cyprus. The military events of the play are based on historical fact. Selim the Second launched the Turkish attack on Cyprus in 1570. His general Mustapha conquered the island a year later. Act I covers the events of one night in Venice, while Acts II–V are set in Cyprus, which was governed by Venice at the time when the play was set. The two settings are symbolically significant. Elizabethan dramatists often used Italianate settings for plays about intrigue, secret love affairs and revenge. This is because foreign courts were stereotyped as being full of villainy, sexual perversion and decadence. Venice had a reputation as a city of wealth and sophistication, but was also perceived as a place of loose morals. Shakespeare is able to use the Venetian setting to establish Othello as an outsider. Although he serves the senate, Othello is not Italian, unlike his cunning adversary, Iago. Iago is a typical Italianate villain: scheming, selfish and amoral. Iago is able to make much of Othello's outsider status, convincing him that he does not understand the society he serves.

Cyprus is an island under occupation. It is described as a 'warlike isle' (II.1.43). The conflict and danger of the setting are **mirrored** in the tragic events that unfold there. Away from the 'civilisation' of Venice, Iago's evil schemes prosper. Cyprus is threatened by the Turks; Othello's peace of mind and marriage are threatened by Iago. Othello is sent to Cyprus to govern and restore peace. Instead of bringing peace, Othello destroys his wife and then himself. Cyprus is also an isolated setting, which is psychologically appropriate for the events of the play. Secure in their love in Venice, Othello and Desdemona are wrenched apart and isolated from one another in Cyprus. It is tragically **ironic** that a once great soldier should die for love in a war zone. Venice and Cyprus are also significant because they are opposites – one a seat of power; the other a vulnerable outpost.

CONTEXT **A04**

A famous sea battle occurred at Lepanto in the Ionian Sea in October 1571, when a coalition of Christian forces, including the Republic of Venice, defeated the main Turkish fleet. The Catholic maritime states had joined forces to prevent the Mediterranean Sea becoming an uncontested highway for the Ottoman Empire.

CONTEXT **A04**

Christian traditions of the Renaissance suggested that Africans were descendants of Noah's son Ham, who was cursed by his father. Thus, it held that they were an accursed race.

STUDY FOCUS: KEY ISSUES IN *OTHELLO* **A03**

- **Conflict and love** Shakespeare deliberately chooses a military man as the tragic lover in *Othello*, drawing our attention to the themes of conflict and love from the first scene. The marriage of Othello and Desdemona provokes very strong reactions in Act I. Some characters oppose the match (Brabantio) while others accept it (the Duke).

- **Race** Objections to Othello's marriage and the early racist descriptions of the hero in Act I draw our attention to the theme of race. The Elizabethans were often prejudiced against foreigners and had particular fears about marriages between black men and white women. They commonly believed that the offspring of such unions would be monsters. The black man had long been associated with the devil in art and literature. In the Renaissance many Christians viewed Moors with suspicion because they considered them heathens, like the Turks. There had been a long-standing conflict between the Muslim Ottoman Empire (the Turks) and the Catholic maritime states of Europe, which sought to hold on to their territories – including Cyprus – in the Mediterranean and prevent the expansion of the Ottoman Empire. As a Moor, Othello would thus have been associated in the Elizabethan mind with a range of ideas and events which provoked anxiety.

- **Gender roles and power** The assertive heroine Desdemona, who chooses her own husband and refuses to be parted from him, draws our attention to gender roles and power in *Othello*. Desdemona's deception of her father also alerts us to the difference between appearance and reality, upon which Iago's evil scheming depends. Ultimately, in spite of her bravery and defence of her own virtue, like so many women in Elizabethan drama, Desdemona does not have the power to determine her own fate; it lies in the hands of the men who abuse her.

CHARACTERS IN *OTHELLO*

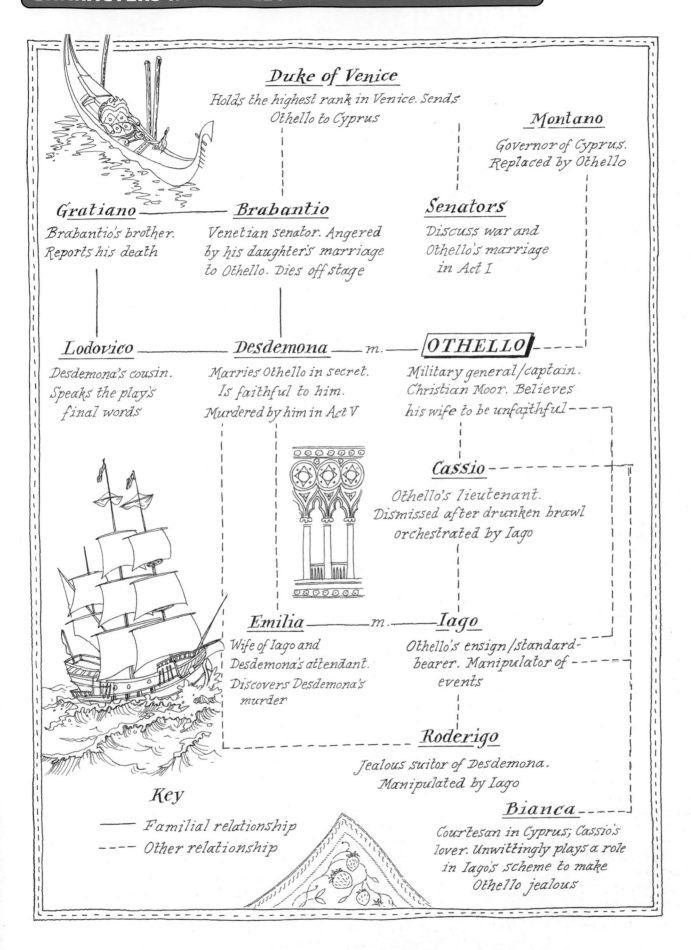

Duke of Venice
Holds the highest rank in Venice. Sends Othello to Cyprus

Montano
Governor of Cyprus. Replaced by Othello

Gratiano
Brabantio's brother. Reports his death

Brabantio
Venetian senator. Angered by his daughter's marriage to Othello. Dies off stage

Senators
Discuss war and Othello's marriage in Act I

Lodovico
Desdemona's cousin. Speaks the play's final words

Desdemona — m. — **OTHELLO**
Marries Othello in secret. Is faithful to him. Murdered by him in Act V

OTHELLO
Military general/captain. Christian Moor. Believes his wife to be unfaithful

Cassio
Othello's lieutenant. Dismissed after drunken brawl orchestrated by Iago

Emilia — m. — **Iago**
Wife of Iago and Desdemona's attendant. Discovers Desdemona's murder

Iago
Othello's ensign/standard-bearer. Manipulator of events

Roderigo
Jealous suitor of Desdemona. Manipulated by Iago

Key
—— Familial relationship
- - - - Other relationship

Bianca
Courtesan in Cyprus; Cassio's lover. Unwittingly plays a role in Iago's scheme to make Othello jealous

SYNOPSIS

ACT I

OTHELLO'S SECRET MARRIAGE

The Moor Othello, a respected general, has secretly married a wealthy Venetian aristocrat, Desdemona. Her father, Brabantio, is informed of this (on the night of the marriage) by Roderigo, who had hoped to marry Desdemona himself. Brabantio goes in search of Othello and then makes his way to the senate where he accuses Othello of bewitching his daughter. Brabantio's accusations are proved false when Othello and Desdemona explain how they fell in love. The Duke of Venice tries to reconcile Brabantio to his daughter's marriage but the angry father disowns Desdemona. The senate sends Othello to defend Cyprus from a Turkish invasion. Desdemona asks to be allowed to accompany her husband. She is put in the care of Othello's ensign, Iago. Iago's wife, Emilia, is to be Desdemona's maid.

IAGO'S REVENGE

Iago is an embittered man. He is angry because Othello has not given him a promotion that he believes was due to him. A young Florentine soldier, Cassio, has been made lieutenant over him. Iago seeks to revenge himself on both Cassio and Othello. Iago has already made trouble for Othello; it was he who persuaded Roderigo to inform Brabantio of Desdemona's elopement in the first scene.

ACT II

CONFLICT IN CYPRUS

The action moves to Cyprus. The threat of military invasion is removed when the Turkish fleet is destroyed in a storm, which Othello, Desdemona and Iago pass through safely. There is a night of festivities to celebrate the destruction of the Turkish fleet and the marriage of Othello and Desdemona. The newly-weds seem secure in their love. However, while there is no longer a military conflict, there is a new threat to the couple's happiness: Iago. Roderigo has been persuaded to follow Desdemona to Cyprus. Iago has promised to help him woo Desdemona, making Roderigo believe that she will soon tire of Othello. Iago now makes Roderigo believe that Cassio is his rival for Desdemona's affections. On the night of the celebrations Iago goads Roderigo into challenging Cassio, whom he has plied with drink. A fight ensues. Cassio is disgraced and Othello dismisses him from his post. Iago tells Cassio that his best chance of winning back Othello's good opinion lies in asking Desdemona to plead for him. Iago plans to persuade Othello that Desdemona has committed adultery with Cassio. Iago has personal motives for his revenge on Cassio and Othello. He claims that they have both cuckolded him (that is, deceived him by having sexual relations with his mistress and his wife, respectively).

CONTEXT A04

The Moors, Islamic inhabitants of Northern Africa, conquered Spain in the eighth century. During the eleventh to fifteenth centuries, Christians reconquered Spain, and many Moors adopted a more European culture. Some became Christians.

CONTEXT A04

Cyprus was one of Venice's colonies, from 1489 to 1571. *Othello* is set in 1570–1, making the hero one of the last men sent to defend the island against the Turks, who, despite their defeat in this play, reasserted their supremacy in the region and gained possession of Cyprus by treaty in 1573.

ACT III

OTHELLO IS OVERCOME BY JEALOUSY

Iago persuades Othello that Desdemona is in love with Cassio and has committed adultery with him many times. He contrives proof of this, making use of a handkerchief belonging to Desdemona, which he claims has been found in Cassio's bedchamber. In fact, the handkerchief was passed on to Iago by Emilia, who picked it up when Desdemona dropped it. Although he is reluctant to believe his wife unchaste, Othello becomes convinced that Desdemona is a whore and is seized by overpowering jealousy. Othello vows to seek revenge on Desdemona and Cassio by killing them. Iago promises to help him. Desdemona is puzzled and frightened by Othello when he questions her about the handkerchief and lies about what has happened to it. Desdemona is unaware of the danger she is in by continuing to plead for Cassio. Cassio gives the handkerchief to his mistress, Bianca, who believes that another woman has given Cassio the handkerchief as a love token.

ACT IV

IAGO'S POISON DESTROYS OTHELLO'S MIND

Iago continues to torment Othello with insinuations about Desdemona and Cassio fornicating. Othello is so overwhelmed by the idea of Desdemona having sex with another man that he falls down in a fit. While he is writhing on the ground, Iago creates another opportunity to 'prove' Desdemona is a whore. He persuades Othello to observe him talking to Cassio. Unable to hear what is being said, Othello believes that Cassio is laughing about committing adultery with Desdemona. Bianca gives the handkerchief back to Cassio, convinced it is proof he has been unfaithful to her. Othello observes what happens between Cassio and Bianca and believes that this is concrete proof of Desdemona's adultery. Othello decides to poison his wife, but Iago suggests smothering her in the marital bed instead. Desdemona is abused physically and verbally in Act IV. Othello refuses to believe her or Emilia's protestations of Desdemona's innocence. Othello calls Desdemona a whore and strikes her in front of Lodovico, who has arrived with a letter from the Venetian senate. Othello has been recalled to Venice and Cassio is to govern in Cyprus in his place. Desdemona is full of foreboding when she asks Emilia to put her wedding sheets on her bed and sings a melancholy song about a woman forsaken in love.

ACT V

THE TRAGIC DENOUEMENT

Othello has asked Iago to kill Cassio. Iago again persuades Roderigo to assist him but the attempt on Cassio's life does not go as planned. Iago wounds Cassio himself and then kills Roderigo. Iago believes removing Roderigo will ensure his safety, but he does not know that Roderigo was carrying letters outlining Iago's evil schemes. These letters are discovered in the final scene. Gripped by jealousy, Othello smothers Desdemona in her bed. She dies protesting her innocence. Emilia comes to inform Othello of the attack on Cassio and finds her mistress dying. Desdemona refuses to blame Othello for her murder. Emilia calls out for help. Montano, Gratiano and Iago come running to find out what has happened. Othello is taken prisoner. Iago's plots are gradually revealed, largely by Emilia, who is killed by her husband for speaking the truth. Iago attempts to escape but is captured and brought back under arrest. He refuses to explain why he has plotted against Othello. Othello realises his terrible folly. He is prevented from killing Iago and turns his weapon on himself. He dies on the bed next to Desdemona, full of remorse. In his final moments, Othello's thoughts are for Desdemona. Cassio is made governor of Cyprus and Iago is led away for torture.

CRITICAL VIEWPOINT A03

In *Othello* (1997), E. A. J. Honigmann claims that *Othello* is 'the most unbearably exciting' of Shakespeare's **tragedies**. What details of the plot do you think led him to say this?

CRITICAL VIEWPOINT A03

Caryl Phillips says Othello's love of Desdemona 'is the love of a possession. She is a prize, a spoil of war'.

ACT I SCENE 1

SUMMARY

- Roderigo is unhappy with Iago for failing to promote his marriage to Desdemona, who has secretly married Othello.
- Iago says that Othello has promoted an inexperienced soldier, Michael Cassio, over him, and that he hates Othello and wants revenge on him.
- To cause trouble, Iago urges Roderigo to wake up Brabantio and inform him of his daughter Desdemona's elopement.
- Brabantio discovers that Desdemona is not in her room. Calling for weapons, he sets out to locate Desdemona and Othello.

ANALYSIS

CONFLICT: PUBLIC AND PRIVATE

From the start of *Othello* the scene is set for conflict. The topic under discussion in the opening lines (marriage) seems of little political significance. However, Shakespeare **juxtaposes** Roderigo's failure to marry Desdemona with Iago's failure to gain promotion, making it clear that private, domestic issues and the public, professional world will collide in *Othello*. The scene ends with an indication that this is not a purely domestic drama. Brabantio arms himself and rouses his neighbours to help him hunt down Othello. He is making his daughter's elopement a public, political affair. The audience realises that the marriage of Othello and Desdemona is going to be at the heart of the conflict in the play. Act I Scene 1 also includes references to the Venetian conflict with the Turks over Cyprus, the setting where Othello's mind and marriage will be destroyed.

STUDY FOCUS: DECEPTION AND DECEIT **A03**

Deception emerges as a key theme. It is established in two ways. Firstly, there are the deceptions that occurred before the events of the play began. Roderigo was deceived into believing he could win Desdemona's hand in marriage. Brabantio has been deceived by both Desdemona and Othello. Iago deceived himself when he believed he would be promoted. Secondly, there is the language of deceit which Iago uses. Iago says that he admires men who make 'shows of service on their lords' (line 51). His reputation as a dutiful subordinate is deceptive; Iago says openly 'I am not what I am' (line 64). Shakespeare has structured the play in such a way that the audience will question the difference between appearance and reality from the start.

MEN TALKING ABOUT WOMEN

The ways in which the male characters discuss women reveal the **patriarchal** context of the play. Iago sneers that Cassio is 'A fellow almost damned in a fair wife' (line 20). This casual sexism helps to establish Iago's misogyny, which he will use to infect Othello's mind. The **imagery** also makes it clear that the male characters view women as their possessions. Iago shouts to Brabantio, 'Look to your house, your daughter, and your bags!/ Thieves, thieves!' (line 80).

Brabantio believes Desdemona has subverted the natural order by eloping. Her decision to choose her own husband is 'treason of the blood' (line 167). The image of Desdemona in 'the gross clasps of a lascivious Moor' (line 124) makes it plain that her 'revolt' (line 132) is outrageous not just because Desdemona has deceived her father, but also because she has

---

CHECK THE FILM **A03**

In the 1952 Orson Welles production, the film opens with the funeral procession of Desdemona and Othello. Iago is seen suspended in a cage, his eyes glinting wickedly. This opening suggests the tragic inevitability of the events that occur. Check Act I Scene 1 for words or events that **foreshadow** a tragic outcome.

CRITICAL VIEWPOINT **A04**

Dr Johnson took a very dim view of Iago. He said that 'the character of Iago is so conducted, that he is from the first scene to the last hated and despised'. Do you think that this is how Shakespeare intended the audience to react to Iago? Are there other ways of responding to Iago?

chosen a Moor. Perhaps because it is too alarming to believe that Desdemona was a willing bride, Brabantio suggests his daughter was a passive victim. Her 'youth and maidhood' have been 'abused' by Othello and his love potions (lines 170–1). This idea reflects the Renaissance stereotype of the black man as cunning sexual predator.

FIRST IMPRESSIONS OF THE VILLAIN

Iago reveals his villainy early on. He seems to have a clear motive for causing Othello harm. Iago tells Roderigo he is bitter because of the way 'Preferment goes by letter and affection/ And not by the old gradation' (lines 35–6). Iago feels Othello has cheated him out of a promotion that was his due. However, should the audience trust what Iago says? Iago stresses that he only follows Othello to 'serve my turn upon him' (line 41).

Iago is good at getting himself out of trouble, or avoiding it altogether: he leaves the stage just as Brabantio discovers Desdemona has gone, knowing that it is 'not meet nor wholesome to my place,/ To be produced' (lines 143–4). The language Iago uses here is a good example of the **irony** that the audience will come to associate with him. Neither his words nor his actions in this scene have been 'wholesome'. There are other examples of **dramatic irony** in this scene, which also centre on Iago. Roderigo fails to see that a man who admits he is a selfish fraud might be using him and Brabantio is unaware of the truth of his words to Iago, 'Thou art a villain!' (line 116). By the end of Act I Scene 1, Shakespeare has established Iago as a powerful, manipulative figure, who instigates and stage-manages chaos efficiently.

THE TRAGIC HERO

Because we do not see him, and he is not referred to by name, Othello is a mysterious figure at this stage. Shakespeare has structured the scene to draw the audience's attention to the role rumour is to play in events. Everything we learn about Othello is second hand. Should we dismiss it as gossip? Iago says Othello is a self-satisfied and bombastic speaker (lines 11–13), who gets his way with the senate in order to promote his own favourites. However, Iago also admits that Othello is an effective soldier, relied on by the Venetian senate (lines 145–51).

REVISION FOCUS: TASK 1   A04

How far do you agree with the following statements?

- The crude sexual imagery in Act I Scene 1 undermines the love of Othello and Desdemona.
- Iago's motives for revenge are plausible.

Try writing opening paragraphs for essays based on these discussion points. Set out your arguments clearly.

GLOSSARY

9	**Off-capped** showed respect by removing hats
13	**epithets** terms or phrases
24	**toged** wearing official dress (togas worn by Roman senators were the garb of peace)
30	**counter-caster** accountant
38	**affined** bound
47	**cashiered** dismissed or cast off
110	**Barbary horse** Arabian thoroughbred (this reference is designed to evoke Othello's barbarism)
112	**jennets** small Spanish horses
156	**Sagittary** the house where Othello and Desdemona are staying, named after the sign of Sagittarius, the centaur

CONTEXT   A04

Venice had a more rigid class structure than England at the time *Othello* was written. The nobility and 'common people' were very distinct from one another. We see evidence of Iago's class envy early in the play when he complains about how promotion goes by 'preferment'. As a man who had risen in society himself, Shakespeare would have understood Iago's resentment.

CRITICAL VIEWPOINT   A03

Many critics have said that the most important theme in Othello is jealousy. Notice how quickly Shakespeare establishes the theme. Iago is jealous of Cassio, and Roderigo feels jealous of Othello for 'beating' him to Desdemona.

EXTENDED COMMENTARY

ACT I SCENE 1 LINES 81–138

A heated exchange between Iago, Roderigo and Brabantio occurs immediately after Iago has informed Roderigo that he hates Othello, and follows the Moor only to 'serve my turn upon him' (I.1.41). We see here how successfully Iago manipulates the way characters perceive each other. Although this is the very first scene and only 80 lines in, the ensign has already succeeded in prejudicing Roderigo's view of Othello's marriage. This is so he can obtain Roderigo's assistance. He wants Roderigo to 'Call up her [Desdemona's] father', 'poison his delight' (I.1.66–7) and 'Plague him with flies' (I.1.70). Iago's use of **metaphors** associates him with poison, corruption and disease throughout the play. Shakespeare has begun to prepare us for the poisoning of Othello's mind, which occurs in Act III.

The location of Act I Scene 1 is significant. It is night-time, and the two levels of the stage used (Brabantio at the window, Iago and Roderigo concealed in the darkness of the street below) signifies disruption and confusion. Brabantio's physical security (his house) is threatened, as well as his peace of mind. Iago refers to Desdemona's elopement using a verb that signifies an assault on Brabantio's property; the old man has been 'robbed' (line 84). Roderigo's descriptions of Desdemona's movements add to the atmosphere of disorder, and establish the danger of Venice at night. 'At this odd-even and dull watch o' the night' Brabantio's daughter has been transported to the 'gross clasps of a lascivious Moor'. We know that the social order has been threatened by the elopement because Desdemona has been taken away from her home in darkness, and by 'a knave of common hire, a gondolier' (lines 121–4).

When he first appears Brabantio assumes the role of angry **patriarch**. We know he is powerful because he speaks of 'my spirit and my place' (line 102) and his property. Further, when he says 'My daughter is not for thee' (line 97) to Roderigo we know that Brabantio looks upon Desdemona as a possession. This idea follows on neatly from the earlier use of 'robbed'. Brabantio dismisses Roderigo in a commanding tone at line 95 and is offended by Iago's presence. He finds Iago's mode of address offensive, asking, 'What profane wretch art thou?' before insulting him as a 'villain' (lines 113–16). Brabantio's social position is undermined in this scene, not just by the 'wheeling stranger' who has eloped with his daughter (line 134), but also by Iago's saucy words and Roderigo's description of Desdemona's 'gross revolt' (line 132). We know that Brabantio's authority is subverted too because his utterances contain questions as well as threats, and his words increasingly show he is alarmed. Instead of directing his social inferiors, Brabantio finds himself acting in response to them.

Roderigo follows Iago's instructions throughout Act I Scene 1. He speaks politely to Brabantio, reinforcing our sense of the father's important social position. The terms in which Roderigo describes Desdemona's elopement, and in particular Othello, echo the negative descriptions of the Moor earlier in the scene. The **images** Roderigo employs focus on the unnatural quality of the match and Desdemona's disobedience. This marriage is a subversion of the natural order. Roderigo is a representative of Venetian society, one of the 'curled darlings' (I.2.68) Desdemona has rejected. His **xenophobic** view of her marriage is one that Brabantio can understand. As we see later in the first act, Brabantio views his daughter's marriage as an incomprehensible rejection of everything she has known.

Iago speaks a different language from the other two male characters. He is crude and mocking. Iago's racist descriptions of Othello are similar to Roderigo's use of 'lascivious Moor' (line 124) and are a key part of the negative black stereotype that is being created. Iago's references to 'an old black ram', 'a Barbary horse' and 'the beast with two backs' (lines 87, 110, 115) reinforce the idea that Desdemona has made an unnatural match and cast Othello in a repugnant role: he is a lustful predator. Iago's imagery suggests race and sex are going to be important issues in *Othello*. The reduction of the Desdemona–Othello match to bestial sexuality is typical of Iago, who is associated with unpleasant animal imagery throughout the play. However, we might already feel that the imagery here tells us more about Iago's character than Othello's because we are aware of Iago's hatred. Earlier in the scene Iago said he wants revenge on the Moor, so we know he is an untrustworthy villain.

We quickly realise that Iago is persuasive and self-confident. He answers Brabantio back and forces his own interpretation of events on him. It is Iago's crude comments which really capture Brabantio's attention in this scene. Roderigo finds it difficult to assert himself, but after Iago's speech at line 107 Brabantio begins to take note of what he is hearing. Act I Scene 1 also reveals Iago's ability to improvise. He sets the pace and controls the drama. It was his idea to wake up Brabantio and he gets the result he wanted; an angry father, appalled by what he hears.

This is an exchange of contrasts and discord which sets the scene for the events that follow. The contrasts are reflected in the imagery and setting, which establish a number of themes and ideas that are going to be important in *Othello*: social disruption, class and power, delusion and knowledge, male and female sexuality and black and white. The rather chaotic feel signifies that disruption has already occurred and we know that the marriage of Othello and Desdemona is going to be the focal point for future disruption because these three characters react to it so strongly and describe it in such negative terms. We are also aware of the difference between Desdemona and her husband: she is the 'white ewe' (line 88) while Othello  is the 'black ram'. Desdemona has been stolen, but we also know she has given herself away because she has chosen to elope secretly. Venice – a civilised place associated with power, prosperity and order – has been assaulted by a 'wheeling stranger' (line 134). We wonder how the tension that has been set up in this scene will be resolved, particularly the evident dislike and disdain Iago, Roderigo and Brabantio feel for Othello. We can see that the villain has already had some success in getting his view of Othello accepted; now we want to see the tragic **protagonist** for ourselves.

CHECK THE BOOK **A03**

For a discussion about the way Shakespeare portrays race in the play, see an essay on *Othello* by Frances Dolan, 'Revolutions, Petty Tyranny and the Murderous Husband' in Kate Chedgzoy (ed.), *Shakespeare, Feminsim and Gender* (2001).

CRITICAL VIEWPOINT **A03**

The actor Dominic West, who played Iago in 2011, commented that *Othello* becomes 'a sexual competition between him [Iago] and Othello' (BBC Radio 4, 'Front Row', 23 December 2011). Do you find this view helpful when considering the relationship between Othello and Iago, and Iago's relationship with Desdemona?

ACT I SCENE 2

SUMMARY

- Iago warns that Brabantio may use his influence to have Othello arrested and his marriage dissolved.
- Othello is confident that his services to the state, his reputation and his royal breeding make him a suitable match for Desdemona.
- Cassio brings a message from the Duke, who urgently requires Othello's presence at a meeting of the Venetian council. On the way there Othello and his soldiers are accosted by Brabantio and his followers.
- Othello commands the men to put away their weapons and denies Brabantio's accusations of bewitching Desdemona.
- Brabantio decides to go to the council meeting too, so that the Duke can be informed of Othello's treachery.

ANALYSIS

OTHELLO'S CONFLICT

Two **images** in this scene highlight the conflict that Othello faces. On the one hand, he is a successful soldier, used to leading armies, as his command to Brabantio's followers makes clear: 'Keep up your bright swords, for the dew will rust them' (line 59). On the other hand, having married, he has now his 'free condition/ Put into circumscription and confine' (lines 26–7). The audience may wonder how Othello will combine his conflicting roles as military man and lover-husband. What do you make of the fact that the military image Othello uses is poetic, while the language he uses to describe his marriage suggests entrapment?

FIRST IMPRESSIONS OF OTHELLO

In contrast to the characters we have seen so far, Othello speaks with a measured calm in **blank verse** in this scene. Othello and Iago are polar opposites: one seeks to resolve conflict while the other revels in it. Iago does his best to stir up trouble when he tells Othello that Brabantio has spoken against Othello in 'scurvy and provoking terms' (line 7), but Othello is unworried. Two brief statements, 'Let him do his spite' (line 17) and 'I must be found' (line 30), suggest he is ready to face the consequences of his actions. When he is accused of evil enchantment Othello pleads for calm and says it is not time to fight (lines 81–3).

Othello's quiet confidence and sincerity about his love for Desdemona are attractive. Othello is not the pompous man Iago described in Act I Scene 1. In spite of his secret marriage, he says he prefers to be open about his actions (lines 30–2). Othello is also brave, dignified and authoritative, as shown by his handling of Brabantio and his followers. We may accuse him of pride when he speaks of his services to the state and insists that his 'parts ... title, and ... perfect soul' (line 31) will 'manifest me rightly' (line 32), but we understand that his reputation has been attacked. By making Othello so different from the version of him described by Iago, is Shakespeare challenging his audience to accept the Moor as a noble, worthy man?

STUDY FOCUS: INSULTS   A02

The coarse imagery Iago used in Act I to describe the sexual union of Othello and Desdemona continues. Iago makes a crude joke when he tells Cassio that Othello has 'boarded a land carrack' (line 50, see **Glossary** for the double meaning). By using a **metaphor** of piracy Iago is degrading Othello, and echoing Brabantio's accusation that he is a 'foul thief' (line 62). Brabantio adds to his earlier insulting comments about enchantment. Othello is 'a practiser/ Of arts inhibited' (lines 78–9). The 'foul charms' he has used to bewitch Desdemona are 'gross'. As if it were not demeaning enough to accuse Othello of practising black magic, Brabantio also makes a racial insult. He cannot believe that Desdemona would 'Run from her guardage to the sooty bosom/ Of such a thing as thou' (lines 70–1). This negative language dehumanises Othello. Will the audience side with the deceived father or the victim of his verbal assault?

CONTEXT   A04

Brabantio suggests the world has been turned upside down by Othello's marriage to Desdemona in the rhyming couplet that closes the scene. In **Jacobean tragedy**, references to the subversion of the 'natural' order are used to warn the audience that there is trouble ahead.

CASSIO'S FIRST APPEARANCE

Just as we will compare the real Othello with Iago's version of him, we will want to see if Cassio is the inexperienced fool Iago portrayed him as in Act I Scene 1. In his first speeches Cassio comes across as trustworthy and reliable. He delivers his urgent summons from the Duke in a way which makes it clear the Cyprus mission is very important. However, Othello has not taken Cassio into his confidence about his marriage: he acted alone when he eloped. Does this mean there is a distance between the two soldiers? The most significant feature of Cassio's presentation in this scene is his failure to understand Iago's sexual joke about Othello's marriage at line 50. His puzzlement suggests Cassio does not share Iago's crude sense of humour, thus distancing him from the villain at this stage. This appears **ironic**, however, as Iago will cast Cassio in the role of seducer in the next scene.

KEY QUOTATION: ACT I SCENE 2   A01

Othello defends his love for Desdemona simply and clearly, stating: 'I love the gentle Desdemona' (line 25).

- This is the first sincere reference to love in the play.
- Othello's positive view of his relationship with Desdemona is in conflict with the way it is perceived by others.
- 'Gentle' is a **pun** which means both kind hearted and of noble birth. By stressing that Desdemona is 'gentle', does Shakespeare reinforce or undermine our view of Othello as a deserving romantic hero?

GRADE BOOSTER   A02

To show your understanding of structure for AO2 you need to have a good grasp of the way Othello's **characterisation** develops. A comparison of your first impression of Othello with the way he is presented in Acts III and V would enable you to explore the dramatic methods Shakespeare uses to chart Othello's downfall.

GLOSSARY

7	**scurvy**	insulting, rude
12	**magnifico**	a title used of Brabantio
17	**cable**	scope (a nautical metaphor)
18	**signiory**	the Venetian state/oligarchy
21	**promulgate**	make known or publish
26	**unhoused**	unconfined, free
33	**Janus**	the two-faced Roman god of beginnings, doorways and passages
50	**land carrack**	either a treasure ship or a slang term for a prostitute
95	**idle**	unimportant or trivial

ACT I SCENE 3

SUMMARY

- Othello is told to prepare for war against the Turks after their invasion of Cyprus.
- Brabantio repeats his accusations of witchcraft against Othello.
- Othello recounts the history of his relationship with Desdemona and she is brought to the council chamber to confirm Othello's words; the Duke urges Brabantio to reconcile himself to the marriage.
- Desdemona asks to be allowed to accompany her husband on his military campaign and Othello places her in Iago's care.
- Brabantio warns Othello against trusting Desdemona.
- Iago says he will help Roderigo seduce Desdemona and cuckold Othello.

ANALYSIS

OPPOSITION AND OTHELLO

Othello faces a great deal of opposition in this scene. He is effectively put on trial in the council chamber when he is forced to defend his character and his actions. When Desdemona backs him up and refuses to be parted from him, we know that Othello has one steadfast ally. However, in spite of the Duke's support, his trials are not over. Shakespeare has structured this scene so that discussions move back and forward between love and war, showing that Othello will constantly be pulled in different directions.

Othello's military skill is established by repeated references to him as 'valiant' early in the scene, while Desdemona's refinement and femininity are emphasised. Iago sneers that Desdemona is a pampered and delicate 'super-subtle Venetian' (line 357), while Othello is 'an erring barbarian' (line 356). Because of their differences, we may wonder whether Othello and Desdemona are a good match. However, Othello is confident that love and war can be combined. An audience may doubt this. Othello has had little experience in matters of the heart. He needed prompting to woo Desdemona. And Othello is a mature man, coming late to love, while Brabantio suggests his daughter is not much more than a girl.

STUDY FOCUS: THE LANGUAGE OF LOVE
A02

An analysis of the language Othello and Desdemona use when describing their love for each other is revealing. Othello says that Desdemona 'loved me for the dangers I had passed/ And I loved her that she did pity them' (lines 168–9). Desdemona was seduced by Othello's story-telling powers, while the Moor was enchanted by the Venetian's sympathetic response to his history: 'She gave me for my pains a world of sighs' (line 160). Later in this scene Desdemona says that she 'saw Othello's visage in his mind' (line 253). There is no question of their deep sincerity, but an audience might wonder whether Othello and Desdemona fell in love with an **image** or idea of the other. Look closely at the other speeches about love in Act I Scene 3. Are the lovers too idealistic?

DESDEMONA

Consider carefully your first impressions of Desdemona. Take into account the conflicting views that the characters and critics have of her. Some critics see her as a victim, while others believe she is partly responsible for what happens to her. In this scene she clearly makes choices for herself.

CONTEXT A04

By 1603 when Shakespeare came to write *Othello*, Venice had been employing paid mercenaries and freelance generals like Othello – who had their own armies – to protect the wealth of the city for quite some time. It was a cosmopolitan place, where personal advancement was possible, in spite of the rigid and hierarchical social structure that existed. Travellers admired Venice because of the sensual pleasures the city provided. While the Venetians were considered hospitable, they also had a reputation for religious zeal.

GRADE BOOSTER A02

To get the best grades you need to show an excellent understanding of the way Shakespeare uses language and other dramatic techniques. Commenting on 'honest' and 'honesty', which are key words in the play, is a good way of showing your understanding of **irony** in *Othello*. In Act I Scene 3, Othello twice refers to Iago's honesty (lines 285 and 290).

There is a contradiction in what Brabantio tells us about his daughter, and the young woman we see. How are we to reconcile the image of a 'maiden never bold;/ Of spirit so still and quiet that her motion/ Blushed at herself' (lines 95–7) with Othello's description of Desdemona as 'half the wooer' (line 176)? How would Shakespeare's audience have reacted to the idea of a woman choosing her own husband and teaching him how to win her heart (see Othello's speech at line 129)?

Think about how an actress playing Desdemona should deliver the lines she addresses to her father, the Duke and her husband. Desdemona seems to speak assertively to her father when he rejects her. She challenges Brabantio when she declares 'I am hitherto your daughter. But here's my husband' (line 184). She also refuses to stay with her father while Othello is away at war. However, Desdemona accepts male authority at the same time that she subverts it. She speaks of transferring her duty and obedience from her father to her husband, just as her mother did. But there is another contradiction to consider. Desdemona claims she is a submissive wife ('My heart's subdued/ Even to the very quality of my lord', lines 251–2) but also demands the right to accompany Othello to Cyprus ('I did love the Moor to live with him … Let me go with him', lines 249–60).

IAGO'S REVENGE

Iago speaks in fast-moving **prose** when outwitting Roderigo, suggesting he is thinking on his feet. Alone on stage, Iago returns to **blank verse**, demonstrating his ability to manipulate his style to suit his audience and purposes. At the start of his **soliloquy** he has not decided how he is going to proceed with his revenge. A few lines later Iago has the outline of a subtle plan. He delights in his quick wits, suggested by the way he thinks aloud, 'let me see now' (line 391). For 'mere suspicion' (line 388) he will destroy Othello's marriage and disgrace Cassio. It is **ironic** that Iago will fabricate a rumour that Cassio is 'too familiar' (line 395) with Desdemona as revenge for the rumour that he was cuckolded.

CRITICAL VIEWPOINT A03

Caryl Phillips has remarked on Othello's lack of confidence as a wooer, pointing to two lines: 'It was my hint to speak' (I.3.143) and 'Upon this hint I spake' (I.3.167). Phillips says that Othello 'feels constantly threatened and profoundly insecure'.

CHECK THE BOOK A03

Iago tells us there is a rumour that Othello has slept with his wife Emilia (lines 68–71). Is this a plausible reason for revenge? For Iago's **characterisation** as 'motiveless malignity', see Coleridge's comments in John Wain (ed.), *Othello* (1971).

REVISION FOCUS: TASK 2   A02

How far do you agree with the statements below?

● Desdemona and Othello are well matched.

● Act I is dominated by hatred rather than love.

Try writing opening paragraphs for essays based on these discussion points. Set out your arguments clearly.

GLOSSARY

1	**composition**	consistency
62	**mountebanks**	people who deceive others
199	**clogs**	shackles used on animals to prevent them from straying
201	**grise**	step
225	**sufficiency**	worth, ability
227	**slubber**	sully or make dirty
238	**exhibition**	financial support
274	**indign**	unworthy
306	**incontinently**	at once
333	**sect or scion**	branch or graft
350	**coloquintida**	a bitter apple used as a purgative
372	**Traverse**	get ready for action (a military term)
384	**snipe**	a bird, this is a term of contempt like 'woodcock'

CONTEXT A04

The Elizabethans used the term 'black' to refer to a range of skin colours; anyone of non-European background might be described as 'black' by Shakespeare's contemporaries during the Renaissance.

ACT II SCENE 1

SUMMARY

- The Turkish fleet is destroyed by a storm, but all the characters arrive safely in Cyprus.
- Iago dislikes the courteous way Cassio greets Emilia.
- Othello is overjoyed to be reunited with Desdemona.
- Iago persuades Roderigo to provoke Cassio into losing his temper in the hope of discrediting him.
- Iago reiterates his desire to be revenged on Othello and Cassio. He suspects them both of cuckolding him.

ANALYSIS

THE CYPRUS SETTING AND THE STORM

The principal characters are now isolated in the 'warlike isle' (line 43) of Cyprus, removed from the orderly social and political scene of Venice. The storm **foreshadows** the passions

that will be unleashed in this new setting. We might also see the storm as being related to Othello and his violent emotions. Othello is associated with sea **imagery** throughout the play (see **Part Four: Language**). Or we may see the storm as representing Iago, whose violence it reflects. The storm is also a device by which Shakespeare can dispose of the Turkish threat, which is no longer necessary to the plot. The external threat (the Turks) is replaced by the internal threat (Iago).

The storm serves other purposes. While it rages, the soldiers cannot see clearly what is happening and are full of fear, enabling Shakespeare to **mirror** the confusion of Act I Scene 1. Montano's concern for Othello's safety indicates his respect for 'the warlike Moor' (II.1.27) and reinforces our esteem for him. **Ironically**, Othello, who is looked upon as Cyprus's saviour, will prove as destructive as any tempest. Equally ironically, Iago, who will destroy Othello's happiness, arrives in Cyprus a week earlier than expected because the storm has helped his progress. It seems that fortune is favouring Iago. Symbolically, Iago lands before Othello, suggesting he will be in charge in this new setting. A final irony to consider: the marriage of Othello and Desdemona is destroyed in the birthplace of the goddess of love, Aphrodite.

IAGO THE PREDATOR

Shakespeare sets Iago in direct opposition with Othello and Cassio in this scene. Because a **soliloquy** by Iago closes the scene, we know the villain will triumph. The differences between Othello and Iago are clear. Othello's speeches are generous and joyful. Iago is full of hatred and contempt for the Moor's 'constant, loving, noble nature' (line 287). Personal and professional jealousy dominate Iago's soliloquy. His admission of 'love' (line 289) for Desdemona is intriguing. Should we believe Iago is in love with Desdemona? Perhaps not. Iago immediately redefines his feeling as 'lust' (line 290), 'partly led to diet my revenge' (line 292). Iago wants Othello to suffer the same torment that rages inside him. Would you agree that there is an undertone of competitive racism in Iago's soliloquy? He cannot accept that Desdemona, an aristocratic white woman, has chosen a black soldier.

When talking to the other characters Iago takes on the role of plain-speaking soldier. Ironically, Desdemona and Emilia are amused by Iago's cynical attitude towards women. We might view his crude delineation of the female character as a sign of Iago's narrow and twisted nature. Unlike Othello, who takes delight in his wife's presence, Iago can only see women as false, inferior creatures.

Cassio's gallantry contrasts with Iago's misogyny. Cassio greets Desdemona like a courtier, 'O, behold,/ The riches of the ship is come on shore:/... Hail to thee, lady!' (lines 83–5). Later he takes Desdemona by the hand. He is also gracious to Emilia. Cassio and Iago are opposites in other ways. Cassio mocks Iago to Desdemona when he says, 'you may relish him more in the soldier than in the scholar' (lines 165–6). Cassio is also clearly proud of his own 'breeding' (line 98) and good manners, while Iago is 'profane' (worldly and crude, line 164). However, the audience knows that Cassio's 'courtesy' (line 175) will be used against him when Iago says he'll 'have our Michael Cassio on the hip' (at his mercy, line 303). This image makes Iago's predatory nature clear.

CONTEXT A04

In Greek myth Aphrodite (Venus), the goddess of love, was thought to have risen from the sea on the west coast of Cyprus near Paphos. Poets have long celebrated Cyprus as the island of Venus.

STUDY FOCUS: OMINOUS SIGNS A02

An audience might be concerned that the tone and content of Desdemona's saucy speeches during her conversation with Emilia and Iago seem very different from Othello's romantic speeches. Does this difference foreshadow the couple's doom?

REVISION FOCUS: TASK 3 A02

How far do you agree with the statements below?

● Iago's hatred is more powerful than Othello's love.
● Othello's love for Desdemona is his greatest weakness.

Try writing opening paragraphs for essays based on these discussion points. Set out your arguments clearly.

CRITICAL VIEWPOINT A03

Writing in 1697, Thomas Rymer dismissed Desdemona as a 'silly Woman' whose virtue was suspect. Rymer was offended by Desdemona's vulgar conversation with Iago, commenting that Desdemona was behaving like 'any Countrey Kitchin-maid with her Sweet-heart'. Do you think Desdemona is silly and vulgar in this scene?

GLOSSARY

9	**mortoise**	joint
14	**burning bear**	a star, the Little Bear, used by sailors when navigating
63	**quirks**	extravagant phrases or praise
77	**A se'nnight's**	by a week
126	**birdlime**	a substance spread on bushes to snare birds
126	**frieze**	woollen fabric
155	**To change the cod's head for the salmon's tail**	to make an unwise exchange
176	**clyster-pipes**	a syringe for enemas or vaginal douches
216	**the court of guard**	guard house
307	**egregiously**	extraordinarily (bad)

EXTENDED COMMENTARY

ACT II SCENE 1 LINES 138–99

The reunion between Othello and Desdemona should be a moment of great happiness, but Iago's presence casts a dark shadow over it. Iago's crude **asides** undermine the couple's joy. While they anxiously await Othello's arrival, Iago acts the role of bluff soldier to divert Emilia and Desdemona. Ironically, the sentiments he expresses when he jokes with the female characters are close to the misogynistic opinions he offers in his **soliloquies**. Is Iago so clever, so in control, that he can even get away with pretending to pretend? Desdemona and Cassio do not really take Iago seriously in this scene. He is a source of amusement to them. The audience knows better. We realise that Iago should be feared. His asides provide an alarming running commentary. The **imagery** Iago uses establishes his deadly power. He speaks gleefully of spinning a 'web' to 'ensnare as great a fly as Cassio' (lines 168–9). It is **ironic** that Cassio mocks Iago at line 165. We know that it is his social and professional inferior who is in control. Iago intends to use Cassio's gallantry and sophistication against him.

Iago will also succeed in misconstruing the playful sexuality that Desdemona displays when she says to Emilia, 'O, most lame and impotent conclusion!' (line 161). An audience might feel uncomfortable about Desdemona participating in this saucy exchange, but Shakespeare deliberately stresses her sexuality for several reasons. Firstly, Desdemona's physical attraction to Othello establishes the hero's innocence of witchcraft, and helps us see the couple as a good match. We need to understand how – as Iago puts it – 'well tuned' Desdemona and Othello are (line 198). This makes the collapse of their marriage truly tragic. Secondly, Desdemona's sexuality is important to the plot. Iago's evil designs rely on Desdemona's sexual attractiveness. Thirdly, Desdemona's confidence and quick wits, shown in her questions at lines 139 and 159, are an important part of her appeal. These qualities will be used against the heroine when Iago makes Desdemona's speech seem unreliable and dishonest. There is a cruel irony in the fact that Desdemona warns Emilia playfully about believing what Iago says; it is she who needs to beware of Iago's words. It is also ironic that Iago's description of 'a deserving woman' (lines 148–58) comes to suit Desdemona perfectly in Acts IV and V, when the heroine displays a submissive character.

Although the other characters do not take Iago's misogyny seriously, we do. As Iago's plots evolve they rely on the heartless manipulation of Desdemona, Emilia and Bianca. Iago also influences the way in which the other male characters think of and respond to these women. However, the audience will question what Iago says about the female sex. Although she has disobeyed her father, Desdemona displays none of the negative traits Iago describes in this scene, and as the drama unfolds, we realise that women are victims rather than fools in *Othello*. Interestingly, the discussion about female faults contains irony that eventually works against Iago, who says that he can only stand a quiet woman who will 'ne'er disclose her mind' (line 156). At the end of the play Iago's villainy is revealed when Emilia refuses to be silent.

Iago does not simply have a low opinion of women. He also wants to degrade them. This idea emerges in Iago's soliloquy at line 284. Iago's reference to 'clyster-pipes' at line 176 is crude. Throughout *Othello*, Iago employs similar vulgar images to describe female sexuality. We know from his earlier descriptions of Desdemona as a 'land carrack' (I.2.50) and his saucy chat with Cassio in Act II Scene 3 that Iago cannot think of the heroine as possessing any real worth. Desdemona's love for Othello is so inexplicable to Iago that he has to dismiss it as lust. However, although we want to reject Iago and his crude world view, the villain keeps drawing us back to him. He butts in, whispers, invites us to collude with him and see through his eyes. We don't hear what Desdemona and Cassio say at line 167, so we are compelled to listen to Iago's interpretation of their conversation. This is precisely what Iago does to all the characters in this play; he forces them to accept his version of events.

It is a measure of Iago's power that he is able to undermine a loving reunion. When they meet in Cyprus, Othello's and Desdemona's kisses suggest the erotic strength of their love. We know just how powerful Othello's emotions are because his first thought is for his 'fair warrior' (line 179). It gives Othello 'wonder great as my content/ To see you here before me'; Desdemona is his 'soul's joy' (lines 181–2). Othello's love and the delight he feels in his marriage are moving. However, even before Iago makes his snide and threatening aside of lines 197–9, we are aware that there is a worrying undercurrent. Othello says – innocently – 'I fear/ My soul hath her content so absolute/ That not another comfort like to this/ Succeeds in unknown fate' (lines 188–91). Othello thinks that he is at the height of happiness, but also mentions an 'unknown fate', hinting unknowingly at the **tragedy** that awaits him. Notice the negativity that creeps into Othello's words. In his next speech he says that his happiness 'is too much joy' (line 195). Desdemona rejects this idea, but perhaps Othello's words undermine the power of the kisses that follow and **foreshadow** the tragedy to come. The sea **metaphor** Othello employs to describe the happiness he feels at lines 183–7 is also worrying. Othello suggests that he would be prepared to come through terrible dangers so long as he had Desdemona to greet him. We wonder how Othello will rise to the challenge of a battle in his personal life because we know he is already overwhelmed by his feelings for Desdemona, and we also know Iago is plotting to destroy the intense faith he has in his wife. Thus even Othello's joy adds to the tension of this scene.

CHECK THE FILM A04

In the 1989 TV film of *Othello* it is clear that Othello idealises Desdemona, and puts her on a pedestal. When he arrives in Cyprus, he lifts her up and places her on top of an upturned case that is being used as a platform. Desdemona seems to tower over her husband, who gazes up at her admiringly. The camera moves around and we see from Desdemona's point of view, as the young bride looks down at Othello. The camera angle clearly suggests that Othello has been disorientated by love, and that he has lost some of his power.

ACT II SCENE 2

SUMMARY

- Peace is restored in Cyprus.
- There is to be a night of revels to celebrate the destruction of the Turkish fleet and Othello's marriage.

ANALYSIS

WAR AND LOVE

War and love are **juxtaposed** once again, as they have been throughout the play. The herald's joyful proclamation marks a return to civil order. This is ironic, because in the very next scene Iago will disrupt the peace, and Cyprus will become the location of drunken street fighting. Notice that war is mentioned before love in the herald's speech, a reversal of what happened in the previous scene, when Othello greeted Desdemona before Montano, putting love before war. Shakespeare is reminding us that Cyprus is a dangerous place.

War and love are also linked in this scene. The public festival planned is intended primarily to celebrate the 'perdition' (line 3) of the Turkish fleet. Othello, however, has decided that the celebration of peace should become a celebration of his marriage. The herald stresses Othello's generosity when he says 'there is full liberty of feasting … till the bell have told eleven' (lines 9–10). Iago will take advantage of Othello's generosity in order to start his own campaign of destruction.

GLOSSARY

3	**mere perdition**	complete destruction
8	**All offices are open**	all the kitchens and cellars are open (for drinking and eating)

ACT II SCENE 3

SUMMARY

- Iago is put in charge of the festivities and Desdemona and Othello leave to consummate their marriage.
- Iago persuades Cassio to join in the carousing and undermines Cassio's reputation by telling Montano that Cassio is a drunkard.
- Roderigo antagonises Cassio, a fight ensues and Othello dismisses Cassio from his post.
- Iago advises Cassio to seek Desdemona's help on his behalf.
- Iago intends to persuade his wife, Emilia, to promote Cassio's cause with Desdemona while he poisons Othello's mind.

ANALYSIS

REPUTATION

The theme of reputation dominates this scene. Two characters lose control and diminish their reputations. Cassio ruins his in a drunken brawl. Othello undermines his reputation as a cool-headed commander by losing his temper. Conversely, Iago enhances his reputation as an honest, conscientious soldier and helpful friend. He has masterful self-control in this scene and is able to control others, for example Roderigo's actions and Cassio's drinking. Iago also controls how others see events. He convinces Montano that Cassio is unfit for his job. More subtly, he increases Othello's disgust at Cassio by seeming reluctant to criticise him. Iago's words are just as devastating as Cassio's actions in destroying the lieutenant's reputation. At the end of the scene Iago moves on to his next victim. By destroying Desdemona's reputation the villain will be able to destroy Othello's sanity, marriage and honour.

LOVE DEGRADED

The consummation of the marriage of Othello and Desdemona is interrupted by brawling and degraded by Iago's coarse discussion with Cassio about Desdemona. As a result the audience knows that their love is not secure. Ominously, Othello has to leave his marriage bed to deal with the fight. Iago makes a number of disrespectful comments about Desdemona. He focuses on her sexuality. She is 'sport for Jove' and 'full of game' (lines 17, 19). These are **images** of lust, not love. Cassio describes her attractions in a positive way: she

is 'fresh and delicate', 'modest', 'perfection' (lines 20, 23, 25). Shakespeare presents these two versions of Desdemona to foreshadow the choice Othello will have to make. Will he choose to believe his love is a faithful wife or a whore? Iago thinks it will be easy to destroy the marriage because Othello is 'so enfettered to her love' (line 340) that Desdemona can 'play the god/ With his weak function' (lines 342–3). There is disgust in these images. To Iago, love is weakness.

CHECK THE FILM **A04**

Compare different versions of the drinking scene. In the 1989 TV production starring Willard White and Ian McKellen, Iago prepares a potent punch, and leads the singing; but he does not force Cassio to drink. The drinking game is essentially good humoured and Cassio chooses to consume a lot of alcohol. In Oliver Parker's 1995 film, Cassio is reluctant to drink, and has to be prompted by Iago, who uses gestures and tone of voice to insinuate that Cassio is not a 'real man' if he fails to drink his share. Which version best reflects the words of the text?

GRADE BOOSTER **A02**

To get the best grades at AS and A2 you need to have an excellent understanding of the way in which Shakespeare uses language in *Othello*. One of the most important words in the play is 'think', which you will find is used in many ways. It is used here to reveal Iago's duplicity. Iago toys with Cassio when he says, '**I think you think I love you**' (line 306).

The portrayal of Iago demonstrates some of the Elizabethans' misunderstandings of the works of the Florentine writer, Niccolo Machiavelli (1469–1527). Today Machiavelli is respected as a political theorist, but Shakespeare and his contemporaries believed that his ideas were immoral. So they created stage **Machiavels** who were devious and unscrupulous.

STUDY FOCUS: OTHELLO'S ANGER A02

This scene is a turning point in the play. Othello's loss of temper is a sign that he is no longer master of himself. 'My blood begins my safer guides to rule' (line 201) he says, trying to discover the cause of the fight. Othello is ruled now by passion rather than judgement. His swift dismissal of Cassio is proof of this: 'never more be officer of mine' (line 245). Cassio doesn't get to defend himself. Othello also sounds vindictive. 'I'll make thee an example' (line 247) he says when he realises that Desdemona has been 'raised up' (line 246) by the brawl. Othello's **idiom** is changing. His measured style now includes oaths – 'Zounds' (line 203) – suggesting Othello's loss of control.

IAGO: STAGE DIRECTOR AND ACCOMPLISHED ACTOR

Iago directs this scene from the start. He skilfully manages a large cast of characters and the events which he has set in motion. A convincing actor, Iago also changes roles in order to manipulate his victims. He reassures Cassio that he must not give up hope, playing the part of friend and adviser. This is the same tactic he has used with Roderigo, who does exactly what he's told by Iago, entering and exiting on cue throughout Act II Scene 3. With Othello, Iago is an 'honest' (line 6) dependable soldier. We see the effectiveness of Iago's manipulation in the fact that at the start of the scene he acted under Cassio's orders, but by the end he is Othello's right-hand man.

RODERIGO: VICTIM OR VILLAIN?

Roderigo plays a minor role in *Othello*, but has a key part in this scene. Up to now he has been thematically significant as a failed lover. Now Roderigo is structurally important as Iago's first victim. He started the play a wealthy landowner, but has now spent most of his money and been 'exceedingly well cudgelled' in a fight (line 361). In some productions Roderigo is played for comedy, to contrast with Othello's tragic downfall. However, Roderigo's intentions and actions are villainous: he wants to cuckold Othello and helps to destroy Cassio's career. But everything Roderigo does is stage-managed by Iago, who tells him where to go, what to do, and when to do it. When Iago dismisses Roderigo at the end of the scene we see how insignificant he really is: 'Away, I say, thou shalt know more hereafter:/ Nay, get thee gone' (lines 376–7).

The visual imagery of Oliver Parker's 1995 film links Iago very explicitly to the devil. He covers his hands in soot when he speaks of the 'Divinity of hell' (line 345), and is seen against a dark background, with a fire burning nearby, on several occasions.

KEY QUOTATION: ACT I SCENE 3 A01

Iago is confident that he can manipulate Othello's thoughts. In his **soliloquy** he says: 'I'll pour this pestilence into his ear' (line 351).

- Iago uses the **imagery** of poison which fits his role as villain.
- Iago has confidence in his powers of verbal persuasion.
- Othello is to be the passive recipient of his 'pestilence'; Iago is in control.

GLOSSARY

51	**pottle-deep**	at the bottom of a 2 litre beer mug
61	**a rouse**	large amount of drink
65	**cannikin**	small drinking can
73	**potent in potting**	mighty drinkers
78	**Almain**	German
88	**lown**	lout
136	**ingraft**	deeply ingrained
150	**mazzard**	head
157	**Diablo, ho!**	what the devil!
202	**collied**	clouded

ACT III SCENES 1 AND 2

SUMMARY

- Cassio hires some musicians to serenade Othello and Desdemona, but Othello sends a clown to pay the musicians to leave.
- Iago says he will divert Othello's attention so that Cassio can speak to Desdemona alone and Emilia agrees to help.
- Othello sets out to inspect the fortifications in the town with Iago at his side.

ANALYSIS

EMILIA'S ROLE

Emilia is Iago's stooge (his puppet) in Scene 1. She comes on stage after Iago, suggesting that her movements and actions have been directed by him, and that she does what her husband tells her. Emilia's support for Cassio is appealing. However, we know that she is unknowingly helping her husband and not Cassio when she agrees to take him to speak to Desdemona. It is ominous and **ironic** that Emilia reports that Othello and Desdemona have already been discussing – perhaps even arguing about – Cassio.

STUDY FOCUS: OMINOUS IRONY — A02

There are two further ominous ironies in the first scene of Act III. In Shakespeare's *Twelfth Night* the nobleman Orsino calls music 'the food of love'. Here, like the previous night's brawl, the music intrudes on the private time for Othello and Desdemona. Othello's dislike of the music may also suggest he is a barbarian, since an appreciation of music was thought to be the sign of a civilised and cultured mind. There is another example of irony involving Iago. Cassio could not be more wrong about 'kind and honest' (line 41) Iago, who is working against Cassio in this scene. The audience might also see it as ironic that Iago talks openly to Cassio about deceiving Othello – 'I'll devise a mean to draw the Moor/ Out of the way' (lines 37–8) – in order to show how loyal he is to Cassio's cause. In Scene 2, Iago's deception continues as we see both Othello's and Desdemona's generous natures being abused. In the ominous clues they contain, therefore, the first two scenes of Act III prepare us for Iago's assault on Othello in Act III Scene 3, the central scene in the play.

REVISION FOCUS: TASK 4 — A02

How far do you agree with the following statements?

- Cassio is to blame for his own downfall.
- Emilia is partly to blame for Desdemona's fate.

Try writing opening paragraphs for essays based on these discussion points. Set out your arguments clearly, making specific references to the text.

GLOSSARY

III.1.23 **quillets** from 'quidlibet', a lawyer's verbal quibble

III.2.1 **pilot** captain

III.2.3 **works** fortifications

CHECK THE FILM — A04

In the 1989 film version of *Othello*, Ian McKellen's Iago is a man motivated by sexual jealousy. He is possessive of his wife, kissing and putting his arms around her when he arrives in Cyprus. He also watches Emilia's behaviour with Cassio closely. We can see why he might believe he has been deceived.

GRADE BOOSTER — A02

In order to show your understanding of Shakespeare's dramatic methods, you need to consider the way in which irony is used throughout *Othello*. How do the examples of the word 'honest' in Act III Scene 1 add to your understanding of Shakespeare's use of irony in the play?

ACT III SCENE 3

SUMMARY

- Desdemona pleads with Othello to reinstate Cassio.
- Iago poisons Othello's mind against Cassio, hinting that he has committed adultery with Desdemona, and Othello begins to doubt Desdemona's love and becomes jealous.
- Desdemona drops her handkerchief, which Emilia picks up and gives to Iago.
- Othello demands proof of Desdemona's adultery.
- Iago describes how Cassio called out for Desdemona in a dream and has been seen wiping his beard with the handkerchief.
- Othello asks Iago to kill Cassio and he promotes Iago.
- Othello intends to kill Desdemona.

CONTEXT   **A04**

During the Renaissance people believed that you could tell whether someone was good or evil by observing their outward appearance. For example, physical defects such as birthmarks could be proof that you were a witch. Because he looks honest, Iago is able to conceal his villainy.

ANALYSIS

THINKING, SEEING AND KNOWING

The **imagery** of thinking, seeing and knowing demonstrates how Iago poisons Othello's mind so effectively. Othello is first made suspicious when Iago draws attention to Cassio's exit early in the scene: 'I cannot think it/ That he would steal away so guilty-like/ Seeing you coming' (lines 38–40). Notice how Iago comments on what looks like physical evidence. He has started to interpret events for Othello, a tactic he uses repeatedly. By refusing to share his thoughts, Iago makes Othello desperate to know what they are. Othello's irritation builds, shown in the way his commands, which are at first simply direct ('Show me thy thought', line 119) become angry ('By heaven, I'll know thy thoughts!', line 164). Iago says he is reluctant to speak because his thoughts are 'vile and false' (line 139), leading Othello to assume the worst and jump to false conclusions.

Othello's false belief in Desdemona's treachery is also reflected in images of seeing and knowing. Othello says to Iago, 'If more thou dost perceive, let me know more' (line 243). Notice how Iago's perception is relied on, that there is evidence already and 'more' to find. We know that Othello's thoughts have been successfully infected when he asks Iago to 'set on thy wife to observe' Desdemona (line 244). Othello is no longer 'well tuned' with his wife, but with Iago. Iago even instructs Othello to spy on Desdemona, suggesting the villain's increasing power over his victim.

Othello's agony in the last part of the scene is reflected in images of seeing and knowing. He demands, 'What sense had I of her stolen hours of lust?/ I saw't not, thought it not' (lines 341–2). The final images that relate to seeing lead Othello to thoughts of murder. Iago wonders if Othello would like to witness Desdemona's adultery with Cassio. Iago makes the suggestion in the crudest and most graphic terms: 'Would you, the supervisor, grossly gape on?/ Behold her topped?' (lines 398–9). Earlier in the scene Othello was secure in his wife's love, declaring, 'she had eyes and chose me' (line 192). The once confident husband now believes he is a cuckold and has been deceived by his wife.

STUDY FOCUS: PROOF A02

Does Othello 'give in' to jealousy too easily? Perhaps not. Iago's 'proofs' are many, varied and plausible. Iago's reinterpretation of prior events is persuasive. Cassio was a go-between when Othello and Desdemona were courting, so he had an opportunity to get to know Desdemona. Desdemona deceived her father, so might well be deceiving Othello. Iago reminds Othello that he is a naive outsider who does not understand the 'country disposition' (line 204) of Venetians. Iago presents himself as an expert with superior knowledge about the behaviour of Italian women, implying that his judgement can be trusted. Iago points out that Desdemona rejected a number of suitable partners before marrying Othello. He suggests that it is only natural therefore that she should be 'recoiling to her better judgement' (line 240) and feeling attracted to Cassio. Iago also makes up compelling stories. Cassio's sexual dream is a fabrication, as is the tale of Cassio wiping his beard with the handkerchief. However, Iago's lies seem like truths because he has the handkerchief in his possession, 'ocular proof' to support his version of events (line 363).

LOVE AND WAR

Love becomes war in this scene. In Act I, Othello was under attack from Brabantio, but he had allies on the Venetian council, and was united with Desdemona. Now he is alone, and feels as if he is being assaulted from all sides. Desdemona blurs the boundaries between domestic and public life when she intercedes for Cassio, making Othello uncomfortable. **Ironically**, Othello does not want to hear his wife's words, and asks to be left alone,

suggesting that he is beginning to see Desdemona as an enemy rather than an ally. Equally ironically, just as Othello begins to feel at odds with Desdemona, Iago speaks to him using the language of love: 'My lord, you know I love you' (line 119). This scene is a battle between Desdemona's true love and Iago's false love. Because it is Iago whose voice Othello wishes to listen to, we know that true love will be defeated by false words.

Othello's words about love are troubling even before Iago's poison takes hold. When Desdemona leaves, Othello says, 'perdition catch my soul/ But I do love thee! and when I love thee not/ Chaos is come again' (lines 90–2). Othello is in the grip of emotions that he cannot handle, even before he becomes overwhelmed by jealousy. Is marriage proving too much for him? Notice the two negative abstract nouns that **foreshadow** tragedy: 'perdition' and 'Chaos'. It is ironic that Othello should use these words at this point in the play. By the end of this scene, Othello will be consumed by dark and chaotic thoughts, and he will be planning a murder which he fears will damn his soul.

STUDY FOCUS: A FALSE LOVE A04

The ritual that closes this scene shows that Iago's false 'love' has triumphed. Othello and Iago kneel and join together in the 'bloody business' (line 472) of revenge. Iago swears allegiance to 'wronged Othello's service' (line 470) in a **parody** of the wedding vow Desdemona made to Othello. There is a horrible irony here. Othello is now united with his enemy, as we know from his words to Iago, 'I am bound to thee for ever' (line 217). When Othello begins to discuss killing Desdemona, we know that the first battle in the war for his mind has been won.

CHECK THE FILM A04

In Oliver Parker's 1995 film, Iago is driven by malice, but there is also a definite suggestion of homoerotic love. When Iago delivers the line 'I am your own forever' (line 482), he embraces Othello tightly, and tears appear in his eyes. In the final scene, Othello fatally wounds Iago, who crawls onto the bed to lie at his dead general's feet, where he himself dies.

CONTEXT A04

Notice the way in which Iago raises the topic of 'Good name in man and woman' (line 158) before he reveals his 'suspicions' about Desdemona and Cassio. This reminds us of the importance of masculine honour in Renaissance society. A wife's chastity was part of her husband's honour. A woman's good name was important in Shakespeare's society. Court records for York *c.* 1600 show that 90 per cent of defamation cases involving female plaintiffs involved the woman's sexual reputation.

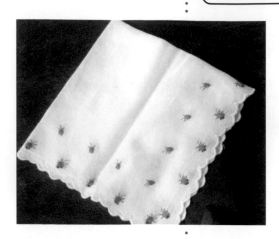

THE HANDKERCHIEF

The handkerchief plays an important role in this scene. In Desdemona's hands it is a symbol of love and faithfulness. Desdemona offers to bind Othello's aching head with it, showing wifely concern. However, Othello will not be comforted, and his rejection of the handkerchief is a sign that he is starting to reject Desdemona. In her anxiety, Desdemona does not realise that she has dropped her handkerchief, which is picked up by Emilia. Emilia informs us that the 'napkin' (line 294) was Desdemona's first gift from Othello and that Iago has been pestering her to steal it. Iago is delighted when Emilia gives him the handkerchief but refuses to tell her how he will use it. Now the handkerchief becomes a sinister object. In Iago's hands it is a symbol of abuse and the misuse of power. Iago won't give it back even when Emilia says that Desdemona will 'run mad' (line 321) when she realises it has gone. Later in the scene Iago turns the handkerchief into false proof of adultery. The love token then becomes a symbol of destruction.

GRADE BOOSTER **A02**

A close analysis of the way in which Shakespeare uses the handkerchief to create meaning would enable you to show your understanding of the dramatist's methods. If you referred to the cultural significance of handkerchiefs in the Renaissance, you would also score highly for AO4.

STUDY FOCUS: STRUCTURE AND PACE **A02**

This is a long scene but on stage it moves swiftly. The pace suits Iago. He needs his poison to work quickly. The pace and structure create a sense of claustrophobia: Othello enters and exits twice but, wherever he turns, he cannot escape Iago's foul words and his own foul thoughts. The way in which the dialogue is structured is significant. During most of the scene there is one-to-one dialogue between Othello and Iago, and Iago comes to dominate: he speaks more words and has more turns than Othello. We will notice how Iago and Othello finish each other's lines, showing that Othello is moving closer to Iago and away from Desdemona. The structure of this scene **mirrors** the structure of Act II Scene 3. In the earlier scene Iago used Roderigo as his stooge. Here the 'fall guy' is Desdemona. Roderigo was physically hurt. In this scene, Desdemona's reputation is wounded.

CONTEXT **A04**

Handkerchiefs were important signifiers of status and wealth in Renaissance Europe. Karen Newman relates the story of a fifteenth-century Venetian who was fined and sentenced to eighteen months' imprisonment after taking a lady's handkerchief. Newman says 'possession of a lady's handkerchief was considered proof of adultery' (see 'Femininity and the Monstrous in *Othello*', in Smith (ed.), *Shakespeare's Tragedies* (2004).)

SILENCE AND SUBMISSION

In this scene the female characters' voices are silenced. Neither Desdemona nor Emilia is listened to. Both submit to their husbands. Emilia gives Iago the handkerchief because he wants it. Her reluctant submission is a sign of danger to come. It **foreshadows** Emilia's silence about the handkerchief in Act III Scene 4, when she unwittingly propels Desdemona towards tragedy. Like Emilia, Desdemona does what she is told. She defends Cassio, but says to Othello before she leaves, 'Whate-er you be, I am obedient' (line 89). Desdemona's submission foreshadows the way in which she will accept responsibility for her own death.

WHAT MAKES OTHELLO VULNERABLE?

There are several reasons why Othello is vulnerable. Firstly, he is inexperienced in dealing with conflict in his private life, demonstrated by his uneasy exchanges with Desdemona. Othello's headache is a symbol of his discomfort. Secondly, as we know from Act II Scene 3, Othello is swift to anger. His resolution is a weakness now. 'No: to be once in doubt/ Is once to be resolved' he tells Iago (line 182). Such decisiveness makes Iago's evil work easier for him. Othello introduces the subject of Desdemona himself when he is warned in general terms about jealousy. Othello also sees things from extreme positions. Desdemona can only be a perfect, submissive wife or a 'whore'. 'She's gone, I am abused' he declares at line 271.

Valerie Traub has suggested that Othello is vulnerable because he internalises Iago's racist view of black men, which undermines his sense of self. In this scene, under Iago's influence, Othello starts to consider the differences between himself and Desdemona as problematic. Othello speaks of his weak merits as a husband. He is 'black ... declined/ Into the vale of years' (lines 267–70). The once confident lover, proud of his royal lineage, military career and fitness as a husband, is slowly being diminished.

OTHELLO THE REVENGER

The change from noble soldier and romantic hero to jealous revenger is signalled when Othello returns to the stage at line 332. Othello's words are increasingly violent, showing his degradation (see line 362), and Othello also grasps hold of Iago. This example of physical violence foreshadows the violence Othello will use against Desdemona. Othello says he does not know what to believe: 'I think my wife be honest, and think she is not' (line 387). However, the violent **images** he uses indicate that Iago is winning: he speaks of 'Poison, or fire, or suffocating streams' (line 392) and then begins to curse, 'Death and damnation! O!' (line 399). At this point Othello's speech begins to break down, signifying the disruption in his mind. The oaths are another example of the 'Iagoisation' of Othello's speech. Othello's words become more disjointed, his thoughts more wild and bloody (see lines 449–53 and 456–65). Othello's most arresting line is the ferocious, 'I'll tear her all to pieces!' (line 434). At the end of the scene Othello speaks like the villain of a **Jacobean revenge tragedy** when he says he will withdraw to 'furnish me with some swift means of death/ For the fair devil' (lines 480–1). Othello is a frightening figure at the end of Act III Scene 3.

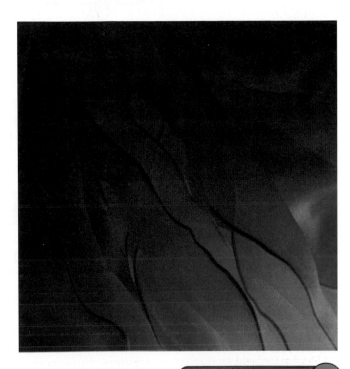

REVISION FOCUS: TASK 5 — A02

How far do you agree with the statements below?

- Othello poisons his own mind.
- Iago's jealousy is greater than Othello's.

Try writing opening paragraphs for essays based on these discussion points. Set out your arguments clearly.

GLOSSARY

24	**a shrift**	place of confession
126	**close delations**	secret thoughts that are shut up inside
143	**leets and law-days**	a leet was a local court of justice presided over by a magistrate
185	**exsufflicate**	puffed up or fly-blown
264	**haggard**	a hawking term; wild, untameable
265	**jesses**	straps on a hawk's legs, used to fasten the hawk to a leash on the falconer's wrist
269	**chamberers**	gallant courtiers; seduction is implied
333	**mandragora**	a sleep-inducing drug from the mandrake plant
349	**Pioneers**	the lowest rank of soldier
359	**Jove's dread clamours**	thunder
390	**Dian**	Diana, goddess of chastity
406	**prime**	lecherous, on heat
456	**Pontic sea**	the Black Sea
459	**Propontic**	Sea of Marmora, between the Black Sea and the Aegean
459	**Hellespont**	Dardanelles Straits

CRITICAL VIEWPOINT — A03

Caryl Phillips remarks that Othello's line 'she had eyes and chose me' reveals Othello's 'gross insecurity'. Do you agree? He also says that the 'fatal mistake' Othello makes is 'to question his own judgment'. Do you agree that this is the cause of Othello's downfall?

CONTEXT — A04

According to **Aristotle**, the tragic hero should not be entirely good or evil. Instead, he should possess a fatal flaw, which will incite pity and fear in the audience. Critics are divided about Othello. Some feel that he is a noble man brought down by a devil, while others think he is too easily moved to jealousy. Based on your reading of this scene, what do you think?

ACT III SCENE 4

SUMMARY

- Desdemona asks the clown to inform Cassio that she has pleaded for him.
- She is uneasy about losing the handkerchief.
- She tries again to promote Cassio's cause.
- Othello is angry with Desdemona because he believes she has lost the handkerchief.
- Cassio's mistress, Bianca, is annoyed with Cassio because he has not visited her recently and he gives Bianca Desdemona's handkerchief, saying he found it in his bedchamber.

ANALYSIS

DESDEMONA THE VICTIM

This unhappy scene focuses on Desdemona. She is not only her husband's and Iago's victim. Here she is also at the mercy of the clown, whose riddling shows how words can be misconstrued. Desdemona's powerlessness **mirrors** her position in the previous scene. In spite of her lies to Othello about the loss of the handkerchief, an audience is likely to sympathise with Desdemona. She is bullied by Othello but does not appreciate the danger she is in when she tries to return to the subject of Cassio. She is understandably alarmed by Othello's description of the handkerchief and his repeated requests to see it. We can understand Desdemona's falsehood here; surely she is simply seeking not to anger Othello further?

Desdemona is abused by Emilia and Cassio too. Emilia knows what happened to the handkerchief but fails to defend or help her mistress. In spite of knowing Othello is angry, Cassio selfishly accepts further offers of help from Desdemona. By the end of the scene we will feel that generous and true-hearted Desdemona is as troubled and isolated as Othello, but more vulnerable because she is a woman. Her vulnerability is indirectly alluded to in Emilia's **metaphor** about food. Emilia tells Desdemona that men soon tire of women: 'They are all but stomachs [appetites], and we all but food' (line 105). She adds that men 'eat us hungerly, and when they are full/ they belch us' (lines 106–7). This **image** of vomiting suggests the danger that Desdemona is in; she will be eaten up and destroyed.

STUDY FOCUS: LIARS AND DECEIVERS **A02**

The lies Iago told in the previous scene lead directly to the deceptions here, all of which are linked to the handkerchief. Othello interrogates Desdemona about it, but fails to share his suspicions openly. Instead, Othello tells what might be considered lies about the handkerchief in that the yarns he spins about the handkerchief's origins are contradictory. Desdemona also panics and resorts to lies, claiming she still has the handkerchief. Emilia lies when she says she does not know where it is. Bianca believes she has been deceived by Cassio when he gives her the handkerchief. Although he tells the truth about how he got it, Cassio is still deceitful. He sends Bianca away because he doesn't want to be seen 'womaned' (line 195). Yet Cassio is happy for Desdemona to work for him behind the scenes.

A MAGIC SYMBOL

The handkerchief is now loaded with ominous significance, and the whole plot hangs on it. It represents different things to different characters. To Othello the handkerchief symbolises Desdemona's honour. The mythic qualities that Othello endows it with represent the Moor himself. The 'magic in the web' (line 71) of the handkerchief represents the 'magic' of Othello's and Desdemona's marriage, which has been destroyed by Iago. For Desdemona the handkerchief is no longer a love token. Instead, it is a frightening object which is linked to discord. The strawberries woven into the handkerchief might represent Othello's passion, or Desdemona's blood, which will be spilt. For Emilia the handkerchief is a test of her loyalty. She has chosen her husband over Desdemona. Cassio treats the handkerchief as carelessly as he treats Bianca. It is a symbol of how Cassio is a user and abuser of women, not unlike Iago. For Iago, the handkerchief is a symbol of his evil power.

JEALOUSY

Emilia introduces the subject of Othello's jealousy. Her comments enable us to appreciate how much faith Desdemona has in Othello. We learn that we can rely on Emilia's judgement, in spite of her lies. Emilia rightly guesses that Othello is eaten up with jealousy which she defines as 'a monster/ Begot upon itself, born on itself' (lines 161–2). In succeeding scenes we will see how true these words are. The exchange between Cassio and Bianca shows us another example of amorous jealousy. Like Desdemona, Bianca has to be satisfied with the treatment she receives from the man she loves; she is powerless to change or direct Cassio. Notice the way in which repetition of the word 'jealous', a noticeable feature of the previous scene, is replaced by repetition of the word 'angry'. Iago's triumph is emphasised by his references to Othello's anger (lines 133, 135, 138). Iago has the power to control the hero's moods now. Othello's anger is a result of his growing jealousy. Arguably, all of the jealousy we see here can be traced back to Iago's jealousy of Cassio and Othello.

CONTEXT A04

Critics have compared Othello to characters who appear in the Romance genre. His wooing of Desdemona with fantastic tales of his past and his travels and, in this scene, his insistence on the magical properties of the handkerchief suggest this. Shakespeare was to write several Romances at the end of his career: *Pericles*, *Cymbeline*, *The Winter's Tale* and *The Tempest*.

GRADE BOOSTER A02

Shakespeare uses the dramatic technique of mirroring in *Othello* to create contrasts and cohesion within the play. Watch out for examples of mirrored events and scenes which you can comment on to demonstrate your understanding of structure and themes for AO2. Here you might consider Bianca's jealousy and anger, and how they mirror Othello's.

KEY QUOTATION: ACT III SCENE 4 A01

Othello asks Desdemona to give him her hand. He says, 'Give me your hand. This hand is moist, my lady' (line 36).

- This command shows Othello physically marking the beginning of his interrogation of Desdemona.
- Othello sees the moistness of Desdemona's hand as proof of her lechery.
- Othello's 'palm reading' can be linked to his pagan ancestry, revealing that he is moving away from the Christian values he adopted. Shakespeare is **foreshadowing** Othello's comments about the magic qualities of the handkerchief.
- Othello will use his hands to kill Desdemona.

GLOSSARY

16	**catechize**	teach by question and answer the principles of the Christian religion
26	**crusadoes**	currency from Portugal, coins which were stamped with Christ's cross
72	**sibyl**	prophetess
76	**mummy**	a fluid derived from bodies that had been embalmed, used for magical or medicinal purposes
202	**be circumstanced**	give in to circumstances or accept things the way they are

ACT IV SCENE 1

SUMMARY

- Iago torments Othello with crude **images** of Desdemona's infidelity and references to the handkerchief, leading to Othello falling down in a fit.
- Iago tells Othello to withdraw so that he can have a conversation with Cassio, and he questions Cassio about Bianca.
- Seeing Desdemona's handkerchief in Bianca's hand and believing Desdemona must have given it to Cassio as a love token, Othello vows to murder his wife.
- Venetian visitors bring news that Cassio is to replace Othello.
- Othello strikes Desdemona.

ANALYSIS

VIOLENCE AND MADNESS

This scene is one of verbal and physical violence, **foreshadowing** the end of the play. Othello gradually becomes overwhelmed by violent thoughts. When Othello falls down in a violent fit, Iago's description of him makes Othello sound like a wild beast. Othello's first thought after spying on Cassio is violent: 'How shall I murder him, Iago' (line 167). He says he would like Cassio to endure an agonising death. The conversation moves to methods of murdering Desdemona. Two come from Othello. He will 'chop her into messes' (line 196) or poison her. Iago suggests strangulation. Is it a sign of madness that Othello accepts this suggestion as 'justice' (line 206)? The verbal violence leads to physical violence as Othello strikes Desdemona. Foreshadowing her grace and dignity in death, she responds passively: 'I will not stay to offend you' (line 246).

STUDY FOCUS: IAGO IN CONTROL A02

Iago controls Othello completely. There is **irony** in his reference to his poisoning as 'medicine' (line 45). Iago's methods are a sadistic repetition of those he used in Act III Scene 3. Iago commands Othello's imagination, conjuring up distressing images of infidelity. He plays devil's advocate when he suggests that Desdemona's honour is hers to give away as she chooses. Iago keeps Othello focused on the handkerchief. Eventually he brings on Othello's fit when he jests about Cassio in Desdemona's bed, 'With her, on her, what you will' (line 34). The casual brutality of these words shows how much Iago enjoys his power. Notice that Iago uses Othello's name when he is in his trance. The villain no longer speaks to his victim with respect.

IAGO'S REVENGE

Iago's control extends to Cassio in their crude discussion about Bianca. Watching this 'play within a play' is uncomfortable. Every word Cassio speaks is infected with Iago's crude world view. Iago is so much the master of events that he even chooses how Desdemona dies when he next speaks to Othello. Iago says it will be best to strangle her in the bed she has 'contaminated' (line 205). There is a horrible irony in Iago, who is the source of infection in this play, using this word. But why does Iago want Desdemona and Cassio dead? It is not simple sadism. They must die before Othello decides to question them. In Act III Scene 3, Othello threatened Iago with death – 'woe upon thy life!' (line 369) – if he could not prove Desdemona to be a whore. Iago's choice of strangulation for Desdemona suits the manipulator's **characterisation**. By having her smothered in her marriage bed Iago is replacing the loving ritual of consummation with a cruel ritual of strangulation.

OTHELLO'S DEGRADATION

Othello's fit is a symbol of his degradation. He is degraded by Iago, but he also degrades himself. His speech style and use of imagery reflect this. Many of Othello's speeches are full of disjointed sentence structures. It is also noticeable that later in the scene Othello uses **prose**, signalling his debasement. Early on, when he is tormented by a theoretical discussion about whether it is possible for man and woman to be 'Naked in bed … and not mean harm' (line 5), Othello uses Christian imagery: 'The devil their virtue tempts, and they tempt heaven' (line 8). Later he speaks of Desdemona being 'damned tonight' (lines 178–9). Othello still has a moral code. However, his speeches are also full of savagery and egotism. 'I will chop her into messes! Cuckold me!' he roars (line 197). The final words he barks at Desdemona are brutal: 'Hence, avaunt!' (line 260).

Othello's degradation is also signified by the way he follows Iago's commands. He becomes Iago's puppet. We will remember how Iago controlled Roderigo's entrances and exits when Othello is set to spy on Cassio. During Iago's play within the play Othello is a pathetic bystander, making helpless comments: 'Look how he laughs already!' (line 110). His lines show how he has been reduced: 'So, so, so, so: they laugh that win' (line 123). This gloating is worthy of Iago. However, the audience knows that it is Iago who will have the last laugh, not Othello.

In spite of the verbal violence, there is much **pathos** in this scene. We sense Othello's pain as he works up to killing Desdemona. He cannot bear the loss of his 'sweet woman' (line 176). Consider this key line: 'But yet the pity of it, Iago – O, Iago, the pity of it, Iago!' (lines 192–3). Othello is torn between thoughts of his wife's sweetness and her treachery. This battle continues for some time, and even after he has decided to kill her 'this night', Othello is worried that Desdemona's 'body and beauty' will 'unprovide my mind again' (lines 202–3).

Further degradation occurs after the Venetian visitors arrive. Othello slips quickly into oaths and savagery. 'Fire and brimstone!' (line 233) he exclaims when he discovers he is to be replaced as governor of Cyprus by Cassio. It seems as if Cassio has supplanted Othello not only in his bed, but also in his military role. We know that Othello has reached rock bottom and destroyed his honour when he strikes Desdemona. This shameful act humiliates everyone. Othello's rude treatment of Lodovico in accusing him of wanting to sleep with Desdemona also reveals how far the hero has fallen (see line 252). His exit line, 'Goats and monkeys!' (line 263), is a long way from the eloquent rhetoric of Act I.

KEY QUOTATION: ACT IV SCENE 1 — A01

Iago torments Othello about the handkerchief. Othello wishes he could forget it: 'O, it comes o'er my memory/ As doth the raven o'er the infectious house' (lines 20–1).

- The plague reference reminds us that Iago is still infecting Othello with poison.
- Notice how passive Othello is; the sentence structure suggests his mind is being acted upon. He is no longer in control of his thoughts.
- Croaking ravens were thought to be birds of ill omen.

GLOSSARY

37	**fulsome**	nauseating, sickening
76	**Confine yourself but in a patient list**	restrain yourself
87	**to cope**	to encounter or copulate with
109	**caitiff**	wretch
145	**fitchew**	polecat (an animal with a strong, musky smell thought to be lecherous) – a derogatory way of referring to Bianca
153	**hobby-horse**	a loose woman

CHECK THE FILM A04

In Oliver Parker's 1995 film, Iago's control of Othello is demonstrated when the ensign locks his master behind bars. It is from this cell that Othello overlooks Iago's conversation with Cassio. The camera occasionally offers the audience Othello's view of events, framed by the bars. We can see how trapped and powerless he is.

CHECK THE BOOK A03

For a discussion of the importance of the handkerchief and its qualities, see Robert B. Heilman's *Magic in the Web: Action and Language in 'Othello'* (1956).

ACT IV SCENE 2

SUMMARY

- Othello questions Emilia but does not believe her when she says Desdemona is true to him.
- Othello confronts Desdemona, trying to get her to confess she has committed adultery, but Desdemona defends her honour.
- Believing that she has assisted Desdemona in her wantonness, Othello offers Emilia money and leaves in disgust.
- Desdemona appeals to Iago for help.
- Iago persuades Roderigo to help in his plot to kill Cassio.

ANALYSIS

OTHELLO'S WAR WITH HIMSELF

Othello's struggle to reconcile the warring emotions of love and jealousy is dramatised through his use of contrasting **images** in this scene. Othello says that 'The fountain' (line 60) of his pure love has been polluted, becoming 'a cistern, for foul toads/ To knot and gender [copulate] in' (lines 62–3). Turning to Desdemona, Othello wonders how she can look so 'lovely fair' while being a 'weed' (line 68). Othello now looks 'grim as hell' (line 65) when faced with the 'rose-lipped cherubin' Desdemona (line 64). These images suggest how much under Iago's influence Othello is. His repetition of the words 'whore' and 'strumpet' indicates how far Othello is removed from the noble hero of the first two acts, even if he still speaks poetically and with a measured tone at times (see lines 48–65). Othello's speech is infected by vile images even when he is eloquent. The insults he offers Desdemona and Emilia as he leaves make it hard to view Othello with much sympathy at this moment. He is a verbal as well as a physical bully.

Yet an audience must sympathise. Desdemona's presence is painful to Othello. When Desdemona defends herself he tries – rather weakly – to send her away. As he leaves he speaks to her contemptuously: 'I cry you mercy then,/ I took you for that cunning whore of Venice/ That married with Othello' (lines 90–2). Notice the way in which Othello dramatises himself using the third person. What is happening is so painful that he has to distance himself from what he is saying. This helps Othello to justify his words and actions. We will see this tendency again later in Act V.

The word 'whore' was the most common term of abuse used to insult women in seventeenth-century England. The word had multiple meanings. For example, it could be used to refer to a professional courtesan or a woman who was dissolute and of bad character.

STUDY FOCUS: TRUTH AND LIES **A02**

Iago has abused the word 'honest' so much that no other character can use it without suspicion falling on them. Both women insist Desdemona is 'honest' and are denounced as liars. We see how far Othello has sunk when he fails to believe either Desdemona or Emilia. They both tell the truth and are abused for it. Emilia's role is similar to Iago's in Act I. However, Emilia is a true rather than a false servant. She defends Desdemona's honour. She is absolutely correct that an 'eternal villain' has slandered her mistress (line 132). For her truthful, plain speaking Emilia is paid off as if she were a brothel keeper. For her honesty, Desdemona is called a whore. Iago has infected Othello so successfully that he misconstrues every true word he hears. Othello turns the truth into lies in this scene.

THE TRIAL OF DESDEMONA

If Othello is suffering, so is his wife. Desdemona is put on trial in this scene. She has become a figure of great **pathos**. It is horribly **ironic** that Desdemona kneels first to Othello, the man who will destroy her physically, and then to Iago, the man who has destroyed her reputation. Desdemona is bewildered by her husband's treatment of her. She asks, 'What horrible fancy's this?' (line 27), revealing how scared she is of Othello. Desdemona tells him plaintively, 'I understand a fury in your words/ But not the words' (lines 32–3). Her words show that Desdemona and Othello no longer 'speak the same language'.

Desdemona's speeches emphasise her innocence and misery. She asks what 'ignorant sin' she has committed (line 71). She says she's 'a child to chiding' (line 116) and cannot bring herself to use the word 'whore'. Notice Desdemona's humility and generosity in this scene. She does not say that Othello is wrong to chide her, just that he could have done it 'with gentle means' (line 114). Desdemona says earnestly that she still loves Othello and will continue to do so however unkindly he treats her; she still calls Othello 'my noble lord' (line 66) and looks for excuses for his behaviour. Desdemona hopes to 'to win my lord again' (line 151), but we know she cannot win because the person she asks to help her (Iago) is – ironically – her deadly enemy.

KEY QUOTATION: ACT IV SCENE 2 — A01

Emilia castigates Othello for believing Desdemona is false. She says, 'Remove your thought, it doth abuse your bosom' (line 14).

- Emilia's open defence of Desdemona prepares us for the role she will play in Act V Scene 2 when she reveals Othello's crime.
- Emilia's disapproval reminds us how far Othello has fallen.
- Ironically, Emilia does not realise Othello's thoughts have been abused – by Iago.

REVISION FOCUS: TASK 6 — A02

How far do you agree with the statements below?

- It is impossible to sympathise with Othello when he bullies Desdemona.
- Desdemona's enduring love for Othello is unconvincing for a modern audience.

Try writing opening paragraphs for essays based on these discussion points. Set out your arguments clearly.

GLOSSARY

28	**procreants**	sexual partners
62	**cistern**	cesspool
123	**callat**	abusive term for a woman
130	**Beshrew**	curse, castigate
134	**cogging**	cheating
177	**doff'st**	put or fob off
190	**votarist**	a nun
196	**fopped**	fooled, duped
229	**determinate**	effective, decisive

GRADE BOOSTER — A04

To get the best possible grades at AS and A2 you need to incorporate critics' views. You could use a critic's view to introduce your own point of view, such as: 'Many critics, including Leavis, perceive Othello's **hamartia** as jealousy. While I agree that Othello becomes jealous, it can be argued that there are other factors that lead to his tragic end, for example pride and naivety.'

CRITICAL VIEWPOINT — A03

G. K. Hunter has said that *Othello* becomes 'a tragedy of the loss of faith'. Do you agree with this assessment? Is loss of faith the cause of Othello's downfall?

CHECK THE BOOK — A03

For comments about the female characters as victims, see Lisa Jardine's chapter on *Othello* in *Still Harping on Daughters* (1983).

ACT IV SCENE 3

SUMMARY

- Othello sends Desdemona to prepare for bed.
- Emilia says she wishes Desdemona had never met Othello, but Desdemona says she still loves her husband.
- Desdemona is unable to dismiss a melancholy song from her mind and sings it.
- The women discuss female infidelity.

ANALYSIS

TWO WIVES

In this scene, the audience is invited to compare the two female characters and their views about men and love. Like her husband, Desdemona is a romantic. Love means everything to her. Now that she believes she no longer has Othello's love, she is lost and melancholy. Desdemona seems unworldly, especially compared with the down-to-earth Emilia. But this is appropriate. Shakespeare is emphasising Desdemona's innocence and the lost romance of her marriage.

Like her husband, Iago, Emilia has a cynical view of human relationships and has a pragmatic approach to sin. Unlike Desdemona, who cannot believe that women can ever be unfaithful to their husbands, Emilia suggests adultery is a 'small vice' (line 69). However, we know Emilia is actually a virtuous woman because she says she would not commit adultery for 'a joint-ring' (a promise of marriage, line 72). In Renaissance society, the wedding ring was a symbol not just of marriage, but also of the wife's chastity, reminding us of the double standards of Shakespeare's time, when codes of sexual conduct for men and women were very different. Emilia takes chastity seriously, as her outrage at Othello's accusations against Desdemona show. It is important that we see Emilia as a virtuous woman if she is to be Desdemona's defender after death. It is appropriate that a woman accuses and condemns Desdemona's masculine abusers.

Emilia offers a realistic – if rather pessimistic – description of marriage. Many of her ideas will strike a chord with a modern audience used to gender equality. It may seem strange that Shakespeare gives so much time to a discussion of sexual politics in a scene which is a pre-death ritual, but giving Emilia a powerful voice in this scene is dramatically significant. Emilia is to become the voice of the audience. She will express the audience's horror in Act V when Othello's crime and Iago's lies are revealed. The audience will contrast the relationship between Desdemona and Emilia with the relationship between Othello and Iago. Unlike Iago, Emilia is a true servant who works hard to support her mistress.

STUDY FOCUS: BAD OMENS

A02

There are several bad omens in this scene. Desdemona is engaged in the ritual of undressing, but instead of preparing for her wedding night, she is preparing for her death bed. Desdemona is full of foreboding. She mentions winding sheets, her eyes itch, she is drawn to Barbary's melancholy song of death. Her lines often seem fatalistic. She says, 'All's one … how foolish are our minds!' (line 21). It does not matter ('all's one') what she does, she cannot change Othello's 'foolish' mind about her. Barbary's song contains references to two trees which are ominous. In *Romeo and Juliet*, Romeo is found wandering in a sycamore grove, suggesting the tree can be associated with forsaken love. In west Scotland sycamores were planted for a sinister purpose. The barons used them to hang their enemies from. The willow was a more traditional symbol for lost or unrequited love.

CHECK THE FILM **A04**

In the 1981 BBC TV production of *Othello*, Penelope Wilton who plays Desdemona seems to have a strong sense of foreboding about her death in this scene. She sits at a dressing table, on which is placed a skull, a Death's Head. In Elizabethan England the Death's Head was a symbol of mortality and melancholy, and was also associated with sexual adventurers and prostitutes.

GRADE BOOSTER **A03**

If you are writing about the theme of love, consider Desdemona's request to Emilia: 'Lay on my bed my wedding sheets' (line 107). Is the heroine preparing to die for love? Or is Desdemona simply trying to win back Othello's love by reminding him of his wedding night? For a high grade at AS and A2 you need to consider alternative views of the text.

THE WILLOW SONG AND WEEPING

Othello and Desdemona have been driven to tears in Act IV. Both have wept – unwittingly – because of Iago's evil influence. Othello has been in mourning for his marriage and his own and his wife's lost innocence. Desdemona has wept because she has lost her love. The mind of Othello has been destroyed and Desdemona is shortly to be tortured, her life snuffed out. It is therefore fitting that the play should be structured so that this quiet scene of sorrow, punctuated by the melancholy willow song, should come at this point. The willow song expresses the meaning of Desdemona's name (ill-starred) and **foreshadows** her terrible fate.

Desdemona's mother had a maid, Barbary, who died singing the willow song which 'expressed her fortune' (line 27). There are clear parallels here with Desdemona. The words of the song refer to accusations of unfaithfulness, reminding us of the heroine's terrible predicament. In the willow song the 'poor soul' sits weeping by the water (line 39). She is able to soften the stones in the 'fresh streams' (line 43). However, unlike the woman in the song, Desdemona has been unable to soften Othello's hard heart with her tears. We learn that the woman in the song 'murmured her moans' (line 43) as she lay by the water. Desdemona will murmur and moan on her death bed as she lies dying.

REVISION FOCUS: TASK 7   A02

How far do you agree with the statements below?

● It is impossible to sympathise with Othello in Act IV.

● Desdemona's love is too passive and she is too much the victim.

Try writing opening paragraphs for essays based on these discussion points. Set out your arguments clearly.

GLOSSARY

10	**incontinent**	immediately
72	**a joint-ring**	a ring made of two separate parts
72	**lawn**	a fine linen fabric
73	**exhibition**	offer, allowance, gift

GRADE BOOSTER   A02

There are strong undercurrents beneath the surface of *Othello* and unlocking Shakespeare's use of symbols and **metaphors** is key to appreciating the play's meanings. The willow song and the handkerchief are obviously key symbols. Watch out for other symbols that you can link to these and comment on.

CONTEXT   A04

In Shakespeare's *Hamlet*, the tragic heroine, Ophelia, like Barbary, goes mad when her lover Hamlet rejects her. Ophelia drowns, having fallen out of a willow tree into the water when the branch she was sitting on broke. Love and madness are often linked together in Renaissance drama.

ACT V SCENE 1

SUMMARY

- Following Iago's instructions, Roderigo tries to wound Cassio but instead Roderigo is wounded by Cassio.
- As Iago steps in and stabs Cassio in the leg, Othello hears cries, believes Cassio has been killed, and is spurred on to his own revenge.
- Lodovico and Gratiano come out when they hear the commotion and attend to the wounded Cassio.
- Iago kills Roderigo.
- Bianca appears. Iago accuses her of involvement in a plot to kill Cassio.
- Roderigo's body is discovered and Iago sends Emilia to inform Othello and Desdemona of what has happened.

ANALYSIS

IAGO IMPROVISES

As in the first scene of the play, we are in a street at night when the action of Act V begins. Iago still seems to be in control, in spite of Roderigo's uneasiness about killing Cassio. The **image** Iago uses to describe Roderigo at line 11 reminds us of the villain's arrogance. Roderigo is simply a 'young quat' (pimple or boil, line 11). And when Iago has finished with Roderigo, 'he must die' (line 22). Iago's ruthlessness and lack of respect for human life prepare us for the violence and brutality of Act V. This scene **mirrors** two others. The confusion and mistaken identities remind us of the storm scene. The street brawling recalls the drunken fight between Cassio and Roderigo on the night of the wedding celebrations. On all three occasions, Iago got the result he wanted. Will he succeed again?

There are signs that Iago will prevail. The action moves swiftly, making a marked contrast with the previous scene. We know that Iago needs events to unfold rapidly if his treachery is to remain hidden. However, Iago is forced to become personally involved in the action, wounding Cassio in an underhand way when Roderigo fails to hit his target. But we see Iago's mastery of the situation when he stabs Roderigo. The violent death of Desdemona's failed suitor **foreshadows** the deaths of much nobler victims in the final scene.

CHECK THE FILM **A04**

In Oliver Parker's 1995 film, Michael Maloney's Roderigo is seen suffering horribly after he is stabbed by Iago. He is gagging on his own blood as he dies. It is visually very clear that he is Iago's victim.

IAGO'S MOTIVES

What motives does Iago offer us in this scene? He has two reasons for wanting Cassio murdered. Firstly, Cassio 'hath a daily beauty in his life/ That makes me ugly' (lines 19–20). Iago cannot bear human virtue in any form and seeks to destroy it. This is a psychological motive. Secondly, Iago needs to kill Cassio for practical reasons. Othello may 'unfold' him to Cassio (line 21). Iago's security is threatened. In spite of his assurance, Iago's urgent final **aside** indicates the danger he is in. Iago repeats an idea that he expressed at the beginning of the scene (see lines 4 and 128–9). The events of this night will make or mar his fortunes. It is appropriate that Iago should use the language of gambling. It might be argued that Iago's closing lines should be delivered in an exultant tone. Even at this critical moment the villain relishes his own evil.

STUDY FOCUS: SETTINGS A04

You need to demonstrate a good understanding of the way in which settings are used for AO4 (Context). For example, you could choose to look at the ways in which the night-time settings for the opening and closing scenes of the play mirror each other, and comment on the dramatic significance of these settings – the street in Venice and the bedroom in Cyprus.

OTHELLO THE AUTOMATON

Othello is little more than an automaton in this scene. Yet again he is an onlooker who fails to see the truth. **Ironically**, it is a misunderstanding that spurs Othello on to his own act of violence. He believes 'brave … honest and just' (line 31) Iago has killed Cassio. It is horrible that Othello acts in direct response to the treacherous example he believes has been set by Iago. Shakespeare is linking Othello's murder of Desdemona with Iago's cowardly wounding of Cassio. Othello's language also links him with the atmosphere of treachery: Othello speaks of blood and lust, blotches and stains. Othello's violent words foreshadow his violent deeds. He talks like a villain, announcing his evil intentions in a dramatic way: 'strumpet, I come' (line 33). But Othello is not taking responsibility for his actions, claiming it is Desdemona's 'unblest fate' that he is fulfilling (line 33). Othello's melodramatic speech style detracts from his heroism but also reminds us how completely his mind has been corrupted by Iago.

STUDY FOCUS: BIANCA THE VICTIM A02

Shakespeare uses Bianca to keep Desdemona in our minds in this scene. Bianca's love for Cassio is honest, but she suffers for it. Like Desdemona before her, she tries to defend herself, but fails to make her voice heard. The way in which Bianca is abused and suffers mirrors Desdemona's downfall. Here Bianca is in danger because of her love for Cassio. By the end of this scene she is falsely suspected of being involved in a murder plot. We could argue that love makes women helpless victims in *Othello*.

KEY QUOTATION: ACT V SCENE 1 A01

Roderigo is the first to recognise Iago's villainy. His dying words are 'O damned Iago! O inhuman dog!' (line 62).

- Iago has used animal imagery to his own advantage and is now recognised as a villain using similar language.

- Imagery of dogs reminds us of how Iago's inhumanity has dehumanised Othello.

- Ironically, Roderigo sees the truth too late, just like Othello.

GLOSSARY

1	**bulk**	stall, shop or a projected part of a building
16	**bobbed**	swindled
54	**spoiled**	hurt, finished
78	**mangled**	wounded

CONTEXT A04

The language Othello uses when he prepares to kill Desdemona is violent and bloody. During Acts IV and V, Othello sometimes sounds like a villain in a **revenge tragedy**. Does this prevent an audience from sympathising with him?

ACT V SCENE 2

SUMMARY

- As Desdemona sleeps in her room, Othello explains he will kill her, then kisses her, thus waking her.
- Desdemona weeps when Othello tells her Cassio is dead and, believing Desdemona loved Cassio, Othello smothers her.
- Emilia is horrified when Desdemona revives briefly and says she caused her own death.
- After Othello explains why he killed Desdemona, Emilia insults him and summons Montano, Gratiano and Iago.
- Iago denies Emilia's accusations of villainy, stabs her and leaves her to die on the bed next to Desdemona.
- Guards return with Iago; Othello wounds him but Iago will not explain his actions.
- Iago's plots are revealed and, realising his folly, Othello kills himself.

ANALYSIS

DEATH

There are three violent deaths in this scene: of Desdemona, Othello and Emilia. There are other 'deaths' too, most notably the death of Othello's reputation. The 'valiant Moor' destroys his good name when he murders Desdemona. Othello's suicide is both retribution and rehabilitation. Othello is destroying the villain he has proved to be, while at the same time trying to resurrect his reputation. Desdemona tries to preserve Othello's good name when she says that she is responsible for her own death. However, Emilia's voice prevails. She insults Othello in language which is racist: 'most filthy bargain', 'As ignorant as dirt' (lines 153, 160). Emilia is correct in her allocation of blame for the death of Desdemona: Othello has proved to be a bad bargain as a husband. The reference to Brabantio's death from grief reinforces this idea. The other fitting 'death' is Iago's unmasking as a villain. Desdemona's and Emilia's sacrificial deaths are clearly undeserved. However, their reputations are enhanced when they die. In death, Desdemona and Emilia prove their honesty and loyalty.

STUDY FOCUS: JUSTICE · A02

Othello uses the language of justice and the law to justify killing Desdemona ('it is the cause', line 1) and demands that she 'deny each article' (line 54) of his accusations before he smothers her. When he realises the truth, Othello takes justice into his own hands and commits suicide. This is **poetic justice**: he kills himself with the sword he used to kill enemies of the Venetian state, which is what Othello proved to be when he took the life of Desdemona. Iago gets his just deserts when his villainy is revealed by Emilia. It is appropriate that one of the women he treated so badly causes his downfall. It is also fitting that Cassio, whom Iago sought to destroy, will be responsible for Iago's torture. But Iago gets away with a great injustice when he refuses to explain himself.

TRAGIC IMAGERY

The tragedy of Desdemona's death is heightened by references to light and religion. These allusions are ominous in the first part of the scene and emphasise the enormity of Othello's crime. Othello enters carrying a light, which **ironically** makes him seem like a priest officiating at a religious ritual. Othello speaks about the 'heavenly' (line 21) sorrow he

CRITICAL VIEWPOINT · A03

In her essay 'The Noble Moor' (1956), Helen Gardner sees the murder of Desdemona as having upon it 'the stamp of the heroic'. Gardner says: 'The act is heroic because Othello acts from inner necessity … The act is also heroic in its absoluteness, disinterestedness, and finality … It must be done.' Do you view Desdemona's murder as heroic? Why 'must' it be done?

CHECK THE BOOK · A03

For a discussion of Iago as an example of supreme, satanic evil, see A. C. Bradley's *Shakespearean Tragedy* (1992 edition).

feels, suggesting he is reluctant to begin the ceremony of death. He repeats the word 'light' several times as he prepares to kill: 'once put out thy light … I know not where is that Promethean heat/ That can thy light relume' (lines 10–13). The words Othello uses to describe Desdemona's body can be linked to the **imagery** of light as her paleness suggests her innocent purity (lines 4–5). Even before she is dead, however, Othello sees her as a funeral monument. When she wakes Othello urges Desdemona to pray because he does not want to 'kill they unprepared spirit … I would not kill thy soul' (lines 31–2). Still obsessed with his masculine reputation, Othello wants to be 'an honourable murderer' (line 291).

When he confronts his crime, Othello again uses religious imagery, but he no longer uses it to justify his actions. Instead he invites God's punishment. Othello addresses Desdemona's dead body: 'When we shall meet at compt [the Day of Judgement]/ This look of thine will hurl my soul from heaven/ And fiends will snatch at it' (lines 271–3). Othello is tortured by what he has done and recognises his guilt: 'Whip me, ye devils,/ From the possession of this heavenly sight!' (lines 275–6). He believes he deserves the torments of hell.

LOVE AND SELF-LOVE

While the constancy of the women's love heightens the tragedy of Desdemona's death, the male characters do not emerge so well from this scene. Othello and Iago can both be accused of excessive self-love. Determined to preserve himself, Iago kills Emilia to silence her. His final lines are gloating and selfish: 'Demand me nothing. What you know, you know./ From this time forth I never will speak word' (lines 300–1). Iago's silence is as cruel as his poisonous words have been and in keeping with the villain's egotism.

We may judge Othello less harshly than we judge Iago. Othello still loves Desdemona. He weeps and kisses her before he smothers her. But his self-love will not allow her to live. Othello insists that he has done nothing 'in hate, but all in honour' (line 292). Throughout the play Othello has been torn between his love for Desdemona, and his regard for his own honour. It is perhaps a combination of overwhelming love for Desdemona and self-love that made his jealousy so extreme. Othello himself says he was 'one that loved not wisely, but too well' (line 342). Unlike the villain, Othello atones for his excessive self-love by destroying himself. Like Desdemona, Othello's last words and actions are loving: 'I kissed thee ere I killed thee: no way but this,/ Killing myself, to die upon a kiss' (lines 356–7). By linking kissing and killing, Othello is suggesting that he cannot live without Desdemona. Cassio's description of Othello is a fitting epitaph. Othello was 'great of heart' (line 359).

REVISION FOCUS: TASK 8   A03

How far do you agree with the statements below?

- Othello's tragedy was that he loved too much.
- Iago's silence is as powerful as his speech.

Try writing opening paragraphs for essays based on these discussion points. Set out your arguments clearly.

GLOSSARY

112	**Promethean heat**	in Greek mythology Prometheus brought life-giving fire to men from Heaven
141	**chrysolite**	topaz
245	**the swan**	it was believed that swans sang before they died
251	**the ice-brook's temper**	a fine Spanish sword, a sword tempered by plunging it into icy water
265	**butt**	target
266	**sea-mark**	beacon or landmark to sail by
283	**I look down towards his feet**	an allusion to the idea that the Devil had cloven hoofs

---

CRITICAL VIEWPOINT   A04

The philosopher Stanley Cavell asserts that Othello's opening speech in Act V Scene 2 is 'part of a ritual of denial'. Do you agree? Does Othello deny he is responsible for his actions?

GRADE BOOSTER   A02

If you are asked to write about the ending of *Othello*, you should consider the dramatic methods Shakespeare uses to ensure Act V Scene 2 is an effective ending to the play as a **tragedy**. For example, you could write about the imagery Shakespeare uses and the language of Othello's final speeches.

CRITICAL VIEWPOINT   A03

Dr Johnson found Act V Scene 2 so moving as to be unendurable. What aspects of the scene do you find moving?

EXTENDED COMMENTARY

ACT V SCENE 2 LINES 222–79

CHECK THE BOOK A03

For comments on Act V Scene 2, in a section called 'The Final Act', see John Russell Brown's *Shakespeare: The Tragedies* (2001).

CHECK THE FILM A04

Othello's fall from grace is conveyed in the final scenes of Oliver Parker's 1995 film when he appears in a black shirt and trousers. All the other male characters wear white shirts in the final scene.

CHECK THE BOOK A03

T. S. Eliot criticised Othello for trying to dramatise himself in a self-aggrandising way in the final scene. See this assessment of Othello in 'Shakespeare and the Stoicism of Seneca', *Selected Essays* (1932). For a further negative reading of Othello's character, see F. R. Leavis's comments about the hero in 'Diabolic Intellect and the Noble Hero', *The Common Pursuit* (1962). For a reading of Othello as noble hero, see A. C. Bradley's *Shakespearean Tragedy* (1992 edition).

The confused physical violence that occurs at the beginning of this extract **mirrors** the confusion of the opening scene. There is a sad **irony** in the fact that Othello the great soldier is now reduced to a failed attempt on the life of Iago, the 'notorious villain' (line 237). Emilia has revealed the truth about the handkerchief, the device that the whole plot has hung on. It is appropriate that 'honest' Iago (e.g. I.3.295) is destroyed by his wife's real honesty. Iago is unmasked as a despicable creature. He curses Emilia before wounding her and running off. This act of unnatural cowardice is the perfect physical expression of Iago's values; yet again he abuses a woman to preserve his own honour. Iago's defiance is unsurprising and typical of him. Even when he is captured Iago remains evasive and selfish: he will not speak.

Emilia's role is to give voice to the audience's outrage at Desdemona's murder. She speaks plainly and passionately, defending Desdemona and guiding our responses to the heroine's death. The repetition in her lines is affecting. Emilia's echoing of Desdemona's willow song as she dies is designed to add to the **pathos** of the scene. Her righteous anger moves Othello towards recognition of his crime. The wretched hero accepts Emilia's harsh words because he knows he deserves them.

The responses of Gratiano and Montano to Othello provide another view of the **protagonist** and his actions. These two characters will provide a sense of closure at the end of this scene. Here they begin to reassert the common-sense, masculine values of the Venetian state by insisting that wicked deeds are punished. The tragic hero has been reduced to the status of base villain. Montano and Gratiano treat Othello like a common criminal: 'let him not pass/ But kill him rather' (lines 239–40). The disarming of Othello is symbolic. Othello is reduced to a nonentity; he is no longer a husband, and now the Venetians have taken his weapon, he is no longer a soldier. In this extract Othello has been degraded. This is fitting given his crime.

But we also see that Shakespeare means to rehabilitate the tragic protagonist. Othello rises above Emilia and the Venetians' reductive versions of him because he readjusts his perception of himself. Othello's desire to be punished (rather than run away from the consequences of his actions as Iago does) goes in his favour. And Othello clearly feels that he deserves not just punishment, but torture: 'Whip me, ye devils … Blow me about in winds, roast me in sulphur/ Wash me down in steep-gulfs of liquid fire!' (lines 275–8). Othello knows he deserves to die. 'But why should honour outlive honesty?' is a key question which needs careful consideration (line 243). We may doubt Othello's conception of himself as honourable at this moment, but not for long. When we realise Othello has another weapon at line 250 we know that he will use this weapon on himself, and inflict the punishment he feels he deserves.

Shakespeare makes Othello impressive again in Act V Scene 2, but his speech at line 257, which begins, 'Behold, I have a weapon', suggests remorse and misery above all else. Othello's desolation comes across strongly in his fatalistic question 'Who can control his fate?' (line 263) and his use of the third person – 'Where should Othello go?' (line 269) – does not so much suggest egotism as dislocation. Othello is lost: he has no wife or profession to sustain him, and as a murderer he is a condemned man. So he turns his weapon on himself and takes control of his own fate, just as he used to determine the fates of his enemies. Othello sees himself in a new and reduced light. He speaks of his 'little arm' and describes the 'impediments' he has made his way through on the battlefield not to boast, but to show that he is diminished (lines 260–1). It is appropriate for Othello to refer back to his earlier life; Shakespeare wants to remind us how far this mighty, noble man has fallen.

The fact that Othello is confined to his bedchamber by others (and by his own actions) shows how he has been reduced. The once great warrior is now a prisoner. The location of this scene suggests claustrophobia and isolation. Although there are other characters on stage we feel that Othello is really alone. He speaks to others briefly, but mostly speaks to himself, to prepare for his self-inflicted fate. If we accept that Othello is speaking of himself and not Iago when he calls out 'O cursed, cursed slave!' (line 274) we have further proof that Othello now feels himself unworthy. He feels the loss of Desdemona agonisingly. Looking at her body Othello is overcome by woe: 'O Desdemon! dead, Desdemon. Dead! O, O!' (line 279). These lines echo Othello's earlier despair. Throughout the play the hero has been inarticulate in moments of extreme pain. When he refers to his wife as an 'ill-starred wench' (line 270) and himself as a man unable to control his own fate we realise that the hero is moving closer to Desdemona and her romantic values again. As in his final speech, Othello's last thoughts here are about the wife he has loved and lost.

This extract prepares us for Othello's final speech: it is the step he must take before killing himself. It is necessary that he explain his thoughts, feelings and remorse so that we will view him as a tragic hero when he dies. The differences between Othello and Iago need to be reasserted. During Acts IV and V, Othello spiralled downwards, becoming more and more like Iago in his words and actions. When he begins to speak in **verse** with some of his former nobility it is a relief: we know that Iago's spell has been broken. Othello's measured calm is deeply affecting, especially given the hysteria and emotional tension of the earlier part of the scene. The 'cruel' Othello whom Emilia describes has died with the maid; now we know the hero's cruelty will be directed against himself because he has acknowledged his folly. Although Othello confronts Iago and will say that he feels he is not entirely to blame for his actions because he was 'Perplexed in the extreme' (V.2.344), we know that the hero accepts responsibility for his crime and will pay for it.

CONTEXT **AO4**

Although suicide is a sin in Christianity, the Ancient Greeks and Romans often saw suicide as patriotic or noble because it was a way of avoiding disgrace and preserving one's honour. In many Greek and Roman **tragedies** the protagonists commit suicide for other reasons as well: to avoid further suffering, end grief or sacrifice themselves for the greater good. Do you feel any of these motives apply to Othello's suicide at the end of the play?

CHARACTERS

OTHELLO

WHO IS OTHELLO?

- Othello is a Moor, a successful mercenary general who works for the state of Venice.
- He is a middle-aged bachelor who elopes with and marries a wealthy young Venetian, Desdemona.
- Othello is posted to Cyprus as governor during the Turkish conflict.
- In Cyprus, Othello believes Iago's false tales of his wife's adultery and smothers her, afterwards killing himself.

OTHELLO: FIRST IMPRESSIONS

Before he appears on stage we are led to believe by Iago that Othello is professionally bombastic and conceited and personally lascivious. But Othello's appearance in Act I Scene 2 contradicts Iago's assessment. Instead we see an impressive figure who displays a number of fine qualities: openness, sincerity and a natural authority. Unlike Shakespeare's other tragic **protagonists**, Othello is not a monarch (King Lear), an aspiring monarch (Macbeth) nor a displaced prince (Hamlet). However, he is a worthy figure and Shakespeare stresses his nobility. The Moor is the descendant of a royal line of kings (Othello refers to his birthright when he defends his right to marry Desdemona) and has been an impressive military commander.

'Valiant Othello' (I.3.49) commands the respect of figures of authority (the Duke of Venice, Governor Montano and even Brabantio). Although we do not see much evidence of his leadership in Cyprus, we know Othello is a conscientious soldier. He attempts to ensure that the carousing at his wedding festivities does not get out of hand and inspects the fortifications in the town in Act III Scene 2. Othello speaks and acts powerfully and in a way that inspires confidence in his character throughout the first two acts of the play (for example his dignity in front of the senate in Act I Scene 3). Othello's positive attributes indicate that we should view him as a hero, as does his customary mode of speech. (Othello speaks in **blank verse** early in the play and is a fine rhetorician, despite his protestations to the contrary.)

CRITICAL VIEWPOINT A04

Caryl Phillips believes that 'the pressures placed upon him rendered his [Othello's] life a tragedy'. Phillips is referring to the pressure of being a black man in a white world. Phillips sees Othello's tragedy as a result of his insecurity and isolation in Venetian society: 'Life for him is a game in which he does not know the rules.'

STUDY FOCUS: OTHELLO AND OPPOSITION   A03

Othello is a play about opposites and opposition, and the many contradictions contained in the play are embodied in the tragic hero. All the characters hold specific, and often opposing views of the Moor. We have to judge Othello in the light of the evidence they present, whilst also taking into account the hero's words, actions and idea of himself (which change). The hero's two contradictory roles also need to be considered. Othello is both military man and lover-husband. There are other contradictions to think about. Othello occupies contradictory personal and political positions. He is a trusted foreign servant (an outsider), wielding power on behalf of the Venetian state, who seeks to become an equal member of and participant in that society through marriage. He is also, of course, a black man in a white world.

OTHELLO'S TRAGEDY: A DOMESTIC TRAGEDY?

The focus in this play is, as has often been suggested, domestic. Othello's previous history, the Turkish invasion and machinations of the Venetian state, provide the backdrop to an essentially private **tragedy**. Although the play focuses on the tragic consequences of sexual jealousy, we must not ignore the wider worldly or political dimension of Othello's tragedy. Othello is proud of his profession and his reputation as a soldier is an essential part of the hero's conception of himself. Othello's desire for revenge is prompted by his need to recover his reputation. A **Jacobean** audience would have understood the weight Othello attaches to his reputation: a man's honour was important and his wife's chastity was an integral part of it. When Othello fears that he has been cuckolded the hero doubts himself and is forced to accommodate a new role, that of duped husband, which his pride will not allow him to accept. It is possible to argue that Othello's marriage is a political act. A black soldier marrying a white aristocrat cannot be viewed in any other way, according to the views of the time.

> **CRITICAL VIEWPOINT A03**
>
> The philosopher Stanley Cavell says that 'tragedy is the place we are not allowed to escape the consequences or price'. How does this statement apply to *Othello*?

OTHELLO'S RACE

Othello's race is a significant part of his **characterisation**. Othello is not the stereotypical immoral, lustful Moor of much Renaissance drama. He is portrayed as such by other characters – notably Iago – but we realise that we cannot trust the judgement of those who make negative comments about Othello's race. Shakespeare encourages the audience to view the Moor's race positively, as Othello does himself in Acts I and II. Race is not an issue for the heroine: as Othello reminds Iago, 'she had eyes and chose me' (III.3.192). Does Othello's race trouble him later in the play? It may make a modern audience uncomfortable, but it seems so. When his mind is poisoned by Iago, Othello comes to doubt his attractions. Othello mentions his blackness, his unsophisticated manners and his advanced age in a speech which suggests diminishing self-confidence as a husband (see III.3.262). Has Iago's racism infected the noble hero? Even if it has, we will never feel that Othello becomes jealous and murderous because he is black. His negative emotions and actions are a result of being 'Perplexed in the extreme' (V.2.344) by Iago, whose racism is a part of his evil, just as Othello's blackness is portrayed by Shakespeare as part of his nobility. (For further comments on Othello's race, see **Part Four: Language**.)

Race is not an issue for the heroine as Othello reminds Iago 'she had eyes and chose me' (Act 3 Scene 3) with his mind poisoned by Iago, Othello does come come to doubt his attraction. Othello mentions his blackness, his unsophisticated manners and his advanced age in a speech which suggests diminishing self-confidence as a husband (Act 3 Scene 2)

- Iago's racism infected Othello?

STUDY FOCUS: OTHELLO AND SLAVERY

Critics have suggested that Othello became 'tawny' rather than black in stag[e] productions in the 1800s. This was to prevent the role from being linked to [the] idea of slavery. At the time that *Othello* was first performed, the African slave[?] trade was already established. In the 1550s, Elizabethan adventurers had set [out] to the coast of Africa, where they raided the villages and kidnapped some of [the] inhabitants, bringing them back to England. Othello himself describes how h[e] was briefly imprisoned as a slave.

OTHELLO THE WOOER AND HUSBAND

The difficulty for an audience comes in accepting Othello as a perfect wooer, lover and husband, partly because Othello married Desdemona in secret – a covert act that sits uncomfortably with Othello's protestation that he has nothing to hide after the marriage. However, we are not encouraged to dwell on the elopement itself because it becomes clear that Desdemona was 'half the wooer' (I.3.176) and the couple speak clearly and honestly about their love, to the council and to each other. Their meeting in Cyprus reveals the intensity and sincerity of their mutual affection, and we are also assured of their sexual attraction.

The Duke of Venice recognises Othello's suitability as a wooer when he says, 'I think this tale would win my daughter too' (I.3.172). He then seeks to reassure Brabantio, 'Your son-in-law is far more fair than black' (I.3.291). However, there are tensions and contradictions that must be considered, as Desdemona's need to live with her husband conflicts with Othello's intention to keep the marriage separate from his duties. We gradually come to question Othello's self-knowledge on this point. He may be a capable general, but the events of the play suggest that Othello is out of his depth in matters of the heart.

OTHELLO'S OVERWHELMING LOVE

When Othello greets Desdemona in Cyprus we get the first hint that the hero is overwhelmed by his love for his wife – almost too happy. Then in Act III Scene 3 he says that he fears chaos when he is away from Desdemona: 'perdition catch my soul/ but I do love thee! and when I love thee not/ Chaos is come again' (III.3.90–2). It seems Othello cannot master his powerful romantic and erotic feelings. Is Othello in the grip of emotions that he cannot control, even before Iago sets to work on him? The successful soldier becomes a blind lover. The qualities that served Othello well as a soldier contribute to his downfall. Othello's decisiveness leads him to seek 'ocular proof' (III.3.363) and then when he is presented with that proof his decision to pursue a bloody course is made swiftly.

But it is not as simple as this. Othello suffers acutely from Act III Scene 3 onwards and does not give into his feelings of jealousy as swiftly as William Hazlitt suggests when he describes Othello as having 'blood of the most inflammable kind'. Othello tries many times to persuade himself that Desdemona is honest; he has second thoughts about murdering her as late as the final scene. And we cannot ignore Iago's presence. Iago is immensely plausible and cunning and Othello has no reason not to trust him. There is a good deal of evidence to indicate that Othello is pushed towards tragedy by a ruthless 'demi-devil' (V.2.298), who takes advantage of his noble nature, and is not simply a jealous booby, as Thomas Rymer claims. We know just how powerful Iago's influence is because Othello begins to speak and think like the ensign when his imagination is polluted. We are forced to come to terms with the idea that Othello is not wholly noble; he is also capable of savagery and crudeness.

OTHELLO'S TRANSFORMATION

The transformation in Othello is troublesome. Why does Othello trust Iago more than he trusts his beloved wife? Why does he believe the worst of Cassio, who has been a trusted friend and colleague? We have to understand that Othello's conception of himself has been challenged. Iago cruelly reminds him that he is an outsider and addresses him as an ordinary, foolish cuckold (see IV.1.65–73). Given his pride, the hero finds this intolerable.

F. R. Leavis has suggested that Othello's readiness to believe Iago is a sign that the hero is rather 'simple minded', inferring that lack of intellect contributes to Othello's **tragedy**. But Othello is much more than a weak fool. By the time Othello descends into murderous jealousy we are well acquainted with his noble character and recognise that he has been 'ensnared' (V.2.299). Surely Othello's preoccupation with honour and chastity are the obsessions of a virtuous, moral character? We might also feel that his desire for revenge is the result of Othello's failure to combine his roles as soldier and lover. When Othello fears that he has been betrayed by Desdemona he says woefully, 'Othello's occupation's gone!' (III.3.360). It is as if Desdemona was the prize Othello earned for his military victories. She has perhaps replaced his career as the source of his pride and honour. No wonder Othello feels her loss so keenly.

OTHELLO'S FINAL SCENE

It is possible to argue that his insistence on the importance of his honour both redeems and damns Othello. His concern for his reputation in the final scene can diminish Othello in the eyes of the audience. Nonetheless, Othello believes he is saving other men's honour and redeeming his own when he smothers Desdemona, calling himself an 'honourable murderer' (V.2.291). Shakespeare reminds us that the hero was a worthy man before he was ensnared by Iago, in order to create **pathos**. When Othello commits suicide he courageously takes his own life to pay for the crime of killing Desdemona. In his final lines and final act Othello is perhaps able to reconcile his two contradictory roles: the soldier kills the faulty lover. So, while it is impossible to condone Othello's actions in Act V Scene 2, it is possible to sympathise with and pity the fallen hero, whose suffering has been extreme.

Readers and critics of *Othello* have responded in many different ways to the **protagonist**. One popular view is that the character of Othello disintegrates psychologically and morally through the play and that this disintegration can be followed in his changing speech style. For example, he uses more oaths in the second half of the play, perhaps indicating moral corruption. Others, such as the scholar Muriel Bradbrook, see Othello as the descendant of the medieval stage devil, a corrupting influence throughout the play. She suggests that Othello should be considered a 'bogeyman'.

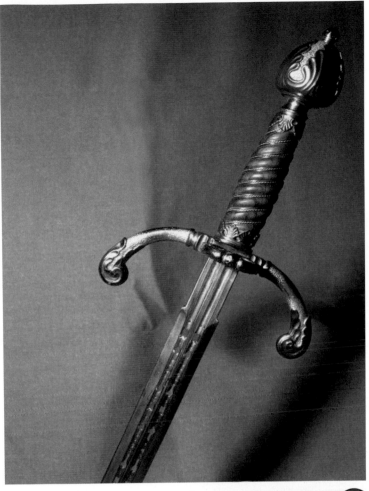

Caryl Phillips, on the other hand, believes Othello to be fundamentally 'an impulsive and insecure man', a vulnerable human being who reacts under pressure ('A black European success', *The European Tribe*, 2000). Some critics go even further and praise Othello's decision to commit suicide, reading it not as a mark of weakness but as a sign of a Stoic hero. Stoics, who followed the teachings of the Greek philosopher Zeno (335–263 BC), were supposedly indifferent to pain, and bore suffering without complaint.

KEY QUOTATION: OTHELLO   **A01**

Othello is proud of his career and character. He says, 'My parts, my title and my perfect soul/ Shall manifest me rightly' (I.2.31–2).

- Othello defends his character. He feels that he is a worthy husband for Desdemona and that he has acted honourably. Has he?
- Some critics suggest that Othello's downfall is caused partly by the sin of pride. Do you agree?
- Compare the positive **imagery** that Othello uses to describe himself in Act I with the imagery in his final speech in the play, where he compares himself with a 'base Indian' and 'circumcised dog' (V.2.345 and 353).

CONTEXT   **A04**

Africans of both sexes were a visible minority in seventeenth-century London, and there were interracial couples. It has even been suggested that Shakespeare knew a black prostitute who lived in the Cripplegate area of the city.

CHECK THE BOOK   **A03**

For a negative reading of Othello's character in the final scene of the play, see T. S. Eliot's 'Shakespeare and the Stoicism of Seneca', *Selected Essays* (1932). Eliot says that Othello's last speech is a 'terrible exposure of human weakness'. Othello turns himself into 'a pathetic figure'. Do you agree with these comments?

DESDEMONA

WHO IS DESDEMONA?

- Desdemona is a wealthy young Venetian woman, the daughter of Brabantio.
- She elopes with Othello the Moor and accompanies him to Cyprus.
- Desdemona is falsely accused of adultery and murdered by Othello.

BRABANTIO'S DESDEMONA

Early in the play Brabantio defines Desdemona as his 'jewel' (I.3.196). He says she is 'A maiden never bold,/ Of spirit' (I.3.95–6), modest and opposed to marriage, afraid to look on Othello. She emerges from her father's descriptions as an innocent, girlish figure. This version of Desdemona proves inaccurate when she speaks in Act I. However, by the end of the play Othello's abusive treatment has turned Desdemona into the fearful girl Brabantio described. This is horribly **ironic**. Desdemona has been silenced and it seems her final role is to be a sacrifice to masculine pride.

CRITICAL VIEWPOINT A03

In *Othello* (1997), E. A. J. Honigmann suggests that it is possible to see Desdemona as 'the strongest, the most heroic person in the play'. Do you agree?

GRADE BOOSTER A01

For the best marks at AS and A2 you need to ensure that you develop clear, well supported arguments about the text. Start your paragraphs with topic sentences. For example, if you are writing about Desdemona as a romantic heroine, an opening topic sentence might be, 'In Act I, Scene 3, Desdemona is portrayed as a determined character with a strong commitment to loving.' Now go to the text to find proof of this.

DESDEMONA THE WIFE

Desdemona asserts her rights as a married woman and insists that she is ready for a sexual relationship. There are other exchanges in the play that suggest Desdemona's sexuality, for example Desdemona's participation in the crude talk with Iago in Act II Scene 1, and her admiring reference to Lodovico in Act IV Scene 3. But the heroine's active sexuality is necessary to the play. Iago is able to make a great deal out of the fact that Desdemona deceived her father in order to choose her own husband, and is therefore untrustworthy.

It is important to remember that although Desdemona has disobeyed her father, she expects to submit to Othello's authority. She states this explicitly when she says, 'My heart's subdued/ Even to the very quality of my lord' (I.3.251–2). When Desdemona urges Othello to reinstate Cassio, she believes she is acting in Othello's best professional interests. Desdemona's 'nagging' can be portrayed on stage as playful and loving, her anxiousness about Othello's health touching.

But Desdemona is not faultless. She lies to Othello about the handkerchief (understandably, for he frightens her with his serious talk about its magical properties). When Othello strikes her publicly Desdemona reproaches him briefly: 'I have not deserved this' (IV.1.240). She then accepts – and defends – his authority over her, as we see from her discussion with Emilia at the start of Act IV Scene 3. Desdemona asserts her loving loyalty and questions Othello bravely in Act IV Scene 2 (see lines 30–89) but is reduced to dumb misery when her husband calls her 'that cunning whore of Venice' (IV.2.91): 'nor answer have I none' she says woefully (IV.2.105), remarking – girlishly – that she is 'a child to chiding' (IV.2.116).

STUDY FOCUS: DESDEMONA'S FINAL WORDS A02

Ultimately Desdemona refuses to blame Othello for her unhappiness: she declares it is her 'wretched fortune' (IV.2.129). Marriage teaches Desdemona that 'men are not gods' (III.4.149) and this is a disappointment to her. But while Desdemona submits willingly to the man she chose to marry, she dies valiantly, fighting to be allowed to live and asserting her honesty. Her final words are intriguing and contradictory. Why does Desdemona take the blame for her own death? Is she trying to protect Othello in death as she sought to defend him in life? Or is she simply a victim asserting her own innocence? However we interpret Desdemona's final words, we will probably feel that the heroine's passivity in Act V Scene 2 contradicts her earlier assertiveness.

CRITICAL VIEWPOINT A03

In *Othello* (1997), E. A. J. Honigmann interprets Desdemona's last words as 'an act of forgiveness'. He claims that 'Love and Goodness defeat Evil' at the end of *Othello*. Do you agree?

DESDEMONA: IAGO'S VICTIM

While we will certainly blame Othello for killing Desdemona, we will also blame Iago. An audience may wonder how he feels about the woman whose reputation he so brutally destroys. In Act II Scene 1, Iago says that he 'love[s]' Desdemona, 'Not out of absolute lust' but 'Partly to diet mine own revenge' (II.1.289–92). He wants to be even with Othello 'wife for wife' (II.1.297). So Iago decides he will 'turn her virtue into pitch' (II.3.355).

Does Iago ever regret what he does to Desdemona? E. A. J. Honigmann argues that Iago finds it difficult to respond to Desdemona in Act IV Scene 2 when he sees how miserable she is. There is one line of Iago that could be delivered with a hint of regret: 'Do not weep, do not weep: alas the day!' (IV.2.126). However, you may feel this is another example of Iago's ability to dissemble and further proof that Iago enjoys turning Desdemona into a victim.

KEY QUOTATION: DESDEMONA A01

Desdemona defends her own honour throughout the play, shown when she says to Othello, 'By heaven, you do me wrong' (IV.2.82).

- Desdemona is still brave and assertive, even when Othello attacks her verbally and physically.
- The reference to heaven reinforces Desdemona's virtue.
- This is an example of irony and **foreshadowing**; Othello will refer to heaven just before he murders Desdemona.

CONTEXT A04

The actor Dominic West, who played Iago in 2011, said that he felt that Iago's 'love' for Desdemona was an important part of the villain's motivation. West said that Iago and the other 'alpha males' in the play were jealous because 'this black guy's come in and stolen the prize girl'. Do you believe West is correct, and that Iago is in love with Desdemona?

Other useful quotations:

- Desdemona actively chose Othello and sees him as a hero: 'I saw Othello's visage in his mind/ And to his honours and his valiant parts/ Did I my soul and fortunes consecrate' (I.3.253).
- Love of Othello makes Desdemona submissive: 'my love doth so approve him/ That even his stubbornness, his checks, his frowns … have grace and favour' (IV.3.17–19).
- Desdemona loves Othello to the bitter end. Her final words are: 'Commend me to my kind lord – O, farewell!' (V.2.122).
- For Othello there are two Desdemonas. She is firstly his 'soul's joy' (II.1.182) but when he thinks she is unfaithful she becomes 'that cunning whore of Venice' (IV.2.91).
- Desdemona is Iago's victim. His intention is to 'out of her own goodness make the net/ That shall enmesh them all' (II.3.356–7).

Iago

Who is Iago?

- Iago is Othello's ensign. He has served with Othello in a number of military campaigns.
- Eaten up by jealousy and hatred, Iago seeks to destroy Othello by poisoning his mind against Desdemona.

Iago the villain

Iago is a compelling and sophisticated villain. He is part **vice**, part **Machiavel** and, like many villains in Renaissance drama, seems to be inherently evil. Shakespeare presents Iago as cynical, quick witted and opportunistic – all qualities of stage villains in **revenge tragedies**. Iago revels in his ability to dissemble and destroy. But while Iago enjoys having an audience and outlines his plots clearly, he is also rather mysterious, especially when he refuses to speak at the end of the play. Iago's silence led Romantic poet and critic Samuel Taylor Coleridge to conclude that the ensign is an example of 'motiveless malignity'. Coleridge also viewed Iago as a 'being next to the devil'. In more recent times, Iago's role has been reassessed. Iago is no longer considered the epitome of evil. Instead he can be seen as an example of an emotionally limited man, driven by petty professional jealousy and class consciousness. Like many stage villains, Iago is a source of **irony** and humour, which makes him appealing to audiences.

GRADE BOOSTER A04

When writing about Iago's evil it is important to refer to it in relation to the literary and historical context of the play if you want to get the best marks. For example, Iago demonstrates several characteristics of a typical **Jacobean** stage villain.

Iago's motives

Professional jealousy is Iago's initial motive for disgracing Cassio. Iago is also envious of the 'daily beauty' in the lieutenant's life (V.1.19). In addition, Iago says that he believes Cassio has committed adultery with his wife, Emilia. Iago's relationship with Roderigo is driven by callous greed and when his 'purse' (I.3.381) becomes a dangerous inconvenience, he kills him. His motives for destroying Othello's happiness are driven by negative impulses. Iago holds a grudge against Othello for promoting Cassio over him. Iago is also eaten up with sexual jealousy. He says he hates Othello because he suspects the general has ''twixt my sheets … done my office' (I.3.386–7). And because of this gnawing paranoia and frustration, Iago determines to use Desdemona's goodness to 'enmesh them all' (II.3.357). It is tempting to add misogyny and racism to these motives. Although Iago never says explicitly that he hates women or foreigners, his low opinion of them is clear in many of his speeches. Iago wants to degrade those he despises.

Why is Iago so successful?

CHECK THE BOOK A03

For a detailed discussion of Iago as alienated, triumphant villain, and an exploration of the villain's motives, see W. H. Auden's essay 'The Joker in the Pack' in John Wain (ed.), *Othello* (1971).

Iago is self-contained, egotistical and confident. These qualities help him in his treacherous quest. Iago is also successful because he can play different roles convincingly, and is able to adapt his style to suit any occasion. He enjoys his ability to hoodwink others into believing he is honest. With Cassio, Iago is coarse and genial. He offers the lieutenant plausible practical advice. He adopts a similar sympathetic approach when he deals with Desdemona in Act IV Scene 2. With Montano and Lodovico he makes a point of stressing that he has Othello's and the Venetian state's best interests at heart. There seems to be an absence of ego in his dealings with these characters, who are socially and professionally superior to him. But this is deliberate and false. Iago can afford to be less cautious with those who are dependent on him. His exchanges with Roderigo reveal the villain as a self-serving and materialistic cynic.

IAGO AND OTHELLO

Iago's dealings with Othello reveal his real skill – his relationship with his general is complex and fascinating. It is possible to argue Iago seeks to replace Desdemona in Othello's affections. Although this is debatable, Iago certainly sets out to prove that he is true to Othello, while Desdemona is false. Gradually, the ensign assumes the control and power we associate with Othello. He is so successful that Othello begins to speak and think like the villain. How does the 'inhuman dog' (V.1.62) destroy the mind, soul and body of the noble, valiant Moor? Iago makes Othello believe that he is loyal, conscientious and noble minded (these are of course – ironically – Othello's best qualities). Iago pretends that he would like to cudgel Othello's detractors in Act I Scene 2 and appears hesitant to describe his 'friend' Cassio's part in the drunken brawl. Iago's show of reluctance in Act III Scene 3 is devastatingly effective. He has an acute eye for his victims' weaknesses and exploits them mercilessly. Iago's role-playing enables him to become stage manager and dramatist, controlling his victims' fates.

IAGO ON STAGE AND SCREEN

Iago has been played by a number of famous actors, including the Victorian actor Henry Irving, who covered his face with his hands at line 393 in Act I Scene 3 when he said 'let's see'. Irving took a long pause before slowly withdrawing his hands to reveal a face which was, according to one spectator, 'all alive with the devilish scheme which had come into his mind'.

Iago's facial expressions are also key in the 1989 and 1995 TV/film productions, in which Iago speaks directly to camera in close-up, drawing the viewer in. Many **soliloquies** are whispered coolly and ferociously, through clenched teeth. The line 'I hate the Moor' (I.3.385) is emphasised slowly and very bitterly by the Iagos of Ian McKellen and Kenneth Branagh.

In a 1995 film, the director Oliver Parker chose to emphasise Iago's brutality towards his wife. During the scene when Emilia gives Iago Desdemona's handkerchief, the villain is lying on top of, and hurting, his wife.

STUDY FOCUS: IAGO'S LIMITATIONS `A03`

In spite of his theatrical and intellectual gifts, perhaps Iago has a limited understanding of those around him. Or maybe Iago recognises others' virtues but perceives them as foolish weaknesses. Iago certainly has no time for love or honesty. Does Iago's crude world view indicate that he is a petty character whose cleverness is superficial? The end of the play proves that you cannot hoodwink everyone all of the time: Iago is foolish to believe that he can. An assessment of Iago must acknowledge his terrible achievements as well as his ultimate failure. The villain succeeds in destroying a marriage and two noble characters, as well as his wife and Roderigo. On the other hand, we must also take into account Iago's refusal to speak at the end of the play. When he takes refuge in silence does Iago reassert his power one last time despite his inevitable fate?

KEY QUOTATION: IAGO `A01`

Iago's plan is to use Desdemona's virtue to destroy Othello. He says 'out of her own goodness [he will] make the net/ That shall enmesh them all' (II.3.356–7).

- The **imagery** suggests that Iago is setting a trap for his prey.
- Iago has contempt for innocence and goodness.

CHECK THE FILM `A03`

A Freudian interpretation of the play might suggest that Iago is subconsciously in love with Othello. This is how Laurence Olivier played the part of Iago. At the line 'I am your own forever' (III.3.482), he kissed his Othello (Ralph Richardson) on the lips. Do you think this is a plausible reading of Iago's character?

GRADE BOOSTER `A03`

The theatre critic Susannah Clapp reviewed a production of *Othello* in 2007. She said that Iago was portrayed as 'the thinker' while Othello was a 'feeler'. Is this how you see these two characters? The actor Dominic West, who played Iago in 2011, said that 'it's much easier to make a devil interesting'. Do you agree that Iago is more interesting than the other characters in *Othello*?

CASSIO

WHO IS CASSIO?

- Cassio is a Florentine soldier, promoted by Othello to the post of lieutenant.
- He acted as go-between during the courtship of Othello and Desdemona.
- Cassio is disgraced when he is involved in a drunken brawl, but is made governor of Cyprus at the end of the play.

CASSIO THE SOLDIER

In Act I Scene 1 we are offered a belittling portrait of Cassio by Iago. Iago presents Cassio as an inexperienced soldier, a mere 'arithmetician' (I.1.18) who has been promoted beyond his deserving. Perhaps this is a case of sour grapes. Iago is jealous of Cassio's promotion. However, there is some evidence that Cassio lacks military judgement. When Othello leaves him in charge, Cassio ends up drunk in a fight. Instead of keeping order and discipline, he creates confusion and alarm. This seems inexcusable, since he has already confessed to having a weak head for drink. Perhaps Cassio's military inexperience is meant to serve as another parallel with Othello, who is an inexperienced lover – despite their inexperience both men take their roles seriously. Because he is made governor of Cyprus at the end of the play, we are encouraged to dwell on Cassio's strengths rather than weaknesses as a soldier.

STUDY FOCUS: CASSIO AND OTHELLO   A03

Michael Cassio's primary function in the play is to offer a point of comparison with Othello. Both soldiers are outsiders who have chosen to serve Venice. Both value their reputations highly. But there the similarities end. Cassio, as an educated Florentine gentleman, is a cultural insider while Othello, due to his race, would have been seen as a cultural outsider. Florence had a reputation as city of culture so, unlike his general, Cassio is a social sophisticate. Othello's relationship with his lieutenant **mirrors** his relationship with his wife. At the start of the play, when Othello is 'well tuned' (II.1.198) with Desdemona, his relationship with Cassio is good. Iago destroys this harmony by creating a fictitious love-triangle. Cassio assisted Othello while he was courting Desdemona but Iago is able to turn this act of loyalty into proof of treachery. At the end of the play Cassio is associated with the restoration of order in Cyprus when he replaces Othello. Cassio's generous tribute to Othello at the end of the play also reminds us how great the hero was. It is fitting that the loyal lieutenant offers the last comment on the 'valiant Moor' (I.3.48).

CASSIO AND IAGO

Cassio's worst qualities are revealed when he is under Iago's influence. This gives us another point of comparison between Cassio and Othello. Iago pretends to be a loyal friend to both men. Iago claims that both men have slept with Emilia, giving him a motive for revenge against both of them. It is to his credit that Cassio is as easy to fool as Othello; to Shakespeare's audience this would have been proof of his honesty.

CONTEXT   A04

Cassio's misery when he fears he has lost his good name reminds us how important reputation was to a man's conception of his honour in the Renaissance. It is a sign of Cassio's worthiness that he feels deeply ashamed of his part in the drunken brawl.

CRITICAL VIEWPOINT   A03

In *Othello* (1997), E. A. J. Honigmann comments that 'one wonders ... whether the men are capable of unselfish love' in *Othello*. Do you think these comments can be applied to Cassio as well as Othello?

Iago is able to play on Cassio's frailties in the same way that he exploits Othello. He takes advantage of the lieutenant's courtesy, recognising that Cassio's weakness lies in the fact that he is 'handsome, young and hath all those requisites in him that folly and green minds look after' (II.1.243–5).

By plying him with drink Iago is able to manoeuvre Cassio out of the way and replace him as Othello's right-hand man. From this position of strength, Iago is then able to make Cassio's virtues look like vices. He uses Cassio's courtesy against him and makes his shame look like guilt. Like Othello, Cassio is a puppet in Iago's hands.

CASSIO THE LOVER

It is possible to feel that Cassio's gallantry is a little overworked at times. However, an audience can see that the lieutenant's praise of Desdemona is innocent and sincere. Later in the play Cassio's gentlemanly exterior seems to conceal some unsavoury qualities. These are revealed through his interaction with Bianca. Cassio's treatment of his mistress is often callous. While he does show her some affection, Cassio also refers to Bianca contemptuously as a 'bauble' (IV.1.134), and compares her to a 'fitchew' (a polecat, IV.1.145). Polecats were considered smelly and lecherous, so this is a very abusive term. It is hard not to judge Cassio harshly when he tells Bianca to be gone because he does not want to be found 'womaned' (III.4.194). Cassio can be accused of using women in the same way that Iago does. Rather than facing up to Othello he enlists the help of Emilia, then Desdemona to plead his case. Cassio may not 'steal away so guilty-like' (III.3.38), as Iago suggests, but is it not spineless to leave Desdemona to defend him?

It is essential that Cassio hang back for the purposes of the plot. And we cannot blame the lieutenant for relying on female intervention. Iago has persuaded Cassio that his best hopes lie in winning over Desdemona first. To Shakespeare's audience Cassio's casual liaison with a young courtesan would not have been enough to detract from his good qualities. We have to remember the 'daily beauty' (V.1.19) of Cassio's life that Iago detests so much. Overall, we may conclude Cassio's worthiness outweighs his weakness. Writing in 1765, Dr Johnson had a very positive view of Cassio's character. He said that 'Cassio is brave, benevolent, and honest'.

KEY QUOTATION: CASSIO — AO1

Cassio is full of shame when he is dismissed from his post by Othello: 'O, I have lost my reputation, I have lost the immortal part of myself – and what remains is bestial' (II.3.258–260).

● Cassio's obsession with his reputation mirrors Othello's obsession.

● Cassio's sorrow over losing his profession **foreshadows** Othello's misery when he thinks he has lost Desdemona's love.

● The reference to being 'bestial' foreshadows Othello's downfall – Othello will become 'bestial' himself when he avenges his masculine honour.

Other useful quotations:

● Cassio's charm and courtesy, welcoming Desdemona to Cyprus: 'O, behold,/ The riches of the ship is come on shore:/ You men of Cyprus, let her have your knees!' (II.1.82-84).

● Cassio's abusive treatment of Bianca: 'I do attend here on the general/ And think it no addition, not my wish,/ To have him see me womaned' (III.4.192–4).

● Cassio's generous tribute to Othello: 'he was great of heart' (V.2.359).

CHECK THE FILM — AO3

In Oliver Parker's 1995 film version of *Othello*, Nathaniel Parker, who plays Cassio, is handsome and genial, but he forgets Bianca's name. What point do you think the director was trying to make?

GRADE BOOSTER — AO3

It is important to show you understand that there are different ways of responding to characters and their actions for AO3, and compare and contrast the ways characters are portrayed in different scenes and why. For example, why is Cassio portrayed as gallant and courteous when he speaks to Desdemona in Act II, but as a reluctant and abusive lover of Bianca?

EMILIA

WHO IS EMILIA?

● Emilia is Iago's wife and Desdemona's maid in Cyprus.

EMILIA'S LOYALTY

Emilia tries to be a loyal wife and servant. Her loyalty is repeatedly tested by the handkerchief. Emilia makes the wrong moral choice when she gives the handkerchief to Iago because he 'hath a hundred times/ Wooed me to steal it' (III.3.296–7). Emilia does this in spite of knowing Desdemona 'so loves the token … That she reserves it evermore about her' (III.3.297–9). Will the audience blame Emilia for putting her husband's 'fantasy' (III.3.303) before her mistress's peace of mind? Emilia's loyalty is tested again when Desdemona wonders how she lost the handkerchief. Emilia's lie – 'I know not, madam' (III.4.24) – makes us uncomfortable. Emilia's loyalty is tested for a final time in Act V. Now Emilia puts Desdemona first. She tells the truth about the handkerchief and betrays Iago. She has chosen good over evil.

EMILIA AND IAGO

Emilia's relationship with Iago is a chilling example of marital disharmony. Whatever love is left is felt by Emilia, who tries to please Iago by giving him the handkerchief. Iago's attitude towards his wife is proprietorial and controlling. Iago is suspicious that Othello has cuckolded him, and dislikes the courtesy Cassio shows Emilia when she first arrives in Cyprus. Iago is jealous not because he loves Emilia, but because he feels his own position is being threatened. We see the couple alone together only once in the play, in Act III Scene 3. Iago treats Emilia contemptuously. He asks her sharply what she's doing alone, implying that her movements should be directed entirely by him. He also insults Emilia as 'a foolish wife' (III.3.308). When Iago realises she has the handkerchief, his tone softens: now Emilia is a 'good wench' (III.3.317). Iago changes his tone because he has something to gain.

It is clear Iago bothers with Emilia only when she can be useful to him. Iago's public treatment of Emilia is as dismissive as the way he speaks to her in private. In Act IV Scene 2, Iago is annoyed when Emilia refers to Iago's false suspicion that Othello cuckolded him. Iago's short lines addressed to his wife sound like threats: 'Speak within doors' (IV.2.146) and 'You are a fool, go to' (IV.2.150). In Act V, Iago's verbal abuse of Emilia intensifies just before he kills her. When she betrays the truth about the handkerchief he calls Emilia a 'Villainous whore!' and 'Filth' (V.2.227, 229). These words encapsulate the disrespect Iago feels for all women. The audience will be pleased that it is his abused wife who brings about her villainous husband's downfall.

EMILIA AND SEXUAL POLITICS

It comes as no surprise that Emilia is cynical about men. Her own match has afforded her little pleasure. Shakespeare gives Emilia a distinctive and increasingly assertive female voice. She uses it to defend herself and her sex. She replies sharply when Iago derides women in Act II Scene 1: 'You shall not write my praise' (II.1.116). In Act III Scene 4 we see that Emilia is more realistic about male–female relationships than Desdemona. Discussing marriage and men she says, ''Tis not a year or two shows us a man./ They are all but stomachs, and we all but food' (III.4.104–5). The audience will appreciate Emilia speaks from bitter experience, and sympathise with her when they see how poorly she is treated by Iago. In the willow song scene Emilia insists that women have the same appetites as men and the same right to 'revenge' if they are badly treated (IV.3.92).

CRITICAL VIEWPOINT A03

In *Othello* (1997), E. A. J. Honigmann suggests that Emilia's final actions prove that love triumphs over hate. He says 'Emilia's love [of Desdemona] is Iago's undoing.' Do you agree that love triumphs over hate in this play?

It is difficult not to agree with some of Emilia's harsh judgements of Othello and we know that she is absolutely right to betray Iago. However, Emilia's pragmatism about men and women is perhaps not far enough removed from Iago's cynicism. We must be cautious about Emilia's defence of adultery in Act III Scene 4. She speaks theoretically here, but her casual acceptance of sin is perhaps an indication that Emilia is too crude a moraliser to be relied on completely as a judge of Othello's character in the final scene. Emilia's female voice is trustworthy, but not infallible.

EMILIA AND DESDEMONA

Emilia is Desdemona's comforter and protector of her honour. She plays the role that Othello should have played for his wife. As Desdemona becomes less assertive in the second half of the play Emilia's role becomes more important. She becomes her mistress's energetic defender, voicing the audience's outrage at the treatment Desdemona receives. In her role as defender she is selfless and sharp witted. She describes Othello's destructive jealousy accurately. Emilia is also wise without knowing it when she says angrily, 'The Moor's abused by some most villainous knave' (IV.2.141). In the final scene Emilia becomes the voice of truth and stops Iago's evil progress. Her final lines reconfirm her own and her mistress's honesty: 'So come my soul to bliss as I speak true!/ So speaking as I think, alas, I die' (V.2.248–9). It seems fitting that Emilia should die beside the mistress she defended with her dying breath.

STUDY FOCUS: EMILIA'S SUSPICIONS   A03

There remain two questions to be asked about Emilia. Firstly, why does she give the handkerchief to Iago when she does not know why he wants it? Emilia regrets giving it to him the moment he takes possession of it, suggesting that she is uneasy about his motives. Secondly, does Emilia suspect her husband before she finally speaks out? Perhaps the answer is yes. When she hears that Iago led Othello to believe Desdemona was false she says, 'I think upon't, I think I smell't, O villainy!/ I thought so then: I'll kill myself for grief!' (V.2.188–9). Her words suggest guilt at keeping quiet about her suspicions. However, Emilia's horrified repeated question 'My husband?' (V.2.138, 142, 145) could be seen as proof that Emilia knew nothing of Iago's villainy. Like Roderigo, whom Iago also brutally silences, Emilia realises the true extent of her husband's evil when it is too late.

KEY QUOTATION: EMILIA   A01

Emilia says 'jealous souls … are not ever jealous for the cause, … [Jealousy] is a monster/ Begot upon itself, born on itself' (III.4.159–62).

- These lines describe Iago's jealousy; he takes revenge on Cassio and Othello without a genuine 'cause'.
- These words suggest Othello's jealousy will feed itself.
- The **personification** of jealousy links it to the handkerchief.
- It is **ironic** that Emilia is the wise expert on jealousy, when she seems to have no clue about Iago's villainy.

GRADE BOOSTER   A02

To get the best grades at AS and A2 you need to make precise points rather than sweeping generalisations. This is especially important when writing about language and **imagery**. For example, rather than saying 'there is a lot of imagery of jealousy in the play', try to comment on a specific example: 'In Act III Scene 4, Emilia defines jealousy as … which shows us that …'

CHECK THE BOOK   A03

For a **feminist** reading of the play, see Marilyn French's essay in John Drakakis (ed.), *Shakespearean Tragedy* (1992).

BRABANTIO

WHO IS BRABANTIO?

- Brabantio is Desdemona's father and a Venetian senator.

BRABANTIO THE SENATOR

Brabantio is an important man used to commanding others. **Ironically**, these are qualities he shares with his son-in-law Othello. We are led to believe that Brabantio is a valuable member of the council, well respected by others. The Duke says that he was missed during the discussions about the Turkish invasion, and takes trouble to reconcile Brabantio to Desdemona's marriage. However, we might feel that Brabantio's professional judgement is questionable. He resolutely refuses to acknowledge Othello's worth, unlike the rest of the Venetian senators. Ironically, like Othello, Brabantio puts his private affairs before affairs of state. Brabantio insists the council put Othello on trial for witchcraft in Act I Scene 3 when they are more concerned with the military fate of Cyprus.

STUDY FOCUS: BRABANTIO THE PATRIARCH A03

Brabantio plays the role of the wronged patriarch. Shakespeare's audience may have felt his wrongs more deeply than we do today. They would have recognised Desdemona's elopement as an assault on **patriarchy**. Like Juliet in *Romeo and Juliet*, the treasured daughter denies her father's right to dispose of her in marriage as he sees fit. Brabantio sees this as a 'gross revolt' (I.1.132) against the natural order. He reminds Desdemona that it is her duty to obey him in Act I Scene 3 (see lines 175–9). Brabantio holds what would have been recognised by Shakespeare's audience as traditional, suspicious views of foreigners. These views come across in Brabantio's descriptions of Othello as a 'foul thief' (I.2.62) who has bewitched Desdemona. To a modern audience these views seem racist. Brabantio suggests that Desdemona's marriage to Othello undermines not just his own authority, but the whole social order.

BRABANTIO'S LOVE FOR DESDEMONA

Brabantio has not been an unsympathetic parent. Until the elopement his home has been a place of family harmony. Othello has been entertained often and Brabantio has been a friendly host. Any audience would understand Brabantio's desire to find a suitable match for his daughter. His paternal love of Desdemona has been wise. He rejected the unworthy Roderigo, as we see when he sternly reminds the failed suitor that Desdemona 'is not for thee' (I.1.97). Brabantio has also allowed Desdemona to reject suitors herself. Brabantio's descriptions of Desdemona in the senate scene may not fit with the confident young woman we see when she appears, but Brabantio recognises his daughter's virtues and cares for her deeply.

Not all of Brabantio's speeches about losing his daughter are unsympathetic. In Act I Scene 3 it clear that the loss of Desdemona weighs very heavily on his soul. He says 'my particular grief/ Is of so flood-gate and o'erbearing nature/ That it engluts and swallows other sorrows' (I.3.57–9). Brabantio's sense of loss is profound. The intense emotion described in this speech **foreshadows** Othello's outraged feelings when he believes he has been betrayed by Desdemona. It is ironic that the reluctant father and his son-in-law are linked by the language of loss they use. Like Othello, Brabantio dies grieving for his lost love. We are told Desdemona's marriage was 'mortal [fatal] to him' (V.2.203).

GRADE BOOSTER A04

For the best grades at AS and A2 you must demonstrate an understanding of the social and historical context of *Othello*. When commenting on the play, remember that Shakespeare lived in a patriarchal society and consider the different ways Elizabethan and modern audiences might respond to Desdemona's 'disobedience'.

CONTEXT A04

Elizabethan society was patriarchal and hierarchical. Fathers expected to control their daughters and marry them off to their own social or financial advantage. Marriage was a means by which men controlled and passed on their property, and women were seen as possessions. Brabantio is more tolerant than many Renaissance aristocrats – he says he was willing to allow Desdemona some choice about whom she married.

WHY DO WE LOSE SYMPATHY WITH BRABANTIO?

Brabantio's immovable unkindness to Desdemona and Othello prevents us from sympathising with the patriarch wholeheartedly. Brabantio refuses to have anything to do

with his daughter after her marriage and he casts Desdemona off. He says cruelly that he would rather 'adopt a child than get it' (I.3.192). Brabantio's final words to Othello are a harsh warning: 'Look to her, Moor, if thou hast eyes to see:/ She has deceived her father, and may thee' (I.3.293–4). The loving, generous father is replaced by a mean-spirited prophet of doom. Brabantio also proves to be too selfishly materialistic. His use of the word 'jewel' (I.3.196) to describe Desdemona suggests that he regards his daughter as a possession. We also come to question Brabantio's judgement when he says it would have been better if Roderigo had 'had' Desdemona rather than Othello. At the same time, it is important to remember that Brabantio is another victim of Iago's manipulation. His unfavourable view of Othello is influenced heavily by the ensign's crude and racist **characterisation** of the Moor.

CHECK THE BOOK **A03**

For a comic treatment of a father trying to marry off his two daughters, see Shakespeare's *The Taming of the Shrew*. In this play there are two daughters, Bianca and Katherina. Bianca is outwardly obedient, but secretly arranges her own marriage, while Katherina is a 'scold' who is married against her will to a fortune hunter, Petruchio.

CHECK THE FILM **A03**

In Oliver Parker's 1995 film Brabantio's bitter lines, 'She has deceived her father, and may thee' (I.3.294), are repeated in flashback late in the play, showing their importance and significance for Othello.

KEY QUOTATION: BRABANTIO **A01**

Brabantio is outraged by the senate's willingness to accept Othello's elopement with Desdemona: 'For if such actions may have passage free/ Bond-slaves and pagans shall our statesman be' (I.2.98–9).

- Brabantio sees Othello as a threat to social order and stability.
- We are reminded of Othello's history – he was taken into slavery before he became a general.
- These words reveal the social attitudes of many people in Shakespeare's society: Brabantio implies slaves and foreigners should not be treated as equals.

REVISION FOCUS: TASK 9 **A02**

How far do you agree with the statements below?

- It is impossible to sympathise with Brabantio.
- The secret nature of the marriage of Othello and Desdemona undermines Othello's heroism.

Try writing opening paragraphs for essays based on these discussion points. Set out your arguments clearly.

RODERIGO

WHO IS RODERIGO?

- Roderigo is a wealthy Venetian gentleman who had hoped to marry Desdemona.
- He is Iago's first victim, and is exploited for his money and in the plot to kill Cassio.

RODERIGO: VICTIM OR VILLAIN?

As a disappointed suitor Roderigo represents the 'curled darlings' (I.2.68) that Desdemona rejected, providing us with a point of comparison with noble Othello.

Roderigo has extremely poor judgement and his actions are generally despicable. Often he seems villainous – he has no concern for Desdemona's feelings, making him a potential abuser of women. He shares responsibility with Iago for prejudicing Brabantio's view of Desdemona's elopement. In Cyprus, Roderigo participates in the attempt on Cassio's life without feeling convinced that his intended victim deserves to die. However, Roderigo is corrupted by Iago and not wholly bad, merely weak and foolish. He lacks resolution or volition and has to be directed off stage many times. Roderigo is suspicious of Iago, but allows himself to be talked round.

It is possible to see Roderigo as another outsider in *Othello*. Iago keeps him on the fringes of the action, ensuring that he remains powerless. Roderigo's miserable end seems a cruel fate. Like Othello he realises the truth about Iago too late. There is some rehabilitation of Roderigo's character in the final scene when his letters are discovered, revealing the truth about Iago's plots. Perhaps Roderigo, like Othello, is both victim and villain?

STUDY FOCUS: RODERIGO AND IAGO

The subplot involving Roderigo is linked very closely to the main plot, so much so that they become interwoven. Roderigo's primary role is to enable the audience to gain insight into Iago's methods. In his exchanges with the 'poor trash of Venice' (II.1.301) the ensign's evil nature is revealed. In the subplot Iago exploits Roderigo for his money, promising his victim that he will be able to enjoy Desdemona's sexual favours. In Cyprus, Iago propels Roderigo into the main plot. Roderigo is used as a pawn in two key scenes: the drinking scene where Cassio is provoked, and then the attack on Cassio's life in Act V. It seems appropriate that Roderigo is the first of Iago's victims to die: he was the first to be taken in.

KEY QUOTATION: RODERIGO   A01

When he dies Roderigo calls Iago an 'inhuman dog' (V.1.61).

- Roderigo realises the truth about Iago too late, and is **ironically** the first to recognise his villainy.
- The **imagery** of dogs is used repeatedly to describe Iago in Act V; it reinforces the audience's sense of Iago's vicious character.
- It is darkly ironic that Othello will also use dog imagery just before he kills himself, linking his evil actions to Iago's influence.

GRADE BOOSTER A02

To get the best grades at AS and A2 you must go beyond description of plot and character. For example, if you are writing about Roderigo's role in the play, you could consider the dramatic significance of his actions and comment on the way in which Roderigo's interactions with Iago contribute to your understanding of the presentation of the theme of deception.

CRITICAL VIEWPOINT A03

In *Othello* (1997), E. A. J. Honigmann says that Roderigo plays two important roles in *Othello*. Firstly, 'Roderigo activates poisonous impulses in Iago'. Secondly, 'Roderigo's over-mastering, self-destructive desire for Desdemona mirrors Othello's'.

BIANCA

WHO IS BIANCA?

- Bianca is a courtesan, who is in love with Cassio.

BIANCA THE VICTIM

Bianca is used and abused in *Othello*. She is seen only in relation to the male characters and is always in a vulnerable position. Cassio is prepared to dally with but not marry her. Iago accuses her of involvement in the plot to kill Cassio to distract attention away from himself. Bianca's vulnerability is a result of her social position, as well as her treatment by the male characters. As a prostitute, Bianca's only power lies in her ability to attract customers. If they choose to abuse her, Bianca's voice counts for nothing because her profession makes her morally dubious. Love also makes Bianca vulnerable. As Iago puts it, ''tis the strumpet's plague/ To beguile many and be beguiled by one' (IV.1.97–8). The irony is that Bianca is more honest and true than the outwardly honourable men who abuse her. Bianca's victimisation by Iago in Act V Scene 1 prepares us for the deaths of the other female victims in the final scene.

CONTEXT **A04**

Venice had a reputation for its courtesans. In Renaissance Venice there were two classes of courtesan: the *cortigiana onesta* (the intellectual courtesan) and the *cortigiana di lume* (lower-class prostitute who lived and practised her trade near the Rialto Bridge). Guidebooks were available, which gave the names, addresses and fees of Venice's most prominent prostitutes. Some courtesans were married women, some were single.

STUDY FOCUS: BIANCA THE LOVER **A03**

Bianca's relationship with Cassio is less idealistic than the Othello–Desdemona match. However, Cassio is clearly more to Bianca than a mere 'customer'. Cassio tells us that 'she haunts me in every place' (IV.1.132–3), suggesting that Bianca is smitten with him. This explains her indignation about the handkerchief, which Bianca believes must be 'some minx's token' (IV.1.152). Bianca's unfounded jealousy **mirrors** Othello's. However, does Shakespeare suggest that Bianca has more plausible reasons for her jealousy than Othello? Notice how Bianca uses the word 'cause' when she complains about Cassio's week-long absence from her. She says woefully, 'To the felt absence now I feel a cause' (III.4.182). Her words **foreshadow** Othello's opening line in the final scene, when he repeats 'It is the cause' (V.2.1) to justify killing his wife. It is worth thinking about why Shakespeare links Bianca and Othello linguistically?

Cassio and Bianca make up, unlike the tragic central couple. We know this because Cassio is dining with Bianca before he is wounded in the final scene. In Act V, Bianca's genuine love of Cassio is seen when she discovers her lover has been stabbed: 'Alas, he faints! O Cassio, Cassio, Cassio!' (V.1.84). Her constancy in love links Bianca to Desdemona. Unlike the stereotypical crude and aggressive prostitute of much Renaissance drama, Bianca is a faithful lover.

KEY QUOTATION: BIANCA **A01**

When Cassio sends her away because he doesn't want to be seen with her Bianca says: ''Tis very good: I must be circumstanced' (III.4.202).

- Bianca's words reveal how powerless she is.
- Bianca has to be content with the way men treat her, just like Desdemona.
- Bianca's acceptance of Cassio's authority over her foreshadows Desdemona's words and actions in Act IV Scene 2.

CRITICAL VIEWPOINT **A03**

It is worth considering the view of women expressed by Iago in relation to all the female characters in *Othello*. Do they provide proof that they are weak minded, foolish, petty or inconstant? There is a strong sense that the women in this play are hapless victims. Bianca, the least powerful figure in the play, is – ironically – the only female survivor.

THEMES

JEALOUSY

THE IMAGERY OF JEALOUSY

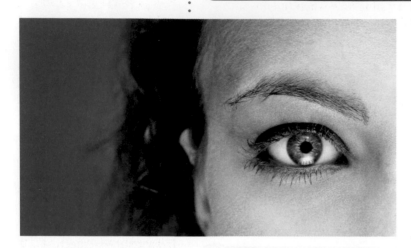

The **imagery** associated with jealousy suggests it is an all consuming, irrational emotion.

It is 'the green-eyed monster, which doth mock/ The meat it feeds on' (III.3.168–9), 'a monster/ Begot upon itself, born on itself' (III.4.161–2). There is a strong sense of devouring and being devoured in these images, which fits in with Iago's description of Othello as being 'eaten up with passion' when he believes Desdemona is unfaithful (III.3.394). Shakespeare explores the monstrous power of jealousy again in *The Winter's Tale*, where King Leontes becomes convinced his wife, Hermione, has been unfaithful. Unlike Othello, whose mind is poisoned by a villain, Leontes's jealousy is fuelled by his own thoughts.

STUDY FOCUS: JEALOUSY AND MADNESS A02

Iago makes explicit connections between jealousy and madness. When Othello is overcome by jealous thoughts he falls down in a fit. Iago observes how 'he foams at mouth, and ... Breaks out to savage madness' (IV.1.54–5). Later Iago feeds Othello's jealousy as Othello watches Iago's conversation with Cassio. Othello believes he is watching Cassio describe his adulterous liaison with Desdemona. Iago comments, 'As he [Cassio] shall smile, Othello shall go mad' (IV.1.101). Emilia also makes a connection between madness and jealousy when she describes how husbands 'break out in peevish jealousies' (IV.3.88). If jealousy is associated with madness, to what extent is Othello responsible for the actions he commits when he is under its influence?

CRITICAL VIEWPOINT A03

F. R. Leavis has claimed that Othello's jealousy 'is unassociated with any real interest in Desdemona as a person'. He says Othello 'slips ... readily into possessive jealousy' because he is 'self-centred'. To what extent do you agree with these comments?

JEALOUSY AND DESTRUCTION

Jealousy is a form of tyranny in *Othello*. It destroys love, honour and nobility in those it afflicts. It makes both male **protagonists** murderous and violent. It also seems that it is the nature of jealousy not to be satisfied. Iago continues plotting against Cassio after he has disgraced him and is not content with disturbing Othello's peace of mind: he must continue until Desdemona is dead. Othello's jealous thoughts are **characterised** by references to acts of violence against Desdemona. He says he will 'tear her all to pieces!' (III.3.434) or 'chop her into messes' (IV.1.197). Othello also wants to torture and kill his supposed rival Cassio. Once his jealousy has been proved false, Othello turns his sword on himself. Jealousy has destroyed him. It also destroys Iago, whose torture is fitting punishment for his jealous crimes.

GRADE BOOSTER A03

For the best grades at AS and A2 you must take into consideration different ways of looking at the text. For example, you might make a **feminist** interpretation of the play, exploring the presentation of gender roles. Or you could take a **new historicist** approach and look at the way ethnicity is presented, taking into account Elizabethan ideas about race (see **Part Five: Historical Background**.)

PROFESSIONAL JEALOUSY

Iago's professional jealousy, which can be linked to the sin of envy, sets the tragic events of the play in motion. Iago envies Cassio primarily because he is promoted to a post Iago has coveted. Iago is also envious of Cassio's superior manners and social status. As late as Act V, Iago is still motivated by jealous thoughts about Cassio. Iago says Cassio must be destroyed because of the 'daily beauty in his life/ That makes me ugly' (V.1.19). Ask yourself whether there is an element of professional jealousy in Iago's treatment of Othello. Does the ensign wish to destroy Othello's military reputation, as well as his marriage?

SEXUAL JEALOUSY

There are three examples of sexual jealousy in the play, all of them unfounded. Bianca, Iago and Othello all believe that they have been betrayed by those they love, and they are all wrong. Does sexual jealousy turn Iago into a villain? Iago's aim is to make Othello and Cassio suffer as he suffers because he fears he has been cuckolded. Unlike Othello, Iago is cool and calculating when he chooses to act on his suspicions, suggesting jealousy follows on naturally from hatred in his characterisation. This is not the case with Bianca and Othello. Their sexual jealousy is a response to feelings of genuine love when they believe their partners have been unfaithful. Perhaps Othello's insistence on proof might suggest that this jealous husband is a nobler man than Iago.

Iago's sexual jealousy is prompted by rumours that 'the lusty Moor/ Hath leaped into my seat' (II.1.293–4). These words suggest sexual jealousy is prompted by competitiveness, as

well as possessiveness. This is something we see again when Othello's overpowering jealousy takes hold. Othello cannot bear the idea of Desdemona's 'stolen hours of lust' (III.3.341). He feels he has been 'robbed'. In Othello sexual jealousy seems to be the 'flipside' of boundless love. What Othello shares with Iago is covetousness: both men feel jealous because they have lost possession of something that they held dear.

Finally, *Othello* suggests jealousy is ridiculous and humiliating, as well as terrifying and corrosive. Iago's motives for revenge are inadequate, and the proofs he provides flimsy. It is horribly humiliating that Othello, a renowned and experienced soldier, should kill his wife and himself because of a handkerchief, which has absurdly come to symbolise his own and Desdemona's honour.

CHECK THE BOOK · A03

Sexual jealousy is an important theme in other plays by Shakespeare. In the comedy *Much Ado About Nothing* the young lover, Claudio, believes his fiancée, Hero, has been unfaithful with another man and rejects her at the altar. His suspicions are proved false and the couple are reunited at the end of the play.

CRITICAL VIEWPOINT · A03

There are several indications in the text that we should not view Othello as a naturally jealous man. When Brabantio warns him that Desdemona may deceive him, Othello is dismissive. He replies, 'My life upon her faith' (I.3.295). Othello trusts his wife completely. It seems that Iago's cunning, Othello's trust in his ensign, and his quick decision-making all conspire to make a jealous man out of him.

KEY QUOTATION: JEALOUSY · A01

Emilia's definition of jealousy suggests how irrational and corrosive it is: 'jealous souls will not be answered ... They are not jealous for the cause,/ But jealous for they're jealous' (III.4.159–61).

- Emilia's words can be applied to both Iago and Othello – neither has a just 'cause' for his actions.
- Iago's jealousy 'will not be answered': Iago's professional grudge against Cassio and Othello turns into a multiple murder plot.
- Othello's jealousy 'will not be answered': he refuses to believe Desdemona's protestations of her innocence.

REVISION FOCUS: TASK 10 · A02

How far do you agree with the statements below?

- Jealousy destroys Othello's marriage.
- The male characters are incapable of unselfish love.

Try writing opening paragraphs for essays based on these discussion points. Set out your arguments clearly.

MEN AND WOMEN

DOUBLE STANDARDS

At the heart of *Othello* is the idea of double standards. Codes of conduct for men and women are very different in this play, as they were in Shakespeare's society. Men have more personal freedom, and women are judged by them and in relation to them. Bianca's vulnerable status as 'strumpet' (IV.1.97) reminds us of the double standard. It is socially acceptable for Cassio to consort with a courtesan, but it is presumptuous for Bianca to expect him to marry her. Iago pretends to help Roderigo in his adulterous pursuit of Desdemona because it enables him to keep hold of his 'purse' (I.3.381). Men toy with and discard women as they choose. Iago's successful vilification of Desdemona is the key example of this. Iago uses the double standard to his advantage when he blackens Desdemona's name. The masculine code of honour is threatened by the idea of active female sexuality, so Iago destroys Othello by making the hero believe his chaste wife has strayed. There are two types of women in Othello's world: chaste wives or whores. If Desdemona is not one, then she must be the other. If she is a whore, she has to be punished.

STUDY FOCUS: GENDER AND POWER · A03

Power is a key factor in all the relationships portrayed. To begin with we are presented with a picture of powerful womanhood: Desdemona has deceived her father and asserted her independence from **patriarchy** by choosing her own husband. The example set by Desdemona shows that male–female relationships are the focus of conflict in this play; they are about opposition and power. Throughout the play we see further power struggles between couples and friends: Iago competes with Desdemona for Othello's ear; Desdemona and Emilia defend themselves against their husbands' suspicions; Bianca tries to assert her rights as Cassio's mistress. The women lose these power struggles. By the end of the play all the female characters are silenced, their fragile power negated. That they ever had any power is debatable. They are only ever seen in relation to the male characters, who have the power to describe, define and kill them.

CONTEXT · A04

During the Renaissance, many people believed that men were intellectually and morally superior to women because of Christian teachings. John Knox, a Protestant clergyman who wrote a diatribe against female rulers called *The First Blast of the Trumpet Against the Monstruous Regiment of Women* (1558), said: 'a woman ought to serve her husband as unto God, affirming that in nothing has woman equal power with man'.

COUPLES

Initially, Desdemona and Othello stand apart from the other couples because they have a harmonious relationship. There is no disillusionment or dissatisfaction here. Bianca and Cassio and Emilia and Iago are not happy couplings. The former is an unequal match between a 'customer' (IV.1.120) who feels a limited affection and a 'bauble' (IV.1.134), whose genuine love makes her unhappy. Cassio reveals the limitations of this relationship – which he clearly feels is unworthy in some way – when he tells Bianca to be gone because he would not be seen in her company. Emilia and Iago are a chilling match. Marriage has made Emilia cynical about male–female relationships. She knows she is merely 'food' (III.4.105) for Iago, acceptable until she disobeys him and refuses to be silent, at which point her husband tries to kill her.

The misogyny of Iago casts a dark shadow over Othello's relationship with Desdemona, which seems so full of optimism and delight at the start of the play. Despite their different social, cultural and racial backgrounds the hero and heroine symbolise a meeting of two minds in Acts I and II. Othello loves Desdemona for her feminine grace and sympathy; she loves him for his masculine heroism. Essentially, Othello and Desdemona love each other harmoniously because of the differences they perceive in each other. These differences become distorted by an interloper, a man who cannot bear to see two lovers 'well tuned' (II.1.198). The envious, unhappily married Iago destroys true love.

OTHELLO, DESDEMONA AND IAGO

In some ways it is possible to see the Othello–Desdemona–Iago relationship as a warped kind of love triangle. Iago seeks to displace Desdemona. What is it that he objects to so strongly when he looks at Othello and Desdemona together? Why does Iago wish to get between them? The text suggests that there is something very complicated going on. Iago's responses to the feminine reveal a mixture of fear and loathing. Part of his contempt for Othello is located in his fear that Desdemona has power. Iago has been sidelined. We know from his mocking reference to Desdemona as Othello's 'general' (II.3.310) that he cannot bear the fact that a female exerts influence. Iago despises Othello for giving into love, which he sees as a feminine, unworthy emotion. Iago's derision of love and the female is also illustrated when he sneers about Desdemona being able to 'play the god' with Othello (II.3.342). Iago loathes the idea of a man being in thrall to a woman, believing Othello is weakened and trapped by love. Othello's soul is 'enfettered' to Desdemona's love, so much so that 'she may make, unmake, do what she list … With his weak function' (II.3.340–3).

Iago responds to this by denigrating Desdemona and by making her voice seem unreliable. The power struggle comes into sharp focus when we consider the vow Iago makes to Othello at the end of Act III Scene 3: 'I am your own for ever' (line 482). Iago's fake love destroys Othello's real love. Othello begins to assert his masculine power in an overbearing way because he believes that Desdemona has begun to assert herself sexually. To any Renaissance husband, this would be unacceptable. We might see the events of Acts IV and V as an attempt by Othello to reassert his own power over Desdemona. Because of this we come to associate masculine love with violence. Iago's misogyny triumphs.

KEY QUOTATION: MEN AND WOMEN A01

Emilia has a disillusioned view of marriage: ''Tis not a year or two shows us a man./ They are all but stomachs, and we all but food' (III.4.104–5).

- These words remind us that the female characters are powerless in *Othello*; they are 'food' for their men.
- Emilia's cynical comments undermine the romance of the marriage of Othello and Desdemona.
- Emilia reminds us of the importance of not judging by first impressions and appearances.

REVISION FOCUS: TASK 11 A02

How far do you agree with the statements below?

- The handkerchief is an unconvincing **catalyst** for **tragedy**.
- *Othello* is essentially a domestic tragedy.

Try writing opening paragraphs for essays based on these discussion points. Set out your arguments clearly.

GRADE BOOSTER A04

If you are asked to write about the ways in which love and marriage are presented in *Othello* you need to link these themes to the cultural and historical context of the play in order to get the best grades at AS and A2. For example, you could consider the status of women in a patriarchal society when commenting on the ways in which Desdemona, Emilia and Bianca are treated by the male characters.

CRITICAL VIEWPOINT A04

In 'The Noble Moor' (1956), Helen Gardner suggests that Desdemona is 'love's martyr'. By dying she wins Othello's love again. Do you find this reading of the end of the play plausible?

CONTEXT A04

In the Renaissance, men expected to command and control their wives. Desdemona submits willingly to Othello's authority. On her marriage day she says, 'My heart's subdued/ Even to the very quality of my lord' (I.3.251–2). Later she obeys Othello even when he strikes her, saying 'I will not stay to offend you' (IV.1.246). Desdemona proves that she is a good Renaissance wife, even if she does deceive her father.

RACE AND COLOUR

OTHELLO'S RACE

It is not possible to define Othello's race exactly. There have been suggestions that he is a Negro, Arabian, Berber or that his Spanish name makes Othello a 'Morisco', a descendant of the Moors of Granada, whose famous palace at Alhambra (see photo) was built in the fourteenth century. It can be argued that Othello's race is irrelevant. If this is the case, why did Shakespeare break with dramatic tradition and present a Moorish hero? Before Othello black characters in Renaissance drama were usually villains. The wealth of **imagery** of black and white and light and dark suggests that colour is significant in this play (see **Part Four: Language**). At the time *Othello* was written there were various stereotypes of the black man, most of them negative. From the medieval period onwards the devil was often depicted in art as a black man surrounded by the flames of hell. Other traditions associated the black man with lust, sin and death. Prior to *Othello*, 'blackamoors' in plays and pageants were usually sinister figures.

CONTRASTING VIEWS OF OTHELLO'S BLACKNESS

There are opposing views about Othello, and his race is at the heart of the way he is perceived. Early in the play positive descriptions of Othello's blackness come from the Moor himself, the Duke of Venice and Desdemona. The fact that Othello has risen to the important and powerful position of general and is accepted as a distinguished member of Venetian society suggests that the state he serves is prepared to see good in foreigners and accept that they have a useful role to play.

However, it is noticeable that even Desdemona, who never regrets marrying Othello, is forced to explain her choice. She defends her marriage by saying she 'saw Othello's visage in his mind' (I.3.253). This suggests either that Desdemona looked past his colour or that Othello's stories and origins excited her. Is Shakespeare suggesting that Othello is the exception to the rule that black is usually bad, or urging us to see that racial differences do not matter in love? If this is the case, Desdemona holds a radical point of view for a **Jacobean** heroine. She is probably the only character in the play who does not view mixed marriages with anxiety. Do the Duke's words to Brabantio suggest caution or racial tolerance? Consider the line, 'Your son-in-law is far more fair than black' (I.3.291). Is this an attempt to excuse Othello's blackness? Does it mean 'Try to accept your daughter's marriage because Othello is virtuous, even though he is black'? Or is this an example of another 'colour blind' white character dismissing race as an irrelevance?

Even when Othello doubts his attractions as a middle-aged black husband, we will recognise that the hero is more noble and impressive than any of the other male characters in the play. Othello is compelling because he is different. His history is fascinating and heroic. It is important to remember that the heroine made an active and positive choice. Othello stresses this when he says 'she had eyes and chose me' (III.3.192). It is Desdemona who insists – publicly – on being allowed to enjoy her marital rights, not Othello.

CRITICAL VIEWPOINT A03

The famous black actor Paul Robeson, who was a notable Othello, said the play was 'a tragedy of racial conflict; a tragedy of honour rather than of jealousy … [I]t is because he is an alien among white people that his [Othello's] mind works so quickly, for he feels dishonor more deeply.' A victim of racial prejudice himself, Robeson saw Othello as an underdog. How do you respond to Robeson's reading of Othello's situation?

There is a very negative view of Othello's blackness, which is undermined because we are not encouraged by Shakespeare to respect the speakers, or we at least question their judgement. To Iago, Roderigo and Brabantio, Othello's colour and racial background – particularly in relation to his marrying a white female – are alarming. Their references to a 'sooty bosom' (I.2.70), 'the thicklips' (I.1.65) and 'an old black ram' (I.1.87) who practises witchcraft construct a negative racial stereotype of Othello. This stereotype would have been very familiar to Shakespeare's audience, even though it makes us uncomfortable today. It is important to remember that the negative racial descriptions of Othello, which dominate the play at times, are essentially inaccurate. The Othello they describe does not exist, although it is possible to argue that the hero begins to display some of the negative aspects of the stereotype when he is persecuted by Iago. Othello is superstitious (the handkerchief), he is passionate (he weeps many times) and he does become violent.

STUDY FOCUS: OTHELLO THE OUTSIDER **A02**

New historicist critics have argued that Othello's tragedy comes about because he can never be anything except an outsider. Othello is in an impossible position as a black man serving a white **patriarchy**. Is Othello foolish to expect his adopted society to accept his marriage to a white woman? There are other ideas of dislocation to consider. We might feel that the hero is dislocated because he marries, turning his back on his profession to become a husband. Othello becomes further dislocated when he views his own race negatively, giving in to Iago's racism. Consideration of Othello's dislocation must include an assessment of his final speeches, which suggest he is not his noble self because he has become a villain. Gratiano and Montano never mention Othello's race when they take him prisoner; they simply want to punish the 'rash and most unfortunate man' for his crimes (V.2.280). References to the devil are reserved for Iago at the end of the play, linking him firmly to the theme of dislocation. In the final scene race is not the cause of Othello's dislocation: his murderous actions are.

KEY QUOTATION: RACE AND COLOUR **A01**

Desdemona views Othello's origins positively. When asked if Othello is jealous she praises her husband's character: 'I think the sun where he was born/ Drew all such humours from him' (III.4.30–1).

- Desdemona's positive view of Othello's race provides a clear contrast with the negative Renaissance racial stereotype of Othello as a cruel, savage black man, which comes across in Iago's speeches.

- Desdemona's positive view of Othello's origins echoes Othello's own early positive descriptions of himself, showing how well matched the couple are, in spite of their racial difference.

- **Ironically**, Desdemona is wrong about Othello: he does become jealous, although Shakespeare does not suggest Othello has a propensity to jealousy because he is black.

CONTEXT **A04**

England and Morocco were closely linked in the late sixteenth century through trade. Elizabeth I set up the Barbary Company, and an embassy of Moroccans was received at court in 1600. At the same time, Elizabeth was responsible for a decree that tried to expel foreigners, specifically negroes and 'blackamoors', from England in 1601. English attitudes to 'foreigners' were clearly contradictory.

STRUCTURE

DRAMATIC STRUCTURE

THE USE OF SETTINGS

CONTEXT   A04

As well as being a setting associated with sophistication and culture, Venice had a reputation as a place of liberty. In particular, foreign visitors noticed the way in which young men were brought up to have loose morals. In his *History of Italy* (1549), William Thomas noted that the Venetians 'bring up their children in so much liberty that … by that time he cometh to twenty years of age' a young man 'knoweth as much lewdness as is possible to be imagined'.

There is a narrow focus in *Othello*. There are two principal locations, Venice and Cyprus, but gradually our attention becomes fixed on a single bedroom, creating a feeling of claustrophobia that is unique in Shakespeare's **tragedies**. The outer world becomes insignificant as Othello becomes obsessed and jealous. The use of Venice as a location is significant. At the end of the sixteenth century, dramatists began to use Italy as a suitable location for **revenge tragedies**. The Italians were thought to be worldly and Venice in particular was associated with everything that was culturally sophisticated. It was a location that suggested power, order and wealth.

It is appropriate that the **Machiavellian** trickster Iago should originate and appear in an Italian setting before being transported to Cyprus. Shakespeare's use of a war with the Turks and the uneasy atmosphere of the garrison town in Cyprus – a 'halfway house' between civilisation and the heathen world – is also dramatically significant. The war isolates Desdemona from everything and everyone she knows; similarly, Othello feels his difference and isolation in Cyprus when he is 'Perplexed in the extreme' (V.2.344). Here, in this unfamiliar setting, with the threat of danger lurking, passions are unleashed and order is destroyed. The storm helps to establish and reflect the fear and violence that the characters will experience in Cyprus, while also being a symbol of the love of Othello and Desdemona.

A SENSE OF CLAUSTROPHOBIA

GRADE BOOSTER   A02

When writing about *Othello* it is important to remember that you are writing about a play. Making references to specific dramatic methods Shakespeare uses, e.g. **mirroring**, **foreshadowing**, will help you to demonstrate your understanding of the genre.

The sense of claustrophobia is heightened by the fact that there is no real subplot in *Othello*. The action of the play focuses on Iago's role and Othello's reactions to his 'reports' (V.2.183). Even the characters who seem to have other 'lives' are closely linked to the married couple: Roderigo's foolish hopes and Cassio's relationship with Bianca provide points of comparison with the Othello–Desdemona match. Our sense of claustrophobia is heightened because we are observing a group of characters who exist in a tightly knit social network, where each character has a clearly defined position and a view of every member of the group. Iago threatens the order and harmony of the network because he is able to manipulate the most powerful group member. The single plot intensifies dramatic tension: we are never given a moment's respite to look away from Iago's progress as he pushes Othello towards tragedy.

REVERSAL AND REPETITION

The structure of the play relies on reversal and repetition. In the first three acts Iago comes to dominate. In Act I he is the underdog, overlooked and irrelevant except as an escort for Desdemona. In Act II, Iago forms his plans and sets up his revenge, so that in Act III he is able to 'triumph' over Othello. Conversely, Othello is at his most secure in Acts I and II, when he defends and then consummates his marriage. In Act III he struggles to resist the jealousy that threatens to overpower his reason, succumbing to it in Act IV. In Act V, Othello sinks further when he smothers Desdemona. He becomes what Iago is: a destructive revenger. At the end of the play the tragic **protagonist** is partially redeemed when he recognises his folly and chooses to destroy himself, while Iago's downfall is assured when he is revealed as a scoundrel. Can you find other repetitions and reversals?

STUDY FOCUS: LONG AND SHORT SCENES   A02

The construction of scenes is extremely effective in *Othello*. Long scenes of painful discussions or confrontation are punctuated by short scenes or moments of violence – verbal and physical. Act III Scene 3 is a good example of how Shakespeare structures a scene for maximum theatrical impact. It is the longest scene in the play, and painful to watch. Iago takes full advantage of the awkwardness that already exists between the married couple. His relentless assault on Othello begins after Desdemona has tried and failed to get Cassio reinstated. When he knows he has hooked Othello, Iago exits. It is safe to leave because Othello has just asked him to set Emilia spying on Desdemona: Iago's poison is working. Othello's first moment of isolation shows his agony. He asks wretchedly, 'Why did I marry?' (III.3.245). After further awkward exchanges between the major characters, Othello is back in Iago's clutches. From line 331 to the end of the scene, 130 lines later, Othello's speeches become explosive and bloodthirsty. By the end of the scene Othello's 'fair warrior' (II.1.179) has become 'the fair devil' (III.3.481). Iago has won the battle of words.

REVISION FOCUS: TASK 12   A02

How far do you agree with the statements below?

- The Roderigo subplot adds very little to the play.
- Love defeats evil at the end of *Othello*.

Try writing opening paragraphs for essays based on these discussion points. Set out your arguments clearly.

CHECK THE BOOK   A03

All the main characters (with the exception of his wife, interestingly) call Iago 'honest', and the ensign makes extensive use of the word himself when deceiving his victims. It is as if Shakespeare is showing Iago's insidious power to 'enmesh them all' (II.3.357) through his ability to get his victims to think of and describe him in the same way. For comments about the fifty two uses of the word 'honest' in the play, see William Empson in John Wain (ed.), *Othello* (1971).

CRITICAL VIEWPOINT   A03

Helen Gardner states that the 'terrible end' of Othello has 'a sense of completeness' which makes it 'the most beautiful end in Shakespearean tragedy'. How would you argue for or against Gardner's viewpoint?

THE TIMESCALE OF OTHELLO

THE 'DOUBLE TIME SCHEME'

The theory of a 'double time scheme' in *Othello* dates from the middle of the nineteenth century. There can be no doubt that there are inconsistencies in the way time is presented in *Othello*. It appears that the disintegration of Othello's mind and marriage occurs extremely fast and Iago recognises that he must move quickly if his plots are to remain concealed; at the same time the characters make statements that suggest time is moving quite slowly.

'LONG TIME'

In Act III Scene 3, Iago describes Cassio's lustful dream, which we are told occurred 'lately' (III.3.416) when Iago shared Cassio's bed. In Act III Scene 4, Bianca complains to Cassio that he has stayed away from her a week, and Othello himself says that he believes Desdemona has committed adultery with Cassio 'A thousand times' (V.2.210). It seems highly unlikely that Lodovico would be sent from Venice to install Cassio as governor within a week of Othello's arrival in Cyprus. These statements which suggest 'long time' are primarily designed to increase the plausibility of Othello's jealousy. But it is also necessary for Shakespeare to present the poisoning of Othello's mind occurring swiftly, without a substantial interval of time. The play would be less dramatic if Iago loosened his grip on his victim once he was in his grasp.

'SHORT TIME'

This brings us to the question of 'short time'. The first act of *Othello* takes place in one night. When the characters have arrived in Cyprus (after a period travelling) time seems to move very quickly, increasing the sense of claustrophobia and heightening the intensity of the drama. The characters land just before 'this present hour of five' (II.2.9–10), the wedding celebrations occur that evening, Cassio is dismissed from his post the same night and we see Iago packing Roderigo off to bed at dawn the following morning. On this day Desdemona pleads for Cassio, having met with him earlier in the morning. Iago sees his chance and moves into action immediately. Between Act III Scene 3 and Act IV Scene 1 there might plausibly be a short interval, but thereafter there can be no break until the curtain falls at the end of Act V. It is this relentlessness that grips us in the theatre, where we do not notice the inconsistencies. It might also be argued that an insistence on 'short time' is a deliberate theatrical decision. Perhaps Shakespeare uses his time scheme to show us how powerful and unreasonable jealousy is. We know that Desdemona has not had the opportunity to commit adultery, and yet her husband becomes convinced she has betrayed him often.

STUDY FOCUS: NIGHT TIME   A02

The majority of the scenes in the play take place at night. The opening scene occurs in the street in Venice at night, and the play ends in Othello's bedroom in Cyprus at night. Cassio's reputation is destroyed at night after a drunken brawl. In Act V he is wounded by Iago in the street at night. Roderigo and Emilia are also stabbed at night, dying of their wounds. Because Iago is present at or has instigated all the violent events that occur at night, we know that night time is associated with his evil progress. Iago has been able to use the cover of darkness to conceal his plots, so it is highly appropriate that he is unmasked at night. However, because so much of *Othello* occurs at night, there is never any doubt that evil will triumph over goodness.

GRADE BOOSTER   A02

In Shakespeare's **tragedies** there is always a key turning point in Act III, after which the play proceeds swiftly towards an inevitable conclusion. Watch out for moments in Acts III–V which suggest Othello and Desdemona are moving inexorably towards their doom. You can comment on these to show your knowledge of structure and genre for AO2 and AO4.

CHECK THE BOOK   A03

The critic A. C. Bradley coined the terms 'long and short time' to describe the timescale in *Othello*. For a fuller discussion of time in the play, have a look at Bradley's *Shakespearean Tragedy* (1992 edition).

FORM

TRAGEDY

THE ORIGINS OF TRAGEDY

Greek tragedy is based on conflict and depicts the downfall of high-ranking characters, who make fatal errors of judgement (**hamartia**) because of their overweening ambition and pride (**hubris**). They are destroyed swiftly by the disastrous consequences of their errors. There is a strong element of fate determining the outcome in Greek tragedy, which the tragic hero dies fighting against. At the end of Greek tragedies justice and order are restored and a new status quo is established. **Catharis** – a purging of the emotions – has taken place. **Aristotle** suggested that tragedy should evoke pity and fear (**pathos**) in an audience.

GREEK TRAGEDY AND *OTHELLO*

Othello fits into the classical mould in a number of ways. Othello is a high-ranking general and is descended from a line of kings. Many believe that he suffers from hubris. What do you think? Is Othello overambitious when he marries Desdemona? Does he overreach himself when he tries to combine the roles of soldier and husband? Is the hero too proud and self-satisfied? It is possible to argue that there is a sense of inevitability about Othello's downfall from the moment he arrives in Cyprus and declares he feels 'too much joy' (II.1.195). Undoubtedly, the tragic denouement in Act V evokes feelings of fear and pity. Emilia performs some of the functions of a Greek **chorus** when she comments on Othello's folly.

STUDY FOCUS: SHAKESPEAREAN TRAGEDY AND *OTHELLO* A02

In his tragedies Shakespeare explores the nature of good and evil, the disintegration of families and the breakdown of law and order within states or countries. In *Othello*, Shakespeare pits good (Othello) against evil (Iago) and we watch as the tragic hero's new family unit is destroyed against the backdrop of the Turkish conflict. As well as observing some of the conventions of Greek tragedy, Shakespeare makes effective use of the theatrical conventions of his own age. By the time Shakespeare came to write *Othello*, it was usual to present tragedies in five acts, with a climax or turning point in Act III and a tragic outcome in Act V.

However, *Othello* is a highly original tragedy. Shakespeare presents the first black hero in English drama, departing from theatrical convention. Shakespeare also subverts tragic conventions by keeping the evil revenger Iago alive at the end of the play. In most **Jacobean** tragedies the villain dies as part of the process of catharsis so that order can be restored. Iago's dominance in this tragedy is also unusual; the villain and hero have equivalent stage time and are equally powerful speakers.

THE INFLUENCE OF COMEDY

Shakespeare makes use of a number of theatrical conventions that his audience would have recognised as belonging to comedy. These borrowings reveal Shakespeare's ability to work innovatively with the tragic form. The central focus in the play – the jealous husband who fears he has been cuckolded – is more often associated with comedy than tragedy. Iago is a descendant of the cunning slaves of Roman comedy, who delight in outwitting their masters. The foolish father Baptista and his wily daughter Bianca, who chooses her own husband in Shakespeare's early comedy *The Taming of the Shrew*, are ancestors of Brabantio and Desdemona. Both – deceived father and deceptive daughter – are stock characters from comedy.

LANGUAGE

STYLES OF SPEECH

OTHELLO'S CHARACTERISTIC SPEECH STYLE

From his opening speeches in Act I Scenes 2 and 3 it is clear that Othello's characteristic **idiom** is dignified, measured **blank verse**. This helps establish his heroism and nobility. Othello's speeches demonstrate authority in Act I Scene 2. There is a sense of danger and beauty in Othello's references to 'bright swords' and 'dew' (line 59), when he is confronted by Brabantio and his followers. Shakespeare makes us aware that Othello is an impressive character and a powerful speaker. This power is reinforced in the next scene when Othello uses words not just to defend his elopement with Desdemona, but also to enable him to keep her. If Othello does not speak persuasively the 'bloody book of law' (I.3.68) may deprive him of his wife. Desdemona acknowledges her husband's rhetorical power when she speaks. She was seduced by his storytelling. Desdemona uses the same dignified and purposeful idiom that Othello employs. Through their shared speech patterns Shakespeare conveys the harmony and mutual affection of Othello and Desdemona. The lovers are, as Iago expresses it, 'well tuned' (II.1.198) at this point.

OTHELLO THE POET

Many of Othello's long speeches can be compared to poems, expressing the nobility and romance we come to associate with the tragic **protagonist**. Othello is Shakespeare's most 'poetic' hero, which seems appropriate because we focus on his experiences of love in this play. But Othello does not just speak of his love poetically; he speaks of his career as a soldier in the same vein, establishing himself as a great military man. The orderliness of Othello's verse suggests not just his confidence as a lover, but also the fact that the senate are wise to trust in Othello's judgement. Because of his measured speech style, we accept the poetic hero as both soldier and husband in the first act of the play.

STUDY FOCUS: THE POWER OF LANGUAGE IN *OTHELLO* A02

Elizabethan and **Jacobean** dramatists used language to establish and build dramatic atmosphere, to define time, place and character. But in *Othello*, language is not simply the medium by which the drama is conveyed: in this play language is action. Othello 'falls' because he believes Iago, whose every utterance is deceptive. Through language, Iago imposes his will on the hero, and creates opposition within Othello's marriage. When Othello is taken in by false words, **tragedy** is the result. This play shows us the power of words. We watch as characters construct their own and others' identities through language, and exert power either by speaking, remaining silent or silencing others.

OTHELLO'S CORRUPTION

When Othello begins to see himself and his wife through Iago's eyes and is corrupted by Iago's false words, his stately style begins to break down. At his lowest point, just before he falls to the ground in a fit, Othello's words convey his agitation. In Act IV Scene 1 lines 35–43 he asks questions and barks out a series of short exclamations. He exclaims 'handkerchief!' three times. Othello's fractured sense of self is conveyed through the words and syntax. His speech ends with these lines: 'It is not words that shakes me thus. Pish! Noses, ears and lips. Is't possible? Confess? handkerchief! O devil!' (IV.1.41–3).

GRADE BOOSTER A02

There are significant differences between the poetic **images** and speech style Othello uses early in Acts I and II in comparison with the violent images and disjointed style he uses in Acts III and IV. For a good AO2 mark, you need to be able to comment closely on specific examples of Othello's 'styles' and explore what they mean, and why Othello's speech style changes.

CRITICAL VIEWPOINT A03

G. Wilson-Knight has described Othello's speech as 'highly coloured … stately … rich in sound and phrase'. He also suggests that Othello's speech displays a 'uniquely soldierly precision' and 'serenity of thought'. His famous lines convey these qualities: 'Keep up your bright swords, for the dew will rust them' (I.2.59).

There is a terrible **irony** in Othello's declaration that 'It is not words that shakes me thus'. The events of the play and the violence of his outburst here suggest that words are the cause of Othello's destruction. Notice the use of disjointed **prose** rather than measured verse: reason has given way to passion. Othello has also begun to use oaths, such as 'Zounds' (II.3.203), which are associated with Iago. This shows Iago's ability to influence the speech styles of others. Right at the end of this speech we struggle to make any sense of Othello's words. These lines suggest the hero's degradation and degeneration.

LANGUAGE AND DISINTEGRATION

From Act III onwards Othello and Desdemona struggle to understand one another's language. The break-up of their marital harmony is conveyed through the disruption in the lines, and Othello's measured calm gives way to verbal bullying (see III.4.80–98). This pattern **mirrors** the disrupted lines of Act III Scene 3 when Iago first started to poison Othello's mind. Desdemona later says, 'I understand a fury in your words/ But not the words' (IV.2.32–3). By this point Othello misconstrues everything Desdemona says. Eventually, failing to see that her words should be taken at face value, Othello smothers and silences Desdemona. When confronted with the truth Othello then recovers, returning to the majestic idiom of his earlier speeches at the end of Act V. His final speech echoes his first speech to the senate, but Othello no longer speaks of himself as a worthy hero. Now he compares himself to 'the base Indian' and 'the circumcised dog' (V.2.345 and 353). Othello's words and syntax recall former glories, but also point towards the 'bloody period' of the hero's death (V.2.354).

IAGO'S SPEECH STYLE

Language is the source of Iago's power, but his characteristic idiom is different from Othello's. It is full of **colloquialisms** and oaths, befitting a cynical soldier. But Iago's use of language is more complicated than this. We quickly notice that the villain slips between prose and verse, adapting his style to suit his different audiences and purposes. The fast-moving prose of his exchanges with Roderigo conveys Iago's crude nature, but the ensign makes use of a loftier style too, as in his **parody** of Othello's speech style in Act III Scene 3 (lines 465–72). This speech is an example of Iago's power: he can manipulate his style effortlessly. Most worryingly for the audience, Othello begins to use Iago's base idiom when he decides to revenge himself on Desdemona, showing Iago's increasing authority over him. When he adopts Iago's style and begins to eavesdrop, Othello shows that he has become 'well tuned' with the wrong character.

Iago's use of **asides** reveals his cunning, destructive nature. The villain is able not only to direct but also to comment on the action of the play. Iago's use of **soliloquies** reinforces his power. In *Othello*, Iago speaks his soliloquies first (Othello's soliloquies occur towards the end of the play), drawing the audience in as he outlines his intentions. Because we know exactly what his plans are, we might feel that Shakespeare forces us to admire the villain: Iago is such an impressive manipulator of language. Iago's soliloquies and asides are also a source of a great deal of the **dramatic irony** of *Othello*, which increases dramatic tension for the audience.

Finally, Iago is able to use silence effectively, as in Act III Scene 3 when he deliberately introduces 'stops' (III.3.123) to infuriate and intrigue Othello. By appearing reluctant to talk, Iago gains the opportunity to speak at length and poison Othello's mind. At the end of the play Iago's defiant and deliberate silence can suggest continued power (the villain refuses to reveal his motives and admit remorse) or power thwarted. It is both ironic and appropriate that Iago is unmasked by Emilia, whose powers of speech he has ignored.

CHECK THE FILM **AO3**

The Hollywood retelling of *Othello*, *O* (2001), is set in an American private high school, where the lead – Ovin – is a gifted black basketball player. The Desdemona figure is the principal's daughter. The director claimed that he wanted to use Shakespeare's play to 'draw attention to the violence that occurs in American high schools'. Do you believe a focus on violence is true to the original play?

CHECK THE FILM **AO3**

In the 1981 BBC Shakespeare production of *Othello*, Bob Hoskins's Iago continues to laugh (as he has done throughout the play) after he refuses to speak. The production ends with the sound of Iago's echoing laughter as he is taken away for torture. Iago clearly feels he has triumphed.

IMAGERY

POISONING

There are a number of **images** of poisoning, which we come to associate with Iago. In Act I Scene 1 the ensign says that he wants to 'poison his [Brabantio's] delight' (I.1.67) so that he can make trouble for Othello. Iago's jealousy of the Moor is so strong that it 'Doth like a poisonous mineral gnaw my inwards' (II.1.295). So Iago resolves to 'pour this pestilence into his ear' (II.3.351). These references to poison are appropriate to Iago, whose actions are swift and deadly. Iago relishes the pain he causes, as we can see from his description of his methods in Act III Scene 3. Iago is gleeful as he describes how his poison will 'Burn like the mines of sulphur' (see III.3.329–32).

Othello describes how he feels tortured by jealousy, using images that recall Iago's words, 'If there be cords or knives,/ Poison, or fire, or suffocating streams,/ I'll not endure it' (III.3.391–3). The most chilling reference to poison comes in Act IV Scene 1 when Othello decides to murder Desdemona:

OTHELLO: Get me some poison, Iago, this night. I'll
not expostulate with her, lest her body and beauty
unprovide my mind again. This night, Iago.
IAGO: Do it not with poison, strangle her in her bed –
even the bed that she hath contaminated. (IV.1.201–5)

His mind poisoned with foul thoughts, Othello now seeks to kill Desdemona in the bed that he thinks she has poisoned with her lust. It is particularly chilling that the real poisoner (Iago) suggests the method of killing Desdemona. Iago's power is underlined at the end of the play when Lodovico looks at the 'tragic loading' of bodies on Othello's bed, commenting that it 'poisons sight'. The final image of poisoning in the play emphasises the terrible consequences of infection in *Othello* (V.2.361–2).

HELL AND THE DEVIL

Shakespeare's use of imagery of hell and the devil subverts the negative stereotype of the evil black man and links Iago firmly to the figure of the **vice** from medieval drama. Iago is associated with images of hell and the devil from the start of the play. He makes the link himself at the end of his **soliloquy** in Act I Scene 3. Outlining his evil intentions Iago says, 'Hell and night/ Must bring this monstrous birth to the world's light' (I.3.402–3). Later there is the **oxymoron**, 'Divinity of hell!', followed by these lines:

When devils will their blackest sins put on
They do suggest at first with heavenly shows
As I do now. (II.3.345–8)

There is delight in these lines. Iago revels in evil. Iago also describes Othello as 'the devil' (I.1.90), but in the context of the play this seems to be a racial slur rather than a comment on Othello's character. Elsewhere Iago's comments on the Moor's natural goodness, which makes his (Iago's) work easier. Iago's hellish designs succeed in making Othello see Desdemona as devilish. Othello makes a 'sacred vow' (III.3.464) to wreak vengeance on her 'by yond marble heaven' (III.3.463), convincing himself that Desdemona is damned and must be stopped in her life of sin. In Act IV Scene 2, Othello attempts to force an admission of guilt from Desdemona:

Come, swear it, damn thyself,
Lest, being like one of heaven, the devils themselves
Should fear to seize thee ... (IV.2.36–8)

In this image we see the enormity of Desdemona's crime from Othello's point of view. As he leaves in disgust, Othello turns to Emilia and accuses her too; she 'keeps the gates of hell' for Desdemona (IV.2.94). Emilia turns these words on Othello in the final scene when

---

GRADE BOOSTER **A02**

To get a good grade consider the way in which images are used to evoke particular audience responses. For example, how does Shakespeare intend us to feel when we hear Lodovico's comment that the image of the bodies on the bed at the end of the play 'poisons sight' (V.2.362)?

she discovers Desdemona's murder: 'thou art a devil' she rages, 'the blacker devil' (V.2.131 and 129). But it is Iago who is revealed as the true devil, where he is described as a 'hellish villain' (V.2.366). When he realises the truth about Iago in Act V Scene 2, Othello is bewildered by the ensign's evil. He asks, 'Will you, I pray, demand that demi-devil/ Why he hath ensnared my soul and body?' (V.2.298–9).

ANIMALS AND INSECTS

There are numerous references to animals and insects which chart Othello's downfall. In Iago's mouth this imagery is reductive and negative. Several images suggest how much the villain despises his victims. In Act I Scene 1, Iago sets out with Roderigo to 'Plague him [Brabantio] with flies!' (I.1.70). When he describes Othello's match with Desdemona Iago uses crude animal imagery: 'an old black ram/ Is tupping your white ewe!' he informs Brabantio (I.1.87–8); his daughter has been 'covered' with 'a Barbary horse' (I.1.110); the couple are 'making the beast with two backs' (I.1.115). Othello is an object of scorn too. Iago is confident that the Moor will 'tenderly be led by th' nose/ As asses are' (I.3.400–1), and made 'egregiously an ass' (II.1.307). Iago is sure that Cassio can be humiliated too: 'With as little a web as this will I ensnare as great a fly as Cassio' (II.1.168–9).

Othello is infected by this imagery. But the animal imagery in Othello's speeches reveals the hero's misery, rather than sneering triumph. In Act III Scene 3, Othello says:

> I had rather be a toad
> And live upon this vapour of a dungeon
> Than keep a corner in a thing I love
> For others' uses. (III.3.274–7)

The image of a toad is repeated in Act IV Scene 2 when Othello describes his sorrow at 'losing' the innocent Desdemona he loved so much. Othello is mortified by corruption. (See IV.2.58–63.)

Iago maintain's Othello's jealousy with images of bestial lust. When the Moor demands proof of his suspicions Iago replies sharply:

> It is impossible you should see this
> Were they [Cassio and Desdemona] as prime as goats, as hot as monkeys,
> As salt as wolves in pride ... (III.3.405–7)

We know that Othello has lost all power of reason and can no longer fight off the terrible sexual images his imagination has been polluted with when he yelps 'Goats and monkeys!' (IV.1.263). Othello has become the 'monster, and a beast' he described earlier in the same scene (IV.1.62). It is horribly **ironic** that Desdemona, who we are informed could 'sing the savageness out of a bear' (IV.1.186), cannot convince Othello that his suspicions are false. Appropriately, the last animal images in the play are applied to Iago, whose evil makes him an 'inhuman dog' (V.1.62) and a 'Spartan dog' (V.2.359).

THE SEA AND MILITARY HEROISM

In stark contrast to the imagery associated with Iago, the imagery commonly associated with the noble Othello of the first half of the play is suggestive of power and bravery. Images of the sea and military heroism abound. Othello describes his illustrious career with dignity in Act I Scene 3 (see lines 82–90 and 129–46). Desdemona echoes him when she says:

> My downright violence and scorn of fortunes
> May trumpet to the world. My heart's subdued
> Even to the very quality of my lord ... (I.3.250–2)

By using the terminology of war to describe her love we see that Desdemona is 'well tuned' (II.1.198) with her husband. It is fitting then that Othello describes Desdemona as his 'fair warrior' (II.1.179). Later, when Othello feels their marital harmony has been destroyed, we

sense how deeply he feels Desdemona's supposed betrayal as he spurs himself on to revenge, the **imagery** suggesting the violence to come:

> Like to the Pontic sea
> Whose icy current and compulsive course
> Ne'er feels retiring ebb but keeps due on
> To the Propontic and the Hellespont:
> Even so my bloody thoughts with violent pace
> Shall ne'er look back, ne'er ebb to humble love (III.3.456–61)

STUDY FOCUS: *OTHELLO* AND THE IMAGERY OF VIOLENCE A02

Violence is implicit in the sea and military imagery associated with Othello. As he prepares to take his own life Othello refers to his military career, but also recognises that he has reached 'my journey's end, here is my butt/ And very sea-mark of my utmost sail' (V.2.265–6). This final image of the sea is poignant. By reverting to the noble imagery associated with him earlier in the play Othello is able to raise himself again in our esteem. It is fitting that the images of blood, which Othello repeatedly used when planning his revenge on Desdemona, are replaced by imagery of self-destruction. Just before he kills himself Othello describes how he once beat a Venetian and then 'took by th' throat the circumcised dog/ And smote him – thus!' (V.2.353–4).

BLACK AND WHITE

References to black and white are important. There are also images of light and darkness, heaven and hell (see **Hell and the Devil** above). These images are related to the central paradox in the play: Othello, who is 'far more fair than black' (I.3.291), is the virtuous, noble man, while white Iago proves to be a devilish creature with a black soul. When Iago blackens Desdemona's character, Othello feels his honour is threatened; he expresses his dismay by referring to his own blackness in a negative way. Up to this point Othello has been proud of his race and secure in his love. Now we sense that the 'black' (in the sense of angry, violent) Othello will supersede the 'fair' Othello:

> I'll have some proof. Her name, that was as fresh
> As Dian's visage, is now begrimed and black
> As mine own face. (III.3.389–91)

We might feel that these lines describe Othello's regret at the corruption of his imagination by Iago. He no longer has a 'fresh' name; instead his mind – as well as his name – is 'begrimed', just as Desdemona's name has been besmirched. Later in the same scene Othello calls for assistance with his revenge: 'Arise, black vengeance, from thy hollow cell' (III.3.450). Here Othello seems to link himself to hell and darkness, even though he also feels that he is serving heaven by making 'a sacrifice' (V.2.65) of Desdemona. The confusion suggested by these images is appropriate: the hero is pulled in two directions for much of the play, wanting to believe that Desdemona is honest, while also believing that she is damned.

Desdemona is associated with images of light, divinity and perfection throughout the play. The final **metaphor** Othello uses to speak of her suggests her purity and preciousness; she is 'a pearl' he threw away like a 'base Indian' (V.2.345). As he prepares to kill her Othello cannot quite believe that Desdemona was false; the metaphor 'Put out the light, and then put out the light!' (V.2.7) expresses this idea clearly. The drama of the play occurs as Othello moves away from the light of Desdemona's love towards the darkness of Iago and his world view, becoming a black villain in the process. Notice how many of the key scenes or events occur at night (see **The Timescale of *Othello*** above). It might be argued that we associate Othello with darkness from the very beginning of the play: his first entrance occurs at night, and his final act, the murder of Desdemona, also occurs at night. Has the Moor fulfilled his tragic destiny when he snuffs out the light on Desdemona and himself?

GRADE BOOSTER A02

Watch out for the imagery of blood in *Othello*. You can relate it to the portrayal of violence and jealousy. For example, Othello repeatedly uses the word 'blood' when his mind is infected and he starts to play the role of revenger.

CHECK THE BOOK A03

All of Shakespeare's **tragedies** include extremely violent acts and deaths. In *Antony and Cleopatra* both the major characters kill themselves for love: Antony runs himself through with a sword and dies in his lover's arms, while Cleopatra poisons herself with an asp (a snake).

IRONY

IRONY AND IAGO

There are various types of **irony** in *Othello*, which relies heavily on **dramatic irony** for its effects. There are also examples of situational and verbal irony which help us to understand the action. Iago is the primary source of dramatic irony. He informs us of his intentions, but his victims do not know that they are being manipulated. The audience knows more than the characters, increasing the tension. Will Iago succeed in his diabolical designs or will he be discovered?

It can be argued that the irony that surrounds Iago and his role forces us to reject the villain. We may marvel at his ingenuity and skill but we cannot approve of Iago. We become increasingly worried by the verbal irony of repeated references to him as 'honest'. There is considerable irony in the use of the word 'love' in this play too. Notice how frequently it is on Iago's lips when he is manipulating his victims. Iago's use of the word 'love' is particularly chilling in the scenes in which we watch the true love of Othello and Desdemona being destroyed by the false and empty love Iago pretends to feel.

An audience might also feel that in some ways the joke is on Iago. He thinks that he is a cunning villain, who can arrogantly conceal his true self and remain aloof while all around him 'lose their cool', but is he not driven by passion? Iago's downfall is ironic. He is brought down by two characters he had no respect for and believed he controlled. Emilia destroys Iago's reputation as an honest man and Roderigo's letters condemn him to torture.

IRONY AND OTHELLO

The many ironies of Othello's situation create his tragedy. The noble warrior is destroyed by his petty-minded subordinate. The great soldier becomes a jealous lover. Othello's military strengths – decisiveness and ruthlessness – are weaknesses in his personal life. The man who roved the world, fighting on its battlefields, dies by his own hand in a bedroom, under armed guard. Othello falls at the very moment that he feels he has reached the height of his success by marrying the 'divine Desdemona' (II.1.73). When his conception of himself is most secure, Othello is undermined. Othello finds that his heroic past counts for nothing: he is forced into the role of villain by the 'inhuman dog' Iago (V.1.62). Having been resolutely sure of Desdemona, Othello finds himself wondering why he has married, convinced that he has united himself with 'the cunning whore of Venice' (IV.2.91). For her own part, Desdemona expects to consummate her marriage in Cyprus, but her marriage bed is transformed into her deathbed. Othello's conviction that his wife has weak morals is heartbreakingly ironic; when he doubts Desdemona, the hero reveals his own weaknesses.

OTHER EXAMPLES OF IRONY

Ironically, other characters reveal their weaknesses when they feel they are on the brink of or have achieved success. Cassio gains promotion only to be disgraced for drunken brawling; Roderigo hopes to kill Cassio and supplant him in Desdemona's affections, but is instead murdered by the man who urged him onto the vile deed, a man whose friendship he believed in. This kind of ironic ignorance is repeated in other relationships in *Othello*. None of the characters truly recognises the real honesty or depravity of those they interact with.

GRADE BOOSTER **A02**

A comparison of the scenes in which songs are sung in *Othello* will help you to understand Shakespeare's uses of dramatic irony and **mirroring**. In Act 2 Scene 3, Iago leads the singing of a bawdy drinking song as part of his strategy to get Cassio drunk. The genial mood Iago establishes hides his poisonous intentions. In Act IV Scene 3, Desdemona sings the melancholy willow song. Iago's bawdy singing – ironically – leads indirectly to Desdemona's song about doomed love.

GRADE BOOSTER **A02**

Dramatic irony is used by many playwrights, but in a play such as *Othello*, in which secrets, lies and people's own words unwittingly condemn them, it is worth mentioning, in relation to AO2, how it is particularly effective in creating tension and tragic momentum.

HISTORICAL BACKGROUND

SHAKESPEARE'S AGE

THE RENAISSANCE

The Renaissance (literally 'rebirth') saw a revival of artistic and intellectual endeavour, which began in Italy in the fourteenth century. It spread gradually northwards across Europe, and is first detectable in England in the early sixteenth century in the writings of the scholar and statesman Sir Thomas More and in the poetry of Sir Thomas Wyatt and Henry Howard, Earl of Surrey. Its keynote was a curiosity in thought which challenged old assumptions and traditions. There was a new confidence in human reason and in human potential which challenged old convictions. Classical texts and the culture of Greece and Rome were rediscovered and, with this rediscovery, the 'golden age' of English literature began, which Shakespeare's plays are part of.

SHAKESPEARE'S DRAMA AND THE RENAISSANCE

Shakespeare's drama is innovative and challenging in exactly the way of the Renaissance. It examines and questions the beliefs, assumptions and politics upon which Elizabethan society was founded. And although his plays conclude in a restoration of order and stability, Shakespeare subverts traditional values, as we see in *Othello*, where the tragic hero is a black man and the heroine an assertive young woman. Critical, rebellious, mocking voices, like Iago's, are heard in Shakespeare's plays. Are characters like Iago given subversive views to discredit them, or were they the only ones through whom a voice could be given to radical and dissident ideas? Was Shakespeare a conservative or a revolutionary?

Because of censorship, any criticism Shakespeare makes of the way those in authority behave, or questions he asks about race and nobility had to be muted or oblique. Direct criticism of the monarch or contemporary English court would not be tolerated. This has something to do with why Shakespeare's plays are always set either in the past, or abroad, as is the case with *Othello*.

NATIONALISM AND XENOPHOBIA

As a student of *Othello*, you need to be aware of the attitudes that existed towards foreigners in Elizabethan England. Italy had what Norman Sanders has called a 'double image'. It was a land of refinement and romance, a model of civilisation. Venice, Europe's centre of capitalism, was a free state, and renowned as one of the most beautiful cities in Italy.

However, at the same time, Italy was a country associated with decadence, villainy and vice. Venice itself was suspect, because it was, as Norman Sanders puts it 'a racial and religious melting pot'. Elizabethans were against mixed marriages and viewed Negroes and 'blackamoors' with suspicion. Elizabeth I issued edicts demanding their removal from England because they were considered an 'annoyance'. Racist views were common, and many believed that black people were fit only to be slaves.

RELIGION IN SHAKESPEARE'S ENGLAND

The nationalism of the English Renaissance was reinforced by Protestantism. Henry VIII had broken with Rome in the 1530s and in Shakespeare's time there was an independent Protestant state church. Shakespeare's plays are free from direct religious sentiment, but their emphases are Protestant. Othello has converted to Christianity and the preoccupation with good and evil in the play suggests its religious context. The central figures of many of Shakespeare's plays, including Othello, are frequently individuals beset by temptation and the lure of evil. Shakespeare's heroes have the preoccupation with self and the introspective tendencies encouraged by Protestantism. We see an example of Othello's introspection in Act III Scene 3 when he is alone on stage and begins to doubt his attractions as a husband (see his speech at line 262).

Shakespeare's tragic heroes are haunted by their consciences; they agonise over their actions as they follow what can be understood as a spiritual progress towards heaven or hell. This is exactly the psychological journey Othello goes on. We see evidence of Othello's tormented conscience both before and after he kills his wife. Desdemona remarks on Othello's inner torment when she says in alarm, 'Alas, why gnaw you so your nether lip?/ Some bloody passion shakes your very frame' (V.2.43–4).

FEMALE SUBORDINATION

Although questions were being asked about the social hierarchy, women remained in subordinate roles, their lives controlled by **patriarchy** during the Renaissance. Women expected to be ruled by men, as Desdemona's submission to Othello demonstrates. Women had few legal rights. They were entitled to inherit property, but if they married, everything they owned passed to their husbands. Many men saw women as possessions, and fathers expected to choose husbands for their daughters, as Brabantio does in *Othello*. Intellectually, women were thought to be inferior to men, and incapable of rational thought. They rarely received an education. Assertive and argumentative women were seen as a threat to the social order and were punished for their behaviour with forms of torture such as the ducking stool, the scold's bridle (an iron framwork placed around the head) or 'carting' (being carted around town and publically mocked).

However, European visitors to England commented that English women had more freedom than was the case in many other European countries. Shakespeare's wife successfully managed a home and property, as well as her family, for twenty years while Shakespeare was pursuing his career in London. Shakespeare's audiences included women, and he wrote a large number of parts for strong-minded female characters, like Desdemona and Emilia.

CONTEXT **A04**

Courtesans and 'bad' women were usually Italian on the **Jacobean** stage. For example, even the central character in *The Dutch Courtesan* (1604) has the Italian name Franceschina. In the comedy *The Fleire* (1606–7) by Edward Sharpham two Florentine cousins discuss their trade as prostitutes. One says that a courtesan 'is for your courtier', while a whore 'is for every rascal'. Which type is Bianca?

SHAKESPEARE'S THEATRE

The form of the Elizabethan theatre derived from the inn yards and animal-baiting rings in which actors had performed in the past. They were circular wooden buildings with a paved courtyard in the middle open to the sky. A rectangular stage jutted out into the middle of this yard. Some of the audience stood in the yard (or 'pit') to watch the play. They were thus on three sides of the stage, close up to it and on a level with it. These 'groundlings' paid only a penny to get in, but for wealthier spectators there were seats in three covered tiers or galleries between the inner and outer walls of the building, extending round most of the auditorium and overlooking the pit and the stage. Such a theatre could hold about 3,000 spectators. The yards were about 80ft in diameter and the rectangular stage approximately 40ft by 30ft and 5ft 6in high.

STAGING PRACTICES

On the Shakespearean stage there was very little in the way of scenery or props – there was nowhere to store them, nor any way to set them up. Anyway, productions had to be transportable for performance at court or at noble houses. The stage was bare, which is why characters often tell us where they are. Location in Shakespeare's plays can be

symbolic. Descriptions of places are used to create a specific dramatic mood or situation. The storm in Cyprus that opens Act II of *Othello* is described verbally by the characters on stage, to create a mood of tension for the audience.

During night-time scenes characters may mention they cannot see what is going on to establish a sense of danger, as happens in Acts I and V of *Othello*. Torches, tapers and candles would have been used to signify night to the audience. The main prop for *Othello* would have been the bed on which Othello strangles Desdemona: it would have dominated the stage. Although Othello's violence against Desdemona is shocking, it needs to be considered in context. The Elizabethans lived in a violent world. Domestic abuse was not uncommon and, except in cases of extreme cruelty, not considered unacceptable.

STAGE HISTORY OF *OTHELLO*

Othello has been one of Shakespeare's most frequently performed plays. The first recorded performance was at the Banqueting House at Whitehall in London (see photo) on 1 November 1604. It was attended by James I, patron of Shakespeare's company, The King's Men. The first actresses to play Desdemona would have appeared on the **Restoration** stage. The diarist Samuel Pepys saw the play twice and noted how the audience called out in horror when Desdemona was killed. In the eighteenth century, partly because of the presence of women on the stage and in the audience, it was felt necessary to make refinements to the text so that *Othello* met contemporary standards of decorum. For example, Desdemona's willow song was removed because it was thought unladylike, and Othello's speeches were cut to emphasise his nobility.

The tradition of cutting the play continued into the nineteenth century, by which time there were two types of Othello on stage: the controlled, dignified Moor or what Norman Sanders describes as the 'blazing portrayal of torrential sexual passion and wild jealousy'. One of the most famous productions of the 1870s involved the Italian actor Tommaso Salvini, who spoke all his lines in Italian while the other characters spoke English. Salvini's Othello was noted for his eroticism and savagery. He prowled around the stage like a tiger, pounced on Desdemona in Act V Scene 2 and 'dashed with her … across the stage and through the curtains … You heard a crash as he flung her on the bed and growls as if of a wild beast over his prey' (see J. R. Towse, *Sixty Years of the Theatre*, 1916). Ira Aldridge, a black American performer who emigrated to England because of racial discrimination against black actors in the USA, was another notable nineteenth-century Othello. He was the first documented black actor to play Othello when he appeared at Covent Garden in London in 1833. He also played Lear, Shylock, Macbeth and Hamlet.

CONTEMPORARY PRODUCTIONS

In the twentieth century *Othello* remained popular on stage, as it is today. There have been three well received productions in the past few years. In 2007, Chitwetel Ejiofor and Ewan McGregor performed the play in period dress. Michael Billington of *The Guardian* commented that Ejiofor 'reminds us that Othello's tragic flaw is less jealousy than an excessive idealisation of his beloved' (5 December 2007). Desdemona was played by Kelly Reilly as possessing 'social bravery' and 'vulnerability'. Billington said 'the intertwined bodies of Othello and Desdemona' at the end of Act V showed how 'something of great potential beauty has been destroyed by the world's ugliness'.

Lenny Henry took on the role of Othello and had a notable success with it in 2009. According to *The Times* (19 February 2009), Henry captured the dignity, anger, bewilderment and pain of Othello. In 2011, Clarke Peters and Dominic West appeared together in Sheffield as Othello and Iago. West played the role of Iago with a Yorkshire accent as 'a bluff, dirty-minded NCO [noncommissioned officer] who is filled with a rancorous, destructive negativity … he has a surface honesty … that yields a lot of laughs' (Michael Billington, *The Guardian*, 21 September 2011). Cassio was played as 'a bit of a rake', making Othello's sexual jealousy plausible, while Emilia was 'raunchy' and 'sex starved', 'with an eye for a young lieutenant'.

CONTEXT **A04**

The nineteenth-century tradition of using Oriental props and costumes when playing Othello has continued to the present day. A notable RSC production of the 1980s featured costumes that bore a resemblance to the garb worn by the Moorish ambassador to Elizabeth I, who was painted in 1600. This portrait has undoubtedly influenced the stage history of the play.

CHECK THE FILM **A04**

Two significant film productions are by Orson Welles (1952) and Oliver Parker (1995); in the latter, Laurence Fishburne is the first big-screen black Othello.

LITERARY BACKGROUND

SHAKESPEARE AND HIS CONTEMPORARIES

Shakespeare had previously portrayed a pair of doomed lovers in *Romeo and Juliet* (c. 1595), which features a young couple (Juliet is only 13, Romeo a little older) from rival Veronese families, the Capulets and Montagues. Because of the feud, the love between Romeo and Juliet is as subversive and unacceptable to their families as Othello's marriage to Desdemona. In both *Romeo and Juliet* and *Othello*, Shakespeare explores the tragic consequences of intense love. In each play the tragic heroine is assertive, but the **patriarch** – Capulet or Brabantio – expects his daughter to make a socially acceptable marriage and is angered when she does not.

'Unequal' and socially unacceptable matches are portrayed frequently by Shakespeare's contemporaries, notably in the plays of John Webster. In *The Duchess of Malfi* (c. 1614), a **revenge tragedy**, the Duchess is cruelly tormented and then murdered on her brothers' orders when they find out about her secret marriage to a servant, a steward called Antonio. Like *Othello*, *The Duchess of Malfi* raises questions about the ways in which men dominate and abuse women.

If you are interested in the way in which race is portrayed in other plays by Shakespeare, you could start by looking at the villainous Moor Aaron in *Titus Andronicus* (1593). He fathers a child with a white woman, Tamora. Their baby is described in these terms: 'A joyless, dismal, black, and sorrowful issue./ Here is the babe, as loathsome as a toad.'

There are a number of **malcontent** and **Machiavellian** villains in Renaissance drama who share Iago's cynicism and abuse others to get what they want. In Shakespeare's *King Lear* (c. 1605), the illegitimate son Edmund plots against his brother and father so that he can get their land and titles. Edmund exploits women in the same way that Iago does. Iago can also be compared with the amoral villain Flamineo in Webster's *The White Devil* (c. 1612). In the hope of advancing his career, Flamineo plots a double murder to bring his married sister Vittoria together with the Duke of Brachiano, who is also married.

LATER TEXTS EXPLORING THEMES OF *OTHELLO*

Later writers have explored the destructive nature of love in a number of texts that can be compared with *Othello*. Emily Brontë's *Wuthering Heights* (1847), Thomas Hardy's *The Mayor of Casterbridge* (1886) and *Tess of the D'Urbervilles* (1891) and Daphne Du Maurier's *Rebecca* (1938) all explore the darker side of obsessive love. Henrik Ibsen's play *A Doll's House* (1879) portrays the disintegration of the marriage of Torvald and Nora Helmer, while Arthur Miller's drama *A View From a Bridge* (1955) portrays the tragic consequences of Eddie Carbone's possessive love for his niece. Robert Browning's dramatic monologues, *My Last Duchess* and *Porphyria's Lover* (1842), offer poetic depictions of obsessive males, who seek to control the women they love. Many of Elizabeth Barret Browning's poems depict idealised love, while Sylvia Plath's collections, *The Colossus* (1960) and *Ariel* (1965), include poems which evoke the sinister, destructive qualities of love.

Finally, you might be interested in looking at the work of Caryl Phillips, who explores themes related to race and dislocation. In *The Nature of Blood* (1997), Phillips rewrites Othello's story in the novel's second major story line. The narrative focuses on Othello's attempts to integrate into Venetian society when he is hired by the Doge to lead the Venetian army against the Turks in the late fifteenth century.

CHECK THE BOOK A03

Othello can be compared with other **tragedies** where the hero is tempted into evil, for example Marlowe's *Doctor Faustus* (c. 1594), in which Faustus makes a pact with the devil, and *Macbeth* (c.1606), who is spurred on to villainy by his wife and his own ambition.

CHECK THE BOOK A03

Love and marriage and gender roles are frequently portrayed in comedy as well as tragedy. Shakespeare's *The Taming of the Shrew* (1593) and *Much Ado About Nothing* (1598) feature strong heroines.

CRITICAL DEBATES

EARLY VIEWS

Thomas Rymer, one of the play's most negative critics, wrote a detailed commentary on *Othello* in *A Short View of Tragedy* (1693). Rymer was outraged by the idea of a black hero and would not accept that the play was a great tragedy, declaring the 'defect' of Othello was that it did not have a moral lesson for the audience. Rymer suggested that Othello might serve only as 'a caution' to maidens not to run away with 'blackamoors' without their parents' consent.

In contrast to Rymer, Dr Johnson's (1765) response to Othello was positive. In Johnson's view Othello was 'magnanimous, artless, and credulous, boundless in his confidence, ardent in his affection, inflexible in his resolution, and obdurate in his revenge'. Johnson also suggested that the play provided a 'very useful moral, not to make an unequal match'.

NINETEENTH- AND TWENTIETH-CENTURY VIEWS

At the beginning of the nineteenth century, Coleridge offered a view of Iago's **characterisation** that has been influential. He argued that Iago is 'A being next to the devil', driven by 'motiveless malignity'. Coleridge suggests that Iago operates without adequate motivation; he is bad because he is bad. Many critics have sought to explain Iago's motivation and commented on his skill as a 'dramatist'. Other nineteenth-century critics shared Rymer's views about Desdemona's marriage to Othello, suggesting she must be a strumpet who lacks morals because she marries a Moor. At the end of the century Swinburne argued that Othello must be seen as 'the noblest man of man's making'.

In 1904, A. C. Bradley presented a positive analysis of Othello, whom he saw as blameless. For Bradley, Othello was 'the most romantic figure among Shakespeare's heroes'. Bradley's Othello is 'so noble … [he] inspires a passion of mingled love and pity' which none of Shakespeare's other heroes inspires. Bradley also argued that the newness of his marriage makes Othello's jealousy credible. Bradley believed that Othello never falls completely and suggested that at the end of the play we feel 'admiration and love' for the hero. Two influential critics rejected Bradley's positive analysis of Othello. Commenting on Othello's final speech, Eliot says the Moor is guilty of trying to cheer himself up and attempting to evade reality. For Eliot this speech is a 'terrible exposure of human weakness'. F. R. Leavis argued that Othello is responsible for his own downfall because he has a propensity to jealousy and possesses a weak character, which is sorely tested by marriage. Othello's love is dismissed. It is 'composed very largely of ignorance of self as well as ignorance of her [Desdemona]'. So far as Iago is concerned, Leavis feels that he has enough of a grievance to explain his motivation.

Critics continued to debate Othello's flaws and nobility. Since the 1950s there have been a number of suggestions that Iago is driven by latent homosexuality. Iago was now considered an example of the typical stage Machiavel who 'personifies … self-interest, hypocrisy, cunning' (Leah Scragg, 'Iago – Vice or Devil?', '*Shakespeare Survey*', 21, 1968). Several twentieth-century critics were preoccupied by the Christianity of Othello. Many noted the Christian signification of certain speeches (e.g. V.2.33 and V.2.24). Othello has been compared to Job, Judas and Adam; Desdemona with Christ; and Iago with Satan. Some critics suggest that Othello is damned when he commits suicide because he has sinned against God's law; he is also accused of other soul-destroying sins, such as murder, despair and entering into a compact with the devil (Iago). Other critics suggest that *Othello* affirms a morality that is consistent with Christianity; the play presents a positive view of love and faith and shows us that vengeance is wicked and pride dangerous.

Desdemona received a good deal of critical attention during the twentieth century. Some commentators suggested she is a goddess and a saint, others saw her as a representative of goodness and purity. Many critics commented on Desdemona's commitment to love.

CRITICAL VIEWPOINT **A03**

Thomas Rymer was as dismissive of the implausible characters as the plot: Othello was a 'Jealous Booby', Iago too villainous to be believed, the Venetians despicable, and Desdemona a woman without sense because she married a 'blackamoor'.

CONTEXT **A04**

John Russell Brown, in *Shakespeare: The Tragedies* (2001), reminds us that the Christian context of the seventeenth century would have had a profound effect on how Iago's evil actions were viewed: 'an audience that believed in devils might see Iago as someone working in close allegiance to an evil power that is greater than any human force.'

CONTEMPORARY APPROACHES

FEMINIST READINGS OF DESDEMONA

Feminist readings of the play explore the gender politics of *Othello*. A feminist critic would consider the roles of the male and female characters in relation to the **patriarchal** context of the play. Many feminist critics have noted how female characters in **Jacobean tragedies** are victims who have limited power and are punished for their sexuality.

Marilyn French (see *Shakespeare's Division of Experience*, 1982) explores the masculine value system at work in *Othello*. In spite of her assertiveness in choosing her own husband, French suggests Desdemona 'accepts her culture's dictum that she must be obedient to males' and is 'self-denying in the extreme' when she dies.

Lisa Jardine (see *Still Harping on Daughters*, 1983) shares French's viewpoint about the misogyny of Othello. She suggests that the stage world of Jacobean drama is wholly masculine and argues that there is only a male viewpoint on offer. Jardine asserts the view that Desdemona proves to be 'too-knowing, too-independent'. Because of her waywardness she is punished by patriarchy. Jardine suggests Desdemona becomes a stereotype of female passivity.

CHECK THE FILM A03

Many famous twentieth-century film and stage productions, including those of Orson Welles and Laurence Olivier, sought to emphasise Desdemona's innocence and purity, and her difference from Othello, by portraying her as a light-skinned blonde.

MARXIST READINGS

A **Marxist critic** would be interested in the political context of *Othello* and power structure of the society in which Othello and Iago operate. Marxist critics also examine the relationships between masters and their servants. Dympna Callaghan considers the cultural significance of Desdemona's wedding sheets and the handkerchief, commenting on how these objects had economic and symbolic value in the Renaissance (see Howard and Shershow, eds., *Marxist Shakespeares*, 2001). Callaghan sees the handkerchief as a 'miniature of the nuptial linens' and suggests it is crucially important to the stability of the marriage of Othello and Desdemona.

CRITICAL VIEWPOINT A03

In 'Othello's Real Tragedy' (1987), Caryl Phillips offers a reading of Othello which stresses the hero's isolation as a black man in a white world. Phillips says Othello is fully aware of his 'tenuous' position and that his tragedy is caused when he 'begins to forget that he is black'.

NEW HISTORICIST READINGS

New historicist critics seek to consider *Othello* in relation to its social and historical context, looking at the play in relation to the ideology and beliefs of Shakespeare's society. New historicists are particularly interested in whether or not *Othello* reinforces or subverts the values of Shakespeare's society. Commenting on the violence against female characters in drama of the Jacobean period, Leonard Tennenhouse (see *Power on Display*, 1986) asserts the view that 'Jacobean tragedies offer up their scenes of excessive punishment as if mutilating the female could somehow correct political corruption. The female in question may be completely innocent … yet in play after play she demands her own death or else claims responsibility for her murder.' Tennenhouse suggests Desdemona has to be destroyed because she is subversive. Unlike many feminist critics, Tennenhouse suggests that Desdemona is 'the embodiment of power' when she appears in Act I and defends her right to choose her own husband.

Frances Dolan (see 'Revolutions, Petty Tyranny and the Murderous Husband' in Kate Chedgzoy, ed., *Shakespeare, Feminism and Gender*, 2001) considers *Othello* in relation to its historical context. She notes how in Shakespeare's society, murdering one's spouse was considered a threat to the social order. Dolan also comments on how Jacobean drama reflects seventeenth-century anxieties about the racial 'other', the traitor 'inside', the plotting subordinate and abusive authority figures. Dolan says that Othello can be linked to all these 'spectres of disorder'. Dolan defines him as a 'domestic tyrant who murders his wife on spurious grounds'. She also suggests Othello is in an ambiguous position because of his race. He cannot hold onto his authority with any confidence or security because he is different from the Venetians. For Dolan, Othello's race would have undermined his heroism: 'By making his protagonist black, Shakespeare prepares his original audience to question Othello's authority, to suspect that he might misuse it groundlessly.'

Nicholas Marsh (see *Shakespeare: The Tragedies*, 1998) considers Iago in relation to his historical context. He suggests that Iago represents a new way of thinking about the world. Iago is a typical **malcontent** or **Machiavel**, a dissatisfied and cynical man who will not stay in his place. He wants to get his own back on a society that thwarts him. Marsh points to Iago's speech in Act I Scene 3, where he outlines his philosophy – ''tis in ourselves, that we are thus, or thus' (line 320) – as proof of his subversive qualities. By way of contrast, Othello 'often conjures the magnificence of a traditional, military order and medieval ideals, such as honour. His love for Desdemona has strong overtones of medieval courtly love where the woman's purity is worshipped and idolized.'

POST-COLONIALISM

A **post-colonial** critique of the play considers the way in which Othello's race is portrayed, and considers the hero's 'outsider' status in a white world.

In *Gender, Race, Renaissance Drama* (1987), Ania Loomba suggests the central conflict in *Othello* is 'between the racism of a white patriarchy and the threat posed to it by both a black man and a white woman'. For Loomba, women and blacks exist as 'the other' in this play. Loomba argues that Othello has a split consciousness and is 'a near schizophrenic hero'; his final speech 'graphically portrays the split – he becomes simultaneously the Christian and the Infidel, the Venetian and the Turk, the keeper of the state and its opponent'. Loomba suggests Othello is an honorary white at the beginning of the play but becomes a 'total outsider' because of his relationship with Desdemona, which ruptures his 'precarious entry into the white world'. Loomba insists, however, that *Othello* 'should not be read as a patriarchal, authoritative and racist spectacle'. Instead the play should be used to 'examine and dismantle' ideas about racism and sexism.

Karen Newman (see '"And Wash the Ethiop White": Femininity and the Monstrous in *Othello*', in Andrew Hadfield, ed., *William Shakespeare's Othello: A Sourcebook*, 1987) says the play exposes the 'fear of racial and sexual difference' of Renaissance culture. Newman argues the white male characters in *Othello*, especially Iago, feel threatened by the 'power and potency of a different and monstrous sexuality' which Othello represents. Newman looks at the play in relation to Elizabethan stereotypes of the black male, in particular, worries about mixed marriages. Shakespeare's contemporaries feared 'the black man had the power to subjugate his partner's whiteness'. This makes the black male monstrous. However, Newman suggests 'by making the black Othello a hero, and by making Desdemona's love for Othello … sympathetic', Shakespeare's play challenges the racist, sexist and colonialist views of his society.

PART SIX: GRADE BOOSTER

ASSESSMENT FOCUS

WHAT ARE YOU BEING ASKED TO FOCUS ON?

The questions or tasks you are set will be based around the four **Assessment Objectives, AO1** to **AO4**.

You may get more marks for certain **AOs** than others depending on which unit you're working on. Check with your teacher if you are unsure.

WHAT DO THESE AOS ACTUALLY MEAN?

ASSESSMENT OBJECTIVES	MEANING?
AO1 Articulate creative, informed and relevant responses to literary texts, using appropriate terminology and concepts, and coherent, accurate written expression.	You write about texts in accurate, clear and precise ways so that what you have to say is clear to the marker. You use literary terms (e.g. tragic **denouement**) or refer to concepts (e.g. **dramatic irony**) in relevant places.
AO2 Demonstrate detailed critical understanding in analysing the ways in which structure, form and language shape meanings in literary texts.	You show that you understand the specific techniques and methods used by the writer(s) to create the text (e.g. **imagery**, **foreshadowing**, etc.). You can explain clearly how these methods affect the meaning.
AO3 Explore connections and comparisons between different literary texts, informed by interpretations of other readers.	You are able to see relevant links between different texts. You are able to comment on how others (such as critics) view the text.
AO4 Demonstrate understanding of the significance and influence of the contexts in which literary texts are written and received.	You can explain how social, historical, political or personal backgrounds to the texts affected the writer and how the texts were read when they were first published and at different times since.

WHAT DOES THIS MEAN FOR YOUR STUDY OR REVISION?

Depending on the course you are following, you could be asked to:

- Respond to a general question about the text as a whole. For example:
  Explore the ways in which Shakespeare portrays jealousy in *Othello*.

- Write about an aspect of *Othello* which is also a feature of other texts you are studying. These questions may take the form of a challenging statement or quotation which you are invited to discuss. For example:
  'Tragedy is concerned with the themes of loss and waste.' Discuss this statement in relation to *Othello*.

- Focus on the particular similarities, links, contrasts and differences between this text and others. For example:
  Compare and contrast how writers explore the presentation of evil in *Othello* **and other text(s) you have studied.**

EXAMINER'S TIP

Make sure you know how many marks are available for each **Assessment Objective** in the task you are set. This can help you divide up your time or decide how much attention to give each aspect.

TARGETING A HIGH GRADE

It is very important to understand the progression from a lower grade to a high grade. In all cases, it is not enough simply to mention some key points and references – instead, you should explore them in depth, drawing out what is interesting and relevant to the question or issue.

TYPICAL C GRADE FEATURES

FEATURES	EXAMPLES
A01 You use critical vocabulary accurately, and your arguments make sense, are relevant and focus on the task. You show detailed knowledge of the text.	*Shakespeare shows the terrible consequences of giving in to jealousy in "Othello". Othello's jealousy is caused by Iago, who makes him believe that Desdemona is unfaithful to him, but it can be argued that Othello is ultimately responsible for her death.*
A02 You can say how some specific aspects of form, structure and language shape meanings.	*Shakespeare carefully manages the action of the plot so that there is no let up in the pace and tension, once Othello's mind has been poisoned against Desdemona. For example, the events in Acts II to V are relentless, creating a sense of drama and claustrophobia.*
A03 You consider in detail the connections between texts, and also how interpretations of texts differ with some relevant supporting references.	*Shakespeare presents Othello as a man overwhelmed by love. In the 1981 BBC TV production of the play the actor playing Othello often weeps, so the audience realise how much he mourns the loss of his love for Desdemona. Leontes, the jealous king in "The Winter's Tale", who falsely suspects his wife has been unfaithful to him, is also saddened when he believes he has lost his Hermione's love. However, his grief is not as passionate as Othello's.*
A04 You can write about a range of contextual factors and make some specific and detailed links between these and the task or text.	*Women in Renaissance society were controlled by their fathers and husbands, so it comes as no surprise that Brabantio rejects Desdemona when he finds out she has married secretly, without consulting him.*

TYPICAL FEATURES OF AN A OR A* RESPONSE

FEATURES	EXAMPLES
A01 You use appropriate critical vocabulary and a technically fluent style. Your arguments are well structured, coherent and always relevant with a very sharp focus on task.	*Shakespeare shows the tragic consequences when a noble hero is overwhelmed by jealousy in "Othello". Othello's jealousy is a direct result of the intense love he feels for his wife Desdemona, whom he tragically comes to believe is a whore when Iago poisons his mind.*
A02 You explore and analyse key aspects of form, structure and language and evaluate perceptively how they shape meanings.	*Shakespeare carefully manages the action of the plot so that the swift pace and dramatic tension are maintained throughout and particularly once the characters arrive in Cyprus in Act II. Time seems to be moving very quickly, favouring Iago's plots, which depend upon his 'poison' working swiftly.*
A03 You show a detailed and perceptive understanding of issues raised through connections between texts and can consider different interpretations with a sharp evaluation of their strengths and weaknesses. You have a range of excellent supportive references.	*Shakespeare presents Othello as a man who is overwhelmed by love. In the 1981 BBC TV production of the play the actor playing Othello often weeps during Acts III and IV. He chokes and breaks down when delivering the words 'the pity of it, Iago!' This makes the audience realise how much he mourns the loss of his idealised love for Desdemona. As A. C. Bradley has noted, Othello is a very romantic figure, who finds it deeply painful to contemplate his wife's infidelity.* *Leontes, the jealous king in "The Winter's Tale", who suspects his wife Hermione has been unfaithful to him, is also saddened when he thinks he lost his wife's love. However, Leontes's grief is never as passionate as Othello's. For example, in Act III Scene 2 ...*
A04 You show deep, detailed and relevant understanding of how contextual factors link to the text or task.	*Renaissance society was patriarchal and women were controlled by their fathers and husbands. Desdemona's elopement is described as 'a gross revolt', an image which suggests the heroine has defied the natural order. Brabantio also says his daughter has made a most unnatural match, choosing Othello's 'sooty bosom', rather than marrying a white aristocrat. These words reveal the Elizabethan fear of black male sexuality and mixed marriages.*

HOW TO WRITE HIGH-QUALITY RESPONSES

The quality of your writing – how you express your ideas – is vital for getting a higher grade, and **AO1** and **AO2** are specifically about **how** you respond.

FIVE KEY AREAS

The quality of your responses can be broken down into five key areas.

1. THE STRUCTURE OF YOUR ANSWER/ESSAY

- First, get **straight to the point or focus in your opening paragraph**. Use a sharp, direct first sentence that deals with a key aspect and then follows up with evidence or detailed reference.

- **Put forward an argument or point of view** (you won't always be able to challenge or take issue with the essay question, but generally, where you can, you are more likely to write in an interesting way).

- **Signpost your ideas** with connectives and references which help the essay flow.

- **Don't repeat points already made**, not even in the conclusion, unless you have something new to add.

TARGETING A HIGH GRADE

Let's take one of the questions from page 86:

'Tragedy is concerned with loss and waste.' Discuss this statement in relation to *Othello*.

Here's an example of an opening paragraph that gets straight to the point:

> Immediate focus on task and key words and example from text

In "Othello", Shakespeare explores the tragic consequences of the hero's loss of honour, and the terrible waste of human potential it leads to. Othello himself sums up his tragedy in Act V when he asks plaintively before he dies, 'why should honour outlive honesty?' So, how and why does Othello lose his honour?

2. USE OF TITLES, NAMES, ETC.

This is a simple, but important, tip to stay on the right side of the examiners.

- Make sure that you spell correctly the titles of the texts, authors and so on. Present them correctly too, with double quotation marks and capitals as appropriate. For example, *'In Act I of "Othello" …'.*

- Use the **full title**, unless there is a good reason not to (e.g. it's very long).

- Use the term 'text' rather than 'book' or 'story'. If you use the word 'story', the examiner may think you mean the plot/action rather than the 'text' as a whole.

EXAMINER'S TIP ✓

Answer the question set, not the question you'd like to have been asked. Examiners say that often students will be set a question on one character (for example, Iago) but end up writing almost as much about another (such as Othello himself). Or they write about one aspect from the question (for example, 'moral corruption') but ignore another (such as 'the nature of evil'). **Stick to the question**, and answer **all parts of it**.

3. EFFECTIVE QUOTATIONS

Do not 'bolt on' quotations to the points you make. You will get some marks for including them, but examiners will not find your writing very fluent.

The best quotations are:

- Relevant
- Not too long
- Integrated into your argument/sentence.

TARGETING A HIGH GRADE   A01

Here is an example of a quotation successfully embedded in a sentence:

Iago starts to poison Othello's mind by warning him against 'the green-eyed monster' jealousy, which he says 'doth mock/ the meat it feeds on.'

Remember – quotations can be a well-selected set of three or four single words or phrases embedded in a sentence to build a picture or explanation, or they can be longer ones that are explored and picked apart.

4. TECHNIQUES AND TERMINOLOGY

By all means mention literary terms, techniques, conventions or people (for example, **idiom** or **Aristotle**) but make sure that you:

- Understand what they mean
- Are able to link them to what you're saying
- Spell them correctly.

5. GENERAL WRITING SKILLS

Try to write in a way that sounds professional and uses standard English. This does not mean that your writing will lack personality – just that it will be authoritative.

- Avoid colloquial or everyday expressions such as 'got', 'alright', 'ok' and so on.
- Use terms such as 'convey', 'suggest', 'imply', 'infer' to explain the writer's methods.
- Refer to 'we' when discussing the audience/reader.
- Avoid assertions and generalisations; don't just state a general point of view (*'Iago is a typical villain because he's evil'*), but analyse closely with clear evidence and textual detail.

TARGETING A HIGH GRADE   A01

Note the professional approach in this example:

Iago has some of the typical qualities of the Machiavellian villain of Jacobean revenge tragedy. For example, he is discontented, cynical and self-serving. He is able to disguise his villainous intentions behind a facade of honesty.

GRADE BOOSTER   A02

It's important to remember that *Othello* is a text created by Shakespeare – thinking about the choices Shakespeare makes with language and plotting will not only alert you to his methods as a playwright but also his intentions, i.e. the effect he seeks to create.

QUESTIONS WITH STATEMENTS, QUOTATIONS OR VIEWPOINTS

One type of question you may come across may include a statement, quotation or viewpoint from another reader.

These questions ask you to respond to, or argue for/against, a specific point of view or critical interpretation.

For *Othello* these questions will typically be like this:

- 'Othello's tragedy is that he gives in to temptation too easily.' Discuss.
- 'Desdemona is self-denying in the extreme when she dies.' How far do you agree with this statement?
- How far do you agree with the idea that race is a central issue in *Othello*?
- To what extent do you agree that Othello is responsible for his own downfall?

The key thing to remember is that you are being asked to **respond to a critical interpretation** of the text – in other words, to come up with **your own** 'take' on the idea or viewpoint in the task.

KEY SKILLS REQUIRED

The table below provides help and advice on answering this type of question.

SKILL	MEANS?	HOW DO I ACHIEVE THIS?
Consider different interpretations	There will be more than one way of looking at the given question. For example, critics might be divided about ... whether Iago has sufficient motivation for his evil.	• Show you have considered these different interpretations in your answer. For example: *It is true that Iago holds a grudge against Othello because he promoted Cassio over him. Another interpretation is that Iago is jealous because a black man has married a white aristocrat. This is further complicated by the fact that Iago says he feels 'love' and 'lust' for Desdemona – it is therefore possible that Iago's grudge is political, racial and sexual.*
Write with a clear, personal voice	Your own 'take' on the question is made obvious to the marker. You are not just repeating other people's ideas, but offering what **you** think.	• Although you may mention different perspectives on the task, you should settle on your own view. • Use language that shows careful, but confident, consideration. For example: *Although A. C. Bradley has claimed that Othello is a romantic figure for whom we should feel 'admiration and love', I believe that Othello is a flawed hero who inspires fear.*
Construct a coherent argument	The examiner or marker can follow your train of thought so that your own viewpoint is clear to him or her.	• Write in clear paragraphs that deal logically with different aspects of the question. Support what you say with well-selected and relevant evidence. • Use a range of connectives to help 'signpost' your argument. For example: *The first point to consider in relation to the presentation of love is the fact that there are three couples to compare in "Othello". Othello and Desdemona are genuinely in love and 'well tuned' at the start of the play. On the other hand, Iago and Emilia do not seem content with each other ...*

ANSWERING A 'VIEWPOINT' QUESTION

Here is an example of a typical question on *Othello*:

Lisa Jardine has said that Desdemona becomes a stereotype of female passivity in *Othello*. To what extent do you agree with this view?

STAGE 1: DECODE THE QUESTION

Underline/highlight the **key words**, and make sure you understand what the statement, quotation or viewpoint is saying. In this case:

- **stereotype of female passivity** = a female character who does not defend herself and accepts her fate without complaining
- To what **extent** do you **agree** = consider whether Jardine's statement is correct, and how far you agree with her
- The **viewpoint/idea** expressed is = Desdemona is a passive victim

STAGE 2: DECIDE WHAT YOUR VIEWPOINT IS

Examiners have stated that they tend to reward a strong view which is clearly put. Think about the question. Can you take issue with it? Disagreeing strongly can lead to higher marks, provided you have **genuine evidence** to support your point of view. Don't disagree just for the sake of it.

STAGE 3: DECIDE HOW TO STRUCTURE YOUR ANSWER

Pick out the key points you wish to make, and decide on the order in which you will present them. Keep this basic plan to hand while you write your response.

STAGE 4: WRITE YOUR RESPONSE

You could start by expanding on the statement or viewpoint expressed in the question.

- For example, in **Paragraph 1**:

  The viewpoint expressed in the question suggests that Desdemona is a passive victim who makes no objection to the way she is treated during "Othello".

This could help by setting up the various ideas you will choose to explore, argue for/against, and so on. But do not just repeat what the question says or just say what you are going to do. Get straight to the point. For example:

  However, I would argue that Desdemona is initially an assertive character, with a strong will of her own. She makes her own choices, and sticks to them.

Then, proceed to set out the different arguments or critical perspectives, including your own. This might be done by dealing with specific aspects or elements of the play one by one. Consider giving 1–2 paragraphs to explore each aspect in turn. Discuss the strengths and weaknesses in each particular point of view. For example:

- **Paragraph 2:** first aspect:

  *To answer whether the critic's interpretation is valid, we need to **first of all** look at …*

  *It is clear from this that …/a **strength** of this argument is*

  *However, I believe this suggests that …/a **weakness** in this argument is*

- **Paragraph 3:** a new focus or aspect:

  Turning our attention to the critical idea that … it could be said that …

- **Paragraphs 4, 5, etc. onwards:** develop the argument, building a convincing set of points:

  Furthermore, if we look at …

- **Last paragraph:** end with a clear statement of your view, without simply listing all the points you have made:

  It is clear therefore, that to say Desdemona is a stereotype of female passivity is only partly true, as I have shown that …

EXAMINER'S TIP

Note how the ideas are clearly signposted through a range of connectives and linking phrases, such as 'However' and 'Turning our attention to …'.

EXAMINER'S TIP

You should comment concisely, professionally and thoughtfully and present a range of viewpoints. Try using modal verbs such as 'could', 'might', 'may' to clarify your own interpretation. For additional help on **Using critical interpretations and perspectives**, see pages 96 and 97.

COMPARING *OTHELLO* WITH OTHER TEXTS

As part of your assessment, you may have to compare *Othello* with or link it to other texts that you have studied. These may be other plays, novels or even poetry. You may also have to link or draw in references from texts written by critics.

A typical linking or comparison question might be:

> **Compare and contrast the presentation of the darker side of love in Shakespeare's *Othello* and another text you have studied.**

THE TASK

Your task is likely to be on a method, issue, viewpoint or key aspect that is common to *Othello* and the other text(s), so you will need to:

> **Evaluate the issue** or statement and have an **open-minded approach**. The best answers suggest meanings and interpretations (plural):
>
> ● What do you understand by the question? Is this theme more important in one text than in another? Why? How? What exactly is meant by 'the darker side of love'?
> ● What are the different ways that this question or aspect can be read or viewed?
> ● Can you challenge this viewpoint? If so, what evidence is there? How can you present it in a thoughtful, reflective way?

> Express **original or creative approaches** fluently:
>
> ● This isn't about coming up with entirely new ideas, but you need to show that you're actively engaged with thinking about the question and are not just reproducing random facts and information.
> ● **Synthesise** your ideas – pull ideas and points together to create something fresh.
> ● This is a linking/comparison response, so ensure that you guide your reader through your ideas logically, clearly and with professional language.

> Know **what to compare/contrast: form, structure** and **language** will **always** be central to your response, even where you also have to write about characters, contexts or culture.
>
> ● Think about the presentation of time, **foreshadowing**, **mirroring**, the use of **asides** and **soliloquies**, the use of contrasting settings; the use of props; and how the scenes are divided, and their length.
> ● Consider different characteristic uses of language: in Shakespeare – **blank verse** and **prose**, characters' **idioms** and use of **imagery**; in other genres – formal/informal style, dialect, accent, balance of dialogue and narration; difference between prose treatment of an idea and poem.
> ● Look at a variety of symbols, images, motifs (how they represent concerns of author/time; what they are and how and where they appear; how they link to critical perspectives; their purposes, effects and impact on the play).
> ● Consider aspects of genre. To what extent do Shakespeare and the author(s) of the other work(s) conform to/challenge/subvert particular genres or styles of writing?

EXAMINER'S TIP ✓

Be sure to give due weight to each text – if there are two texts, this would normally mean giving them equal attention (but check the exact requirements of your task). Where required or suggested by the course you are following, you could try moving fluently between the texts in each paragraph, as an alternative to treating texts separately. This approach can be impressive and will ensure that comparison is central to your response.

WRITING YOUR RESPONSE

The depth and extent of your answer will depend on how much you have to write, but the key will be to **explore in detail**, and **link between ideas and texts**. Let us use the same example:

> Compare and contrast the presentation of the darker side of love in Shakespeare's *Othello* and another text you have studied.

INTRODUCTION TO YOUR RESPONSE

- Discuss quickly what 'the darker side of love' means, and how well this applies to your texts. You may wish to draw on dictionary definitions, but only do so briefly if it is really necessary.

- Mention in support the aspects of love you will focus on in *Othello* and the other text.

- You could begin with a powerful quotation that you use to launch into your response. For example:

> *In the Greek tragedy "Medea", Euripides says 'when love is in excess it brings a man no honour nor worthiness'. This statement helps to illuminate the obsessive love of Othello and Leontes in Shakespeare's "Othello" and "The Winter's Tale".*

MAIN BODY OF YOUR RESPONSE

- **Point 1:** start with the presentation of the darker side of love in *Othello*. What do the critics say? Whose views will you use? Are there contextual/cultural factors to consider?

- **Point 2:** now cover a new factor or aspect through comparison or contrast of this theme with other plays you are writing about. How is this theme presented **differently or similarly** by the writer(s) according to language, form, structures used? Why was this done in this way? How does it reflect the writer's interests? What do the critics say? Are there contextual/cultural factors to consider?

- **Points 3, 4, 5, etc.:** address a range of new factors and aspects, for example, other tragic heroes or other aspects of the darker side of love **either** within *Othello* **or** in both *Othello* and another text. What different ways do you respond to these (with more empathy, greater criticism, less interest) – and why? For example:

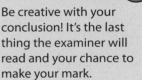

EXAMINER'S TIP

Be creative with your conclusion! It's the last thing the examiner will read and your chance to make your mark.

> *In addition to exploring the psychology of obsession, it can be argued that Shakespeare presents another element of the darker side of love in "Othello" and "The Winter's Tale". Desdemona and Hermione are both sympathetic figures, whose self-sacrificing love leads audiences to pity them. Their steadfastness in the face of darkness and jealousy provides a counterpoint to the tragic elements of the plays.*

CONCLUSION

- Synthesise elements of what you have said into a final paragraph that fluently, succinctly and inventively leaves the reader/examiner with the sense that you have engaged with this task and the texts. For example:

> *To conclude, the darker side of love leads to both tragedy and heroism. Obsession and jealousy are destructive, but those who feel them are redeemed when they realise their folly and come to appreciate the nobility and self-sacrifice of those they have accused and abused.*

RESPONDING TO A GENERAL QUESTION ABOUT THE WHOLE TEXT

You may also be asked to write about a specific aspect of *Othello* – but as it relates to the whole text. For example:

> **Explore the dramatic use Shakespeare makes of ideas about corruption and infection in *Othello*.**

This means you should:

- **Focus** on *both* **corruption** *and* **infection specifically** (not other themes).
- **Explain their 'dramatic use'** – **how** they are used by Shakespeare in terms of action, character and furthering ideas/themes. Consider the dramatic conventions linked to them; for example, the way the tragic outcome is signposted by the imagery of corruption and infection.
- **Look** at aspects of the **whole play text**, not just one scene.

STRUCTURING YOUR RESPONSE

You need a clear, logical plan, as for all tasks that you do.

It is impossible to write about every section or part of the text, so you will need to:

- Quickly note 5–6 key points or aspects to build your essay around:
  Point a *Iago is associated with the imagery of corruption and infection.*
  Point b *Iago is corrupted by his personal ambition and cynical world view.*
  Point c *Iago infects Othello's mind by convincing him Desdemona is false and making him jealous.*
  Point d *The infection of Othello's mind makes him cruel and jealous.*
  Point e *The outcome of corruption and infection is violent death.*
- Then, decide the most effective or logical order. For example, point **c**, then **b**, **a**, **d**, **e**, etc.

You could begin with your key or main idea, with supporting evidence/references, followed by your further points (perhaps two paragraphs for each). For example:

Paragraph 1: first key point. *Othello's mind is infected by Iago, who poisons his thoughts.*

Paragraph 2: expand out, link into other areas. *Iago is a corrupt, evil character, who is driven by personal ambition and jealousy.*

Paragraph 3: change direction, introduce new aspect/point. *As well as being driven by personal ambition, Iago is a misogynist who wants to corrupt Othello's idealised love for Desdemona.*

And so on.

- **For your conclusion:** use a compelling way to finish, perhaps repeating some or all of the key words from the question: For example, either:

End with your final point, but **add a last clause** which makes it clear what you think is key to the answer e.g.:

Shakespeare's presentation of corruption and infection makes it clear that jealousy is a disease which overwhelms and destroys those who feel it. Or:

End with a **new quotation** or **aspect that's slightly different from** your main point e.g.:

Finally, as Frances Dolan says, Othello becomes a 'domestic tyrant who murders his wife on spurious grounds'. Iago's evil has corrupted the tragic protagonist to such an extent that Othello cannot be considered a hero at the end of Act V.

Or, of course, you can combine these endings.

EXAMINER'S TIP ✓

You may be asked to discuss other texts you have studied as well as *Othello* as part of your response. Once you have completed your response on the play you could move on to discuss the same issues in your other texts. Begin with a simple linking phrase or sentence to launch straight into your first point about your next text, such as:
'The same issue/idea is explored in a quite different way in "Othello" … Here …'

WRITING ABOUT CONTEXTS

Assessment Objective 4 asks you to 'demonstrate understanding of the significance and influence of the contexts in which literary texts are written and received ...'. This can mean:

- How the events, settings, politics and so on **of the time when the text was written** influenced the writer or help us to understand the play's themes or concerns. For example, to what extent Shakespeare might have been influenced by his society's attitudes towards race and gender.

or

- How events, settings, politics and so on **of the time when the text is read or seen** influence how it is understood. For example, would audiences brought up in a world of greater racial and gender equality respond differently to the marriage of Othello and Desdemona than Shakespeare's audience?

THE CONTEXT FOR *OTHELLO*

You might find the following table helpful for thinking about how particular aspects of the time contribute to our understanding of the play and its themes. These are just examples – can you think of any others?

POLITICAL	LITERARY	PHILOSOPHICAL
Military situation In Cyprus; conflict between Christian and Muslim states and nations	Use of Machiavellian villain and Italianate setting	Beliefs about the nature of evil

SCIENTIFIC	CULTURAL	SOCIAL
Understanding of medicine i.e. the 'humours' and 'disease' of jealousy	Attitudes towards mixed-race marriages and foreigners	Attitudes towards women

GRADE BOOSTER **A03**

To get the best grades at AS and A2 you need to demonstrate an excellent understanding of the contexts that lie behind *Othello*. Commenting on the cultural and historical associations of Venice and the Turkish invasion of Cyprus will help you to show your knowledge.

TARGETING A HIGH GRADE **A04**

Remember that the extent to which you write about these contexts will be determined by the marks available. Some questions or tasks may have very few marks allocated for **AO4**, but where you do have to refer to context the key thing is not to 'bolt on' your comments, or write a long, separate chunk of text on context and then 'go back' to the play. For example:

Don't just write:

The situation in Cyprus when "Othello" is set was very precarious. Venice had controlled the island for many years, but it was under attack from the Ottoman Empire in 1570. Venice signed a treaty with the Turks in 1573 and Cyprus was then controlled by the Ottoman Empire for the next 300 years.

Do write:

The setting of Cyprus is significant. In 1570, when the play is set, Cyprus was under siege from the Ottoman Empire. It is therefore a location associated with danger, uncertainty and chaos. Many members of Shakespeare's audience would have been aware that the Turks gained control of the island in 1573, and understood the dark irony of Othello's position. Othello would have been one of the last governors sent by Venice to defend the island. Ironically, the tragic protagonist finds himself in the same vulnerable state as the island he is sent to protect.

USING CRITICAL INTERPRETATIONS AND PERSPECTIVES

THE 'MEANING' OF A TEXT

There are many viewpoints and perspectives on the 'meaning' of *Othello*, and examiners will be looking for evidence that you have considered a range of these. Broadly speaking, these different interpretations might relate to the following considerations.

1. CHARACTER

What **sort/type** of person Othello – or another character – is.

- Is the character an 'archetype' (a specific type of character with common features)? (For example, Thomas Rymer, in *A Short View of Tragedy*, suggests Othello belongs in 'a Bloody Farce' because he is the archetype of a foolish cuckold.)
- Does the character personify, symbolise or represent a specific idea or trope (the noble hero brought down by a fatal flaw; how evil preys on goodness)?
- Is the character modern, universal, of his/her time, historically accurate etc? (For example, is Iago the embodiment of Renaissance ideas about evil or, like many modern villains, driven by selfish, petty motives?)

2. IDEAS AND ISSUES

What the play tells us about **particular ideas or issues** and we can interpret these. For example:

- Themes and ideas that obsessed **Jacobean** dramatists e.g. the nature of good and evil; the difference appearance and reality; corrupt authority figures
- The role of men/women in Jacobean society and within marriage
- What **tragedy** means to Jacobean audiences
- Moral and social attitudes towards sexuality and race

3. LINKS AND CONTEXTS

How the play **links with, follows or pre-echoes** other texts, ideas. For example:

- Its influence culturally, historically and socially. Do we see echoes of the characters or genres in other texts? How similar to other stage villains is Iago and why? Does his **characterisation** share features with the **vice** of the medieval mystery plays, for example?
- How its language links to other texts or modes, such as religious works, myth, legend, etc.

4. DRAMATIC STRUCTURE

How the play is **constructed** and how Shakespeare **makes** his narrative.

- Does it follow a particular dramatic convention?
- What is the function of specific events, characters, theatrical devices, staging, etc. in relation to narrative?
- What are the specific moments of tension, conflict, crisis and **denouement** – and do we agree on what they are?

5. AUDIENCE RESPONSE

How the play **works on an audience**, and whether this changes over time and in different contexts.

- Are we to empathise with, feel distance from, judge and/or evaluate the events and characters?

6. CRITICAL REACTION

And, finally, how different audiences view the play. For example:

- Different **theatre critics over time**
- Different **audiences** in earlier or more **recent** years

WRITING ABOUT CRITICAL PERSPECTIVES

The important thing to remember is that **you** are a critic too. Your job is to evaluate what a critic or school of criticism has said about the elements above, and arrive at your own conclusions.

In essence, you need to: **consider** the views of others, **synthesise** them, then decide on **your perspective**. For example:

EXPLAIN THE VIEWPOINTS

Critical view A about the presentation of Othello's race:

> *Frances Dolan feels that Othello's race would have been problematic to Shakespeare's audience and they would have felt suspicious of and mistrusted the hero because he is black.*

Critical view B about the presentation of Othello's race:

> *Karen Newman does not feel that Othello's race is presented in a derogatory way. She feels that Shakespeare challenges the racist assumptions of his society by making his hero a noble Moor.*

THEN SYNTHESISE AND ADD YOUR PERSPECTIVE

Synthesise these views whilst adding your own:

> *While Frances Dolan's idea that Othello's race is problematic could be considered persuasive given what we know about the negativity of Elizabethan attitudes towards black men, Karen Newman's comment that Othello is 'represented as heroic and tragic at an historical moment when the only role blacks played onstage was that of a villain of low status' provides an alternative angle. However, I feel that, in fact, Shakespeare's presentation of Othello's race is neither problematic nor subversive, but instead is used as a means by which the dramatist can explore ideas about opposition.*

TARGETING A HIGH GRADE **A03**

Make sure you have thoroughly explored the dramatic conventions (some of which – such as denouement – are mentioned above). Critical interpretation of drama is of necessity different from critical interpretation of other modes of writing – not least because of audience response, and the specific theatrical devices in use. Key critics are theatre critics – look at what they have to say about recent productions. See the adjacent margin for just two examples of recent reviews of the 2011 Sheffield Crucible Theatre production of *Othello*. They offer, in fact, different 'readings' of the characterisation of Iago.

CRITICAL VIEWPOINT **A03**

In *The Guardian* theatre critic Kate Kellaway said of Dominic West's performance of Iago: 'You can see he has a chip on his shoulder, an angry edge that suggests psychosis is not far away.' However, Kellaway also suggested that Iago was presented as a limited man: 'At the end, Iago seems not an evil enigma but – like many a crook in the dock – an inadequate with nothing to say.'

CRITICAL VIEWPOINT **A03**

In *The Independent* theatre critic Paul Taylor felt that West's Iago was a chilling figure, whose evil was powerful: 'There are moments ... that freeze the soul, as when he [Iago] suddenly advises Othello not to poison Desdemona, but to strangle her in her wedding sheets, as though it were just a helpful piece of advice about an impersonal problem of logistics.'

ANNOTATED SAMPLE ANSWERS

Below are extracts from two sample answers to the same question at different grades. Bear in mind that these are examples only, covering all four Assessment Objectives – you will need to check the type of question and the weightings given for each AO when writing your coursework essay or preparing for your exam.

Question: **To what extent is the corruption of human nature central to *Othello*?**

CANDIDATE 1

AO1 Should try to avoid repetition of the same word; could say 'is a central issue' in the first sentence instead of 'important'

The corruption of human nature is important in "Othello". The most important example of corruption is Iago's poisoning of Othello's mind. This happens in Cyprus, when Iago makes Othello believe that Desdemona is unfaithful to him. Iago corrupts Othello by using the handkerchief as proof that Desdemona has slept with Cassio. He makes Othello believe that Desdemona gave Cassio the handkerchief as a love token, when really she dropped it by mistake, and Emilia passed it on to Iago. The handkerchief, which is a symbol of Desdemona's honour, becomes a symbol of evil. When he believes Desdemona has given it away, Othello thinks his wife has been corrupted. This leads Othello to destroy Desdemona to regain his own honour.

AO2 Immediate focus on task and identification of key example, but could be more precise about the acts/ scenes being referred to

AO1 Style could be more formal – this sounds like a spoken phrase

AO4 Links handkerchief to the theme of corruption successfully; could make more of the theme of honour by relating it to Shakespeare's historical context

AO2 Again, too vague to show understanding – what is meant by corruption?

AO2 Has a grasp of Iago's role and Othello's characterisation

When his mind is corrupted, Othello is different. In Acts I and II he was a noble character, who had faith in Desdemona and her love for him. Infected by Iago's poison, Othello becomes jealous, and his jealousy makes him cruel. For example, Othello verbally abuses Desdemona as 'that cunning whore of Venice' and strikes her in Act IV. When he uses crude language, Othello sounds like Iago. Othello's fit is evidence that the hero has been corrupted. Othello cannot cope with his jealousy, and falls over in a trance. When Othello comes round, he says 'a horned man's a monster and beast'. Because he feels humiliated, Othello becomes obsessed with revenge.

AO4 Clear reference to the correct act, but which scene does this occur in? Could be more precise about context

AO2 Sound comment, but could offer more examples to illustrate the idea more fully

AO2 Needs to comment on this image more fully; becoming narrative

AO1 'leads him' is too vague – what exactly does it mean?

However, we know that Othello is not in control of himself in the second half of the play because Iago leads him throughout Acts IV and V. Because of this, the audience will not blame Othello for what he does. I pity Othello when he eavesdrops on Cassio and gets ready to kill Desdemona. Othello is very distressed in Act V Scene 2. I know this because he has second thoughts about killing Desdemona. Othello believes that his wife's death is a 'sacrifice' and after Desdemona is dead refers to himself as an 'honourable murderer'. Some people might think Othello is making cowardly excuses. But other people will think that the 'noble Moor' has been 'perplexed in the extreme' by evil Iago.

AO3 Shows awareness of likely audience responses, but this is a sweeping statement. It needs to be qualified, e.g. 'an audience **might** not blame Othello **entirely**...'

AO2 Needs textual evidence to support this claim

AO3 Considers alternative audience responses to Othello, demonstrating an open-minded approach

A01 Attempt at signposting – but does this sentence really follow on effectively from the last point in the previous paragraph? Why use 'also'?

A01 First few sentences in this paragraph are rather general and need to be linked together more cohesively

A03 Asserts own viewpoint clearly throughout this paragraph and arrives at a sense of overview, incorporating a critic fruitfully

It is also important to consider Iago's role. Iago enjoys corrupting others. Coleridge suggested Iago is 'a being next to the devil'. Iago is a lone villain in "Othello". The characters he corrupts reject him. Emilia shows he is a villain, Roderigo dies calling him an 'inhuman dog' and Cassio says Iago's actions are 'most heathenish and most gross'. Lodovico says that the bodies of "Othello", Desdemona and Emilia are a 'tragic loading' which 'poisons sight'. This final reference to poison shows the audience how destructive Iago's corruption of Othello has been.

I believe that although Iago's corruption of Othello is important, Shakespeare has other points to make about human nature. In spite of the tragic ending, "Othello" is not just about defeat. Othello recognises he has been corrupted and makes up for it by killing himself. As the critic A. C. Bradley has suggested, Othello never falls completely. When he picks up his sword to commit suicide, I believe that Othello redeems himself and regains his nobility.

A04 Apt reference to a critic, but could link Iago's evil to the context of the play more thoroughly, and also explain what Coleridge meant more fully

A02 Links corruption successfully to destruction and the tragic denouement, showing a grasp of structure

A01 Again, the style is a little bit too close to speech – and too vague

GRADE C

Comment

A01 The material covered is relevant, and arguments make sense, but there is a tendency towards narrative description of events at times. Some helpful signposting, e.g. however, it is important to... Clear concluding paragraph which returns to the terms of the question.

A02 The candidate has a grasp of some aspects of structure e.g. how Othello's **characterisation** changes from Act I to Act V. There are specific references to and appreciation of some aspects of language and **imagery**, e.g. symbolism of the handkerchief.

A03 There are some well chosen quotations and there is a grasp of different interpretations of Othello's actions in Act V. Some apt references are made to critics. There is a strong sense of personal engagement at times.

A04 More could be made of Shakespeare's cultural and historical context.

For a B grade
- Instead of describing events, focus on commenting on them consistently for AO1.
- Make more detailed comments on language, structure or imagery for AO2.
- Make further, more detailed references to critics and different interpretations for AO3.
- Make references to Shakespeare's context for AO4 e.g. Elizabethan attitudes to women/race/ the nature of evil.

CANDIDATE 2

A02 Raises an important question in relation to the key theme of the essay

The corruption of the 'noble Moor' Othello by Iago is a central theme in the play. It leads directly to the tragic outcome. However, is Iago entirely to blame for what happens? I believe it is necessary to assess a range of factors in order to arrive at a conclusion about the extent to which human nature is corrupted in "Othello". These factors include the role of Iago, Othello's characterisation and the Elizabethan context of the play.

A01 Clearly outlines what the focus of the essay will be

A04 Contextualises Iago's villainy

Iago is a cynical Machiavel, a villainous archetype. Stage villains were portrayed as so cunning that noble, virtuous characters could easily be taken in. This makes Othello's corruption by Iago plausible and detracts from the tragic protagonist's responsibility for his actions. Shakespeare portrays Iago as a man who delights in his ability to corrupt others, as Coleridge noted when he described Iago as 'a being next to the devil'. This is how the other characters in "Othello" see him. When his plots are revealed Iago is referred to as a 'demi-devil' and a 'damned slave'. The imagery of hell associated with Iago lends him a terrible corrosive power. However, by the time that Shakespeare wrote "Othello", people were beginning to question traditional assumptions about religion. Protestants believed that man was responsible for his own actions and Shakespeare makes it clear that Iago's victims are morally responsible for the choices they make. Iago is wicked, but his victims are also culpable.

A03 Links critic's comment to examples from the text

A04 Context referred to here, but it is rather general, and could link more to the play

A03 Incorporates a range of critics' views successfully, and then goes on to assess and challenge them

So, if Iago cannot be blamed entirely for the corruption of human nature in "Othello", to what extent is Othello responsible for his own tragedy? Some critics see Othello as 'the noblest man of man's making' (Swinburne) while others claim he is easily corrupted because he is deficient. I believe that the truth about Othello lies somewhere between Swinburne's idealised view of the hero, and Thomas Rymer's condemnation of him as a fool. It is true that Othello finds it difficult to combine the roles of soldier and husband, although I reject Leavis's claim that Othello is a weak and 'unfit' character. In fact, Shakespeare presents his tragic protagonist as a strong and resolute man. Eventually, however, Othello's strength of character becomes a weakness, when his intense feelings of love turn into overwhelming jealousy – he wants to 'tear [Desdemona] all to pieces'.

A01 Needs evidence of Othello's strength/resolution to support this claim

A02 Shows an understanding of the structure and pace of the play, but could offer textual support to expand on these ideas

A02 Focus on language, with well chosen quotations

In spite of his weakness, Othello is not easy to corrupt. Iago does not leave Othello alone for more than a few minutes on stage in Acts III and IV, anxious to see whether his 'poison' is working. Iago needs not only false words but also physical evidence of Desdemona's adultery. This is because Othello continually doubts Desdemona is dishonest. His absolute horror at the idea of his wife deceiving him is revealed in these lines, 'If she be false, O then heaven mocks itself,/ I'll not believe't'. This aligns Desdemona with heavenly forces, which demonstrates the awe in which he holds her. In Act III Scene 3, Othello catches hold of Iago and threatens him with death, demanding 'be sure thou prove my love a whore'. These words are proof that Othello is not easily corruptible, and put the onus on Iago to catch Desdemona out.

AO4 Puts Othello's jealousy in context – ideally cite a text in support

Othello is not only corrupted by Iago. He is also the victim of the cultural beliefs of the society he operates in. During the Renaissance women were seen as the property of men, and their chastity was a badge of male honour. Othello's conception of his own honour is challenged when he comes to believe Desdemona is 'that cunning whore of Venice'. Othello's obsessive jealousy is a direct result of his wounded honour. The Elizabethan audience would have recognised jealousy as a powerful force, which had its own momentum. In "Othello" it is described as a disease, 'a monster / Begot upon itself, born on itself'. This imagery suggests Othello is a powerless victim. However, a modern audience might feel that Othello has a choice about whether he 'gives in' to the 'monster'.

AO3 Remaining open-minded; has a balanced approach and considers alternative responses to the text

AO1 Helpful signposting to provide cohesion

There is one other factor to consider in relation to the corruption of human nature in "Othello". To what extent is Othello's race important when considering whether he is a victim of corruption or responsible for his own actions? The Elizabethans held stereotypical and racist views of black men, believing them credulous, savage and lustful. So perhaps Shakespeare's audience would have believed that Othello is not so much corrupted by Iago, as reverting to type. Othello resorts to cruelty and violence because that is what they thought was 'natural' for a black man.

AO4 Interesting new angle on corruption, linking it clearly to the Elizabethan context and views about race

AO2 Could challenge this idea. Is there textual evidence that proves Othello is naturally violent?

We need to consider the final moments of the play before deciding whether Othello is wholly corrupted. Just before he kills himself, Othello makes it clear that he is destroying the evil part of himself; he compares himself with the 'base Indian' who threw way a 'pearl' (Desdemona). Othello knows he deserves the torments of hell for murdering his innocent wife, demonstrated when he says, 'Wash me in steep-down gulfs of liquid fire!' This powerful language subverts the idea of baptism and that shows that he is preparing to commit suicide, which was held to be a sin. T.S. Eliot has accused Othello of showing 'terrible human weakness' in the final scene. However, I would argue that Othello redeems himself here and that his suicide is a noble act.

AO3 Uses critic successfully to introduce counter argument

GRADE A

AO1 Asserts own view strongly and succinctly to close

Although the corruption of human nature is a central theme, "Othello" is also a play which proves that true nobility cannot be destroyed. Othello has been corrupted, but is not corrupt when he dies.

Comment

AO1 Arguments are well structured and lead on logically from the opening paragraph, which outlines the focus of the essay clearly. Material covered relates to the question, which is kept in mind throughout the essay. The essay is technically fluent, with appropriate critical vocabulary.

AO2 A conceptualised grasp of language and structure are demonstrated, with perceptive analysis of the impact of key aspects of language, e.g. **imagery** relating to evil and jealousy.

AO3 A wide range of critics are referred to, with sharp evaluation of some interpretations, e.g. Leavis. There is close consideration of how different audiences might respond to the presentation of key aspects of the play, with a wide range of supporting references and quotations.

AO4 There is detailed and relevant understanding of how several contextual factors link to the text and task, e.g. Elizabethan attitudes to evil, black men, masculine honour.

For an A* grade

- Make more extensive use of literary terms, e.g. **oxymoron**, **prose**, simile, **metaphor**, for AO1.

- Develop more detailed analysis of language and structure; closer textual analysis of some quotations. Support some points with further comment and textual evidence for AO2.

- Ensure the views of all critics referred to are evaluated sharply for AO3.

- Incorporate discussion of other contextual factors that could help illuminate the play for AO4, e.g. the nature of **tragedy**; the way jealousy/ corruption/ human nature are portrayed in other texts of the period.

WORKING THROUGH A TASK

Now it's your turn to work through a task on *Othello*. The key is to:

- Read/decode the task/question.
- Plan your points – then expand and link your points.
- Draft your answer.

TASK TITLE

'Destruction and loss are the main impressions the audience are left with at the end of *Othello*.' How do you respond to this idea?

DECODE THE QUESTION: KEY WORDS

How do you respond ..?   = what are **my** views?

destruction   = damage that cannot be repaired

loss   = the feeling that someone/something of value has been destroyed

PLAN AND EXPAND

- Key aspect: evidence of destruction?

POINT	POINT EXPANDED	EVIDENCE
Point a Othello's peace of mind is lost	Iago undermines Othello's conception of himself, specifically his manhood	'Would you would bear your fortune like a man!' (IV.1.61)
	Iago undermines his faith in Desdemona	'She did deceive her father, marrying you' (III.3.209)
	Iago makes him feel his race is problematic, and that it is natural for Desdemona to turn away from him	Othello: 'Haply for I am black/ And have not those soft parts of conversation/ That chamberers have ...' (III.3.267–8)
		Rex Gibson on Elizabethan attitudes to race: 'the thought of interracial marriage was abhorrent to most English man and women' (p. 50, *Shakespearean and Jacobean Tragedy*) vs Anita Loomba and Othello as 'an honorary white'
Point b Desdemona's reputation	Different aspects of this point expanded *You fill in*	Quotations 1–2 *You fill in*
Point c Black–white harmony	Different aspects of this point expanded *You fill in*	Quotations 1–2 *You fill in*

- Key aspect: evidence of loss?

POINT	POINT EXPANDED	EVIDENCE
Point a *You fill in*	Different aspects of this point expanded *You fill in*	Quotations 1–2 *You fill in*
Point b *You fill in*	Different aspects of this point expanded *You fill in*	Quotations 1–2 *You fill in*
Point c *You fill in*	Different aspects of this point expanded *You fill in*	Quotations 1–2 *You fill in*

CONCLUSION

POINT	POINT EXPANDED	EVIDENCE
Key final point or overall view *You fill in*	Draw together and perhaps add a final further point to support your view *You fill in*	Final quotation to support your view *You fill in*

DEVELOP FURTHER

Now look back over your draft points and:

- Add further links or connections between the points to develop them further or synthesise what has been said, for example:

> *Ania Loomba suggests that Othello's race does not cause the hero problems early in the play. She suggests Othello is treated by the Venetians as an 'honorary white'. Othello certainly sees himself as Desdemona's equal. However, while this may be true, it is clear that, as Rex Gibson suggests, Othello's marriage to Desdemona may have caused the Elizabethan audience anxiety because 'the thought of interracial marriage was abhorrent' to them.*

- Decide an order for your points/paragraphs – some may now be linked/connected and therefore **not** in the order of the table above.

- Now draft your essay. If you're really stuck you can use the opening paragraph below to get you started.

> *Destruction and loss are central themes in "Othello". In Act I a new marriage destroys Brabantio's family harmony. Othello's elopement with Desdemona occurs against the backdrop of a threatened invasion of Cyprus, which the 'valiant Moor' is sent to defend. In Cyprus, a setting associated with danger and disorder, Iago plots to destroy Othello's reputation and marriage. He achieves this by poisoning Othello's mind. Iago begins by ...*

Once you've written your essay, turn to page 112 for a mark scheme on this question to see how well you've done.

FURTHER QUESTIONS

1) 'Othello is above all a victim of his own jealousy.' Discuss.
2) Explore the ways in which manipulation is portrayed in *Othello*.
3) Coleridge has claimed that Iago is 'a being next to the devil' driven by 'motiveless malignity'. How far do you agree with this view of Iago?
4) The female characters in *Othello* are 'too weak and passive to be convincing'. To what extent do you agree with this view?
5) To what extent is Othello responsible for his own downfall?
6) Leonard Tennenhouse has argued that Desdemona is 'the embodiment of power' when she first appears in *Othello*. Do you agree? Explore the presentation of Desdemona in the light of this comment.
7) Karen Newman suggests that 'by making the black Othello a hero, and by making Desdemona's love for Othello ... sympathetic', Shakespeare challenges the racist and sexist and views of his society. To what extent to you agree?
8) Othello is the first black hero in Renaissance drama. To what extent do you believe race is a central issue in *Othello*?
9) '*Othello* is a domestic tragedy about love.' Explore the presentation of love in *Othello* and another play of your own choosing.
10) T. S. Eliot has said that Othello's final speech is 'a terrible exposure of human weakness'. To what extent to you agree with this comment? Is Othello portrayed as a weak character?

ESSENTIAL STUDY TOOLS

FURTHER READING

THE TEXT

E. A. J. Honigmann, ed., *Othello*, The Arden Shakespeare, Nelson, London, 1997

  The edition of the text used in the preparation of these Notes; includes a helpful introduction to the play which covers sources, characters and themes as well as some extracts from a translation of Cinzio's source novella

Norman Sanders, ed., *Othello*, The New Cambridge Shakespeare, Cambridge University Press, 1984

  Has a useful introduction to the play which includes a stage history and interesting coverage of Shakespeare's sources

CRITICISM

CONTEMPORARY CRITICISM

Harold Bloom, ed., *Othello*, Bloom's Shakespeare through the Ages, Infobase Publishing, New York, 2008

  Includes an analysis of key passages, and critical views from the seventeenth century to the present day, including Rymer, Coleridge, A. C. Bradley and T. S. Eliot

John Russell Brown, *Shakespeare: The Tragedies*, Palgrave Macmillan, Basingstoke, 2001

  Written in a style that makes it accessible to A Level students and split into short sections for ease of use, includes a chapter on Othello called 'Sexuality and Difference'; covers various aspects of the play

Kate Chedgzoy, ed., *Shakespeare, Feminism and Gender*, New Casebooks, Palgrave, Macmillan, 2001

  Includes an essay on Othello by Frances Dolan, 'Revolutions, Petty Tyranny and the Murderous Husband'

Rex Gibson, *Shakespearean and Jacobean Tragedy*, Cambridge Contexts in Literature, Cambridge University Press, 2000

  An excellent, comprehensive and accessible guide to a wide range of tragedies, and their social and historical contexts; also covers critical approaches

Jean E. Howard and Scott Cutler Shershow, eds., *Marxist Shakespeares*, Psychology Press, 2001

  Contains a **Marxist feminist** essay 'Looking Well to Linens: Women and Cultural Production in *Othello* and Shakespeare's England' by Dympna Callaghan

Claire McEachern, ed., *The Cambridge Companion to Shakespearen Tragedy*, Cambridge Companions to Literature, Cambridge University Press, Cambridge, 2003

  Covers ten plays in thirteen essays, including cultural and literary background, the origins of sub-genres of Shakespeare's tragedies, e.g. love, revenge and classical tragedy, critical and theatrical reception of the plays

Lois Potter, *Othello: Shakespeare in Performance*, Manchester University Press, Manchester, 2002

Traces acting traditions and how they affected interpretations of the central roles in the play; looks at various stage and screen versions of the play, with detailed examination of Paul Robeson's portrayal of Othello. Useful for students who are interested in cultural approaches to studying Shakespeare

Nicholas Potter, ed., *'Othello': A Reader's Guide to Essential Criticism*, Readers Guides to Essential Criticism, Palgrave Macmillan, Basingstoke, 2000

  Traces the critical history of the play from the earliest critics up to the present day; also covers the historical context of the play, the most significant themes and recurring critical concerns. Includes Wiliam Hazlitt's 'Characters of Shakespeare's Plays', Valerie Traub's 'Desire and Anxiety: Circulations of Sexuality in Shakespearean Drama' and Stanley Cavell's 'Othello and the Stake of the Other'

Emma Smith, ed., *Shakespeare's Tragedies*, Blackwell Guides to Criticism, Blackwell, 2004

  Includes an overview of criticism of Shakespeare's tragedies, and two contemporary essays on *Othello*, including 'Femininity and the Monstrous in *Othello*' by Karen Newman

LATE TWENTIETH-CENTURY CRITICS

John Drakakis, ed., *Shakespearean Tragedy*, Longman, New York, 1992

  A collection of contemporary criticism with a range of views of *Othello* by different critics: Marilyn French (a feminist reading), Stephen Greenblatt (a **new historicist** reading). Challenging but offers a good range of current views

Marilyn French, *Shakespeare's Division of Experience*, Jonathan Cape, 1982

  Offers a feminist reading of several of Shakespeare's plays, including *Othello*

Andrew Hadfield, ed., *William Shakespeare's Othello: A Sourcebook*, Routledge, 1987

  A broad-ranging guide to critical responses and contexts, from the seventeenth century to the present day; includes critics Karen Newman and Lisa Jardine, who discuss race and gender roles

Lisa Jardine, *Still Harping on Daughters: Women and Drama in the Age of Shakespeare*, Harvester Press, Brighton, 1983

  Persuasive writing about the sexual politics of *Othello*

Ania Loomba, *Gender, Race, Renaissance Drama*, Manchester University Press, 1987

  Explores the sexual and racial politics of *Othello* and comments on Elizabethan attitudes towards race and colour

Nicholas Marsh, *Shakespeare: The Tragedies*, Palgrave, Macmillan, Basingstoke, 1998

  An accessible guide to Shakespeare's tragedies, split into sections that make it easy to use; includes commentary on several aspects of *Othello* and a very useful chapter on the literary and historical contexts of the tragedies

Virginia Mason Vaughan, *Othello: A Contextual History*, Cambridge University Press, Cambridge, 1996

Examines contemporary writings and explores them in relation to the play, e.g. representations of Africans and 'blackamoors', other tales involving jealous husbands, plus a history of *Othello* in performance in England and the USA from 1660 to the 1980s

Caryl Phillips, 'Othello's Real Tragedy', *The Guardian*, 7 February 1987, p. 19

An accessible and thought-provoking piece focusing on Othello as a black man in a white world; also published in a collection of Phillips's essays, *The European Tribe*, Vintage, 2000 under the title 'A Black European Success', pp. 45–51

Leonard Tennenhouse, *Power on Display: The Politics of Shakespeare's Genres*, Methuen, London, 1986

In the chapter 'The Theater of Punishment: Jacobean Tragedy and the Politics of Misogyny', Tennenhouse explores the representation of the female body and female sexuality in Jacobean drama, making some interesting comments about *Othello*

EARLIER CRITICS

A. C. Bradley, *Shakespearean Tragedy*, Macmillan, London 1904, 3rd edition by J. R. Brown, Macmillan, Basingstoke, 1992

Focusing on character and motivation, this text was influential in the twentieth century

T. S. Eliot, 'Shakespeare and the Stoicism of Seneca', *Selected Essays*, 1932

Eliot considers Seneca's influence on Shakespeare and comments on Othello's self-dramatisation and weakness in the final scene of the play

Helen Gardner, 'The Noble Moor', *Proceedings of the British Academy*, XLI, 1956

In exploring the heroism of Othello and the nature of his love for Desdemona, suggests that the hero and his love are flawed

R. B. Heilman, *Magic in the Web: Action and Language in 'Othello'*, Kentucky University Press, Lexington, 1956

Discusses language, symbolism, theme and character in a detailed analysis of the play

G. K. Hunter, '"Othello" and Colour Prejudice', *Proceedings of the British Academy*, LIII, 1967, pp. 139–63

Sheds light on Elizabethan attitudes towards colour and race; also covers the portrayal of Othello and Iago

F. R. Leavis, 'Diabolical Intellect and the Noble Hero', *The Common Pursuit*, Chatto & Windus, London, 1962

A response to Bradley's ideas about Othello, arguing that Othello is responsible for his own downfall because of his deficient character

John Wain, ed., *Shakespeare: 'Othello'*, Casebook series, Macmillan, 1971

Includes comments and essays by Rymer, Samuel Johnson, Coleridge, Bradley, Eliot, Leavis, G. Wilson-Knight and other critics, up to the 1960s

SHAKESPEARE'S THEATRE

For anyone interested in the history of the Elizabethan playhouses, staging practices and acting companies the following book is invaluable:

Andrew Gurr, *The Shakespearean Stage*, Cambridge University Press, 1980

LITERARY TERMS

Aristotle a Greek philosopher (384–322BC) who discussed tragedy in his Poetics. Aristotle observed that tragedy represented a single action of a certain magnitude, that provoked audience reactions of pity and terror which were then resolved by the **catharsis** of the play's climax. Tragedies worked on a process of the reversal of fortune, with the **protagonist** making an error of judgement and then learning the truth about his folly, gaining insight into himself and his situation as a consequence.

aside a dramatic convention in which a character speaks in such a way that some of the characters on stage do not hear what is said, while others do. It may also be direct address to the audience, revealing the character's inner thoughts or motives, as is the case with Iago.

blank verse unrhymed iambic pentameter: a line of five iambs. One of the commonest English metres, the popularity of blank verse is due to its flexibility and relative closeness to spoken English. It allows a pleasant variation of full strong stresses per line, generally four or five, while conforming to the basic metrical pattern of five iambs. Shakespeare uses blank verse when he wants to convey the intensity of characters feelings. Heroes generally speak in verse in Shakespeare's plays, so it is significant when Othello speaks in prose.

catalyst a person or thing that brings about an event or change

catharsis in tragedy, the purging of the effects of pent up emotion and repressed thoughts by bringing them to the surface of consciousness

characterisation the way in which a writer creates characters so as to attract or repel our sympathy. Different kinds of literature have certain conventions of characterisation. In **Jacobean** drama there were many stock dramatic 'types' (see **Machiavel**) whose characteristics were familiar to the audience.

chorus a group of characters in the tragedies of Ancient Greece who represent the ordinary people in their attitudes to the action. They witness and comment on events, but do not participate in them.

colloquialism a casual form of expression used in speech

denouement the final unfolding of a plot; the point at which the audience's expectations, be they hopes or fears, about what will happen to the characters are finally satisfied or denied

dramatic irony a feature of many plays, it occurs when the development of the plot allows the audience to possess more information about what is happening than some of the characters themselves have. Iago is the source of much of the dramatic irony in *Othello*, informing the audience of his intentions. Characters may also speak in a dramatically ironic way, saying something that points to events to come without understanding the significance of their words.

feminism broadly speaking, a political movement claiming political and economic equality of women with men. Feminist criticism and scholarship seek to explore or expose the masculine 'bias' in texts and challenge traditional ideas about them, constructing and then offering a feminine perspective on works of art. Since the late 1960s feminist theories about literature and language, and feminist interpretations of texts have multiplied enormously. Feminism has its roots in previous centuries: early texts championing women's rights include Mary Wollstonecraft's *A*

Vindication of the Rights of Women (1792) and J. S. Mill's *The Subjection of Women* (1869).

foreshadowing a technique used to hint at and prepare the reader for the later events or a turning point in the action

hamartia a Greek term meaning an error of judgement

hubris the self-indulgent confidence that causes a tragic hero to ignore the decrees, laws and warnings of the gods, and therefore defy them to bring about his or her downfall

idiom a characteristic mode of expression for a character

image, imagery in its narrowest sense an image is a word picture, a description of some visible scene or object. More commonly, imagery relates to the figurative language in a piece of literature (**metaphors** and similes) or all the words which refer to objects and qualities which appeal to the senses and feelings. Thematic imagery is imagery which recurs throughout a work of art. For example, in *Othello* Shakespeare's images of the devil and infection underpin the theme of evil.

irony in speech, consists of saying one thing while you mean another (many of Iago's speeches to his victims include examples of this kind). However, not all ironical statements in literature are as easily discerned or understood; the patterns of irony – of situation, character, structure and vocabulary – in *Othello* need careful unravelling. In certain cases the context will make clear the true meaning intended, but sometimes the writer will have to rely on the reader sharing values and knowledge in order for his or her meaning to be understood. Ironic literature characteristically presents a variety of possible points of view about its subject matter.

Jacobean Jacobean drama refers to the plays written during the reign of James I (1603–25).

juxtapose in literature, to place ideas, **images** or events side by side so that they can be compared

Machiavel a villainous stock character in Elizabethan and **Jacobean** drama, so called after the Florentine writer Niccolo Machiavelli (1469–1527), author of *The Prince* (written 1513), a book of political advice to rulers that recommended the need under certain circumstances to lie to the populace for their own good and to preserve power. Embellishment of this suggestion (which was only one small part of his analysis of political power and justice) made Machiavelli almost synonymous with the Devil in English literature. Machiavels are practised liars and cruel political opportunists, who delight in their own manipulative evil. The topic of dissembling and disguising one's true identity amount almost to an obsession in plays in the early seventeenth century. Iago is one of the most sophisticated Machiavellian villains in Jacobean drama.

malcontent a stage archetype who is disaffected, melancholy, dissatisfied with or disgusted by society and life. Iago is not a true malcontent, but he demonstrates some of these qualities.

Marxist criticism emphasises the role of class and ideology and seeks to establish if a text reflects or challenges the current social order. Marxist critics view texts as products which should be understood in relation to their historical contexts. Marxism began with Karl Marx, the nineteenth-century German philosopher who wrote *Das Kapital* (1867), which is considered the seminal work of the communist movement. Marx was the first Marxist literary critic, writing critical essays in the 1830s on Goethe and Shakespeare.

metaphor goes further than a comparison between two things by fusing them together; one thing is described as being another, thus carrying over its associations. References to Iago as being a dog and a devil help Shakespeare portray the villain's evil.

mirroring in literature, a character or event mirrors another character or event when the two follow similar plots, act in similar ways or contain similar elements or traits. Shakespeare uses mirroring in *Othello* to increase the audience's appreciation of the characters and their situations.

new historicism the work of a loose affiliation of critics who discuss literary works in terms of their historical contexts. In particular, they seek to study literature as part of a wider cultural history, exploring the relationship of literature to society.

oxymoron a figure of speech in which contradictory terms are brought together in what is at first sight an impossible combination. There are a number of examples in *Othello*, e.g. Cassio is said to be 'damned in a fair wife' (I.1.20); Iago speaks of 'honest knaves' (I.1.48) and also informs us 'I am not what I am' (I.1.64).

parody an imitation of a work or style devised so as to ridicule its characteristics. Iago mocks Othello by imitating his speech style.

pathos moments in works of art which evoke strong feelings of pity are said to have this quality

patriarchy a community or family under the authority of a patriarch. The patriarchal system places the man at the head of the household or government.

personification a type of metaphorical language in which things or ideas are treated as if they are human beings, with attributes and feelings

poetic justice Thomas Rymer devised this term in 1678 to describe how literature should always depict a world in which virtue and vice are eventually rewarded and punished appropriately.

post-colonialism criticism explores the ways in which texts carry racist or colonial undertones

prose the most typical form of written language, which sounds like the natural flow of speech rather than the more formal rhythmic structure of poetry and verse. Prose is traditionally associated with 'low' and comic characters in Renaissance drama, but Shakespeare uses it for other purposes as well. In *Othello*, Shakespeare uses prose when he wants the dialogue to sound urgent and fast moving.

protagonist a main character in a play

pun usually defined as a play on words: two widely differing meanings are drawn out of a single word, usually for comic, playful or witty purposes. In the sixteenth and seventeenth centuries puns were often used for serious purposes in serious contexts.

Restoration Charles II was restored to the throne in 1660. The English Restoration (1660–89) refers to the final years of the reign of the Stuart kings.

revenge tragedy a special form of tragedy in which a **protagonist** pursues vengeance against those who have done wrong. These plays often focus on the moral confusion caused by the need to answer evil with evil. The Elizabethan interest in the tragedies of Seneca gave rise to many revenge tragedies. Bloodthirsty scenes and every kind of sensational horror typify revenge tragedy.

soliloquy a dramatic convention which allows a character in a play to speak directly to the audience, as if thinking aloud about motives, feelings and decisions. The use of the soliloquy enables the dramatist to give characters psychological depth. Part of the convention of the soliloquy is that it provides accurate access to the character's innermost thoughts.

tragedy Shakespeare's tragedies concentrate on the downfall of powerful men and often illuminate the resulting deterioration of a whole community. The protagonists in Shakespeare's tragedies are not necessarily good. In *Othello* the protagonist is noble, but becomes cruel and vicious when he is jealous.

verse see **blank verse**

vice, the a figure in morality plays of the fifteenth and sixteenth centuries who tempts humankind in a half-comic, half-unpleasant manner. Many critics argue that Iago is modelled on this stock character.

xenophobic fearing or hating foreigners

TIMELINE

WORLD EVENTS	SHAKESPEARE'S LIFE (DATES FOR PLAYS ARE APPROXIMATE)	LITERATURE AND THE ARTS
1492 Columbus sails to America		
		1513 Niccolò Machiavelli, *The Prince*
1534 Henry VIII breaks with Rome and declares himself head of the Church of England		
1556 Archbishop Cranmer burnt at the stake		
1558 Elizabeth I accedes to throne		
	1564 Born in Stratford-upon-Avon	
		1565 Giambattisa Cinzio Giraldi, *The Hecatommithi*
		1565–7 English translation, by Arthur Golding, of *Ovid's Metamorphosis*
1568 Mary Queen of Scots taken prisoner by Elizabeth I		
1570 Elizabeth I excommunicated by Pope Pius V		
1571 The Battle of Lepanto		
		1576 Erection of the first specially built public theatres in London – the Theatre and the Curtain
1577 Francis Drake sets out on round-the-world voyage		
		1581 Barnabe Rich, *Farewell to Military Profession*
1582 Outbreak of the Plague in London	**1582** Marries Anne Hathaway	
	1583 His daughter, Susanna, is born	
1584 Raleigh's sailors land in Virginia		**1584** French translation, by Gabriel Chappuys, of Cinzio's *The Hecatommithi*
	1585 His twins, Hamnet and Judith, are born	
	late 1580s–early 90s Probably writes *Henry VI (Parts I, II, III)* and *Richard III*	
	c.1585–92 Moves to London	
1587 Execution of Mary Queen of Scots after implication in plot to murder Elizabeth I		**1587** Christopher Marlowe, *Tamburlaine the Great*
1588 The Spanish Armada defeated		
1589 Accession of Henri IV to French throne		**c.1589** Kyd, *The Spanish Tragedy* (first revenge tragedy)
		1590 Edmund Spenser, *The Faerie Queene*
1592 Plague in London closes theatres	**1592** Writes *The Comedy of Errors*	**1592** Marlowe, *Doctor Faustus*
	1593 Writes *Titus Andronicus, The Taming of the Shrew*	
	1594 onwards Writes exclusively for the Lord Chamberlain's Men; writes *Two Gentlemen of Verona, Love's Labours Lost, Richard II*	
	1595 Writes *Romeo and Juliet, A Midsummer Night's Dream*	
1596 Drake perishes on expedition to West Indies	**1596** Hamnet dies; William granted coat of arms	
	1598 Writes *Much Ado About Nothing*	**1598** Marlowe, *Hero and Leander*

WORLD EVENTS	SHAKESPEARE'S LIFE (DATES FOR PLAYS ARE APPROXIMATE)	LITERATURE AND THE ARTS
	1599 Buys share in the Globe Theatre; writes *Julius Caesar, As You Like It, Twelfth Night* **1600** *The Merchant of Venice* printed **1600–1** Writes *Hamlet, The Merry Wives of Windsor* **1601** Writes *Troilus and Cressida* **1602** Writes *All's Well That Ends Well* **1602–4** Probably writes **Othello**	**1599** Translation, by Sir Lewes Lewkenor, of Cardinal Contareno's *The Commonwealth and Government of Venice* **1600** John Parry, *History and Description of Africa*
1603 Death of Queen Elizabeth I; accession of James I	**1603 onwards** His company enjoys patronage of James I as The King's Men **1604** *Othello* performed; writes *Measure for Measure*	**1603** John Marston's *The Malcontent* first performed
1605 Discovery of Guy Fawkes's plot to blow up the Houses of Parliament	**1605** First version of *King Lear* **1606** Writes *Macbeth* **1606–7** Probably writes *Antony and Cleopatra* **1607** Writes *Coriolanus, Timon of Athens*	**1605** Miguel de Cervantes, *Don Quijote de la Mancha* **1607** Cyril Tourneur's *The Revenger's Tragedy* published
	1608 Writes *Pericles*; The King's Men acquire Blackfriars Theatre for winter performances	
1609 Galileo constructs first astronomical telescope **1610** Henri IV of France assassinated; William Harvey discovers circulation of blood; Galileo observes Saturn for the first time	**1609** Becomes part-owner of the new Blackfriars Theatre	
	1611 *Cymbeline, The Winter's Tale* and *The Tempest* performed **1612** Shakespeare retires from London theatre and returns to Stratford **1613** The Globe Theatre burns down **1616** Dies **1623** *The First Folio* published	**1611** King James's translation of the Bible **1612** John Webster, *The White Devil* **1613** Webster, *Duchess of Malfi*

REVISION FOCUS TASK ANSWERS

TASK 1

The crude sexual imagery in Act I Scene 1 undermines the love of Othello and Desdemona.

- Yes – images such as 'an old black ram is tupping your white ewe' make Othello seem like an animal and sexual predator.
- No – we realise Iago hates Othello, so we might have our doubts about whether the crude images can be applied to the couple.
- No – we need to know more about the elopement before we can make up our minds about the couple's love.

Iago's motives for revenge are plausible.

- Yes – Iago says that he hates Othello because he promoted Cassio over him – this is plausible.
- Yes – Iago hates Cassio because he thinks he is undeserving – this is plausible.
- Yes – Iago is discontented with his position in life, 'the curse of service' – this is plausible.

TASK 2

Desdemona and Othello are well matched.

- Yes – they share the same measured speech style and both defend their love assertively; they were equal wooers.
- Yes – the lovers both idealise each other: Othello appreciates Desdemona's feminine charm and sympathy; Desdemona appreciates Othello's heroism and nobility.
- No – the differences (in age and background) between them may suggest that Othello and Desdemona are a vulnerable couple.

Act I is dominated by hatred rather than love.

- Yes – Iago's **soliloquies** and exchanges with Roderigo are full of hatred, and cast a shadow over the love between Othello and Desdemona.
- Yes – Brabantio's objections to the marriage of Othello and Desdemona continue the theme of hatred.
- No – Othello and Desdemona speak movingly of their love, so there is a clear counterpoint to hatred.

TASK 3

Iago's hatred is more powerful than Othello's love.

- Yes – Iago's hatred has intensified: now he says he has been cuckolded by Othello and wants to get even 'wife for wife'.
- No – Othello is still secure in his love; he greets Desdemona as his 'fair warrior'; she is his 'soul's joy'.
- Yes – because Iago is the last to speak in the scene in a soliloquy full of hatred, he seems more powerful than Othello.

Othello's love for Desdemona is his greatest weakness.

- Yes – Othello's love starts to seem fragile: he says he feels 'too much joy' when he greets Desdemona in Cyprus.
- Yes – Othello has been overwhelmed by his feelings for Desdemona; she is his 'soul's joy'.
- No – Othello's love is not a weakness; Iago's desire to destroy it is the real threat.

TASK 4

Cassio is to blame for his own downfall.

- Yes – he knows he has a weak head for drink so is at fault in the brawl when he gets drunk and rises to Roderigo's challenge.
- Yes – he is supposed to be keeping peace in Cyprus, but instead neglects his military duties and causes alarm and chaos.
- No – his downfall is engineered by Iago.

Emilia is partly to blame for Desdemona's fate.

- Yes – she chooses to keep silent about the whereabouts of the handkerchief.
- No – Emilia cannot be blamed for Iago's plot against Desdemona; she does not know how cunning and evil her husband is.
- No – Emilia is not responsible for Othello's actions; Othello determines Desdemona's fate, not Emilia.

TASK 5

Othello poisons his own mind.

- Yes, to an extent – Othello introduces Desdemona into the conversation when Iago mentions jealousy in general terms.
- No – Iago poisons Othello's mind by making insinuations about Desdemona and Cassio.

- No – Iago takes advantage of Othello's 'free and noble' nature.

Iago's jealousy is greater than Othello's.

- Yes – Iago is driven by personal jealousy (sexual jealousy).
- Yes – Iago is driven by professional jealousy.
- No – Othello's jealousy is just as great; but he has only one motive for his jealousy, whereas Iago is jealous of Cassio, Othello and Desdemona.

TASK 6

It is impossible to sympathise with Othello when he bullies Desdemona.

- Yes – Desdemona is bewildered and cannot understand what she has done to lose Othello's love.
- Yes – Othello is cruel to Desdemona.
- No – we understand how much Othello is suffering.

Desdemona's enduring love for Othello is unconvincing for a modern audience.

- No – Desdemona said that she would submit to and obey Othello's authority, and her love for her husband is great; she continues to try to find excuses for him which are plausible (e.g. bad news from Venice, professional worries).
- No – we have seen enough of the couple happy together to be convinced that Desdemona made the right choice when she married Othello.
- Yes – a **feminist** reading of the play would point to the way in which women are made into passive victims in *Othello*. What happened to the assertive Desdemona we saw in Act I? Her change in character is unconvincing.

TASK 7

It is impossible to sympathise with Othello in Act IV.

- Yes – calling his wife a whore with only the proof of the handkerchief is troublesome for the audience.
- Yes – striking Desdemona publicly is deeply humiliating.
- No – Iago is so cruel and merciless, we can see how Othello has become a victim himself.

Desdemona's love is too passive and she is too much the victim.

- No – Desdemona is not passive, she points out that she does not deserve to be treated so cruelly.
- No – Desdemona hopes to win back her husband's love actively. She has the wedding sheets put on her bed to remind Othello of their wedding night.
- Yes – by the end of Act IV she has been abused so often that Desdemona is clearly powerless.

TASK 8

Othello's tragedy was that he loved too much

- Yes – Othello's last thoughts are of Desdemona, showing the tragic intensity of his love.
- No – Othello's tragedy was that he was 'perplexed in the extreme' by Iago.
- No – Othello's tragedy was his obsession with his masculine honour and reputation.

Iago's silence is as powerful as his speech.

- Yes – the villain refuses to explain his motives to Othello, mocking the tragic hero.
- No – Iago may still be alive, but we know he will be tortured until he confesses.
- No – words were the source of Iago's power, so when he stays silent we know he has been defeated.

TASK 9

It is impossible to sympathise with Brabantio.

- Yes – Brabantio verbally abuses Othello and casts off Desdemona in a cruel way.
- No – Brabantio is abused himself by Othello and Desdemona when they elope.
- No – in a **patriarchal** society like Shakespeare's the actions of Desdemona and Othello are socially unacceptable.

The secret nature of the marriage of Othello and Desdemona undermines Othello's heroism.

- Yes – Othello says he is honest and trustworthy, yet he elopes without permission to marry Desdemona; this is not the action of an honourable man.
- No – Desdemona was 'half the wooer' and the elopement adds to the air of romance about the couple.
- No – we know that Brabantio would never have given Othello permission to marry Desdemona; Othello is proving his heroism by risking all for love.

TASK 10

Jealousy destroys Othello's marriage.

- Yes – Othello kills Desdemona because he is overwhelmed by jealous thoughts of her with other men.
- No – Iago destroys Othello's marriage.
- No – obsessive male pride (Iago's and Othello's) destroys Othello's marriage.

The male characters are incapable of unselfish love.

- Yes – the minor male characters – Roderigo and Cassio – both abuse women for their own selfish gratification.

- Yes – Iago and Othello are both too possessive of their wives.
- No – Othello's love was generous and unselfish before Iago poisoned Othello's mind.

TASK 11

The handkerchief is an unconvincing **catalyst** for **tragedy**.

- Yes – it comes to symbolise too much, i.e. Desdemona's chastity.
- No – because it is part of Othello's personal heritage and history, we can understand the tragic hero's distress when Desdemona loses it.
- No – the proofs that Iago contrives are all convincing, and the handkerchief is compelling physical evidence.

Othello is essentially a domestic tragedy.

- Yes – unlike in Shakespeare's other great tragedies, e.g. *Macbeth*, *King Lear*, *Hamlet*, the hero's private tragedy does not have wider ramifications for the political and social order.
- No – there is a political dimension to the tragedy because it is set against the backdrop of war and Othello is a military commander whose death represents a military loss to Venice.
- No – because of the theme of race and the mixed marriage of Othello and Desdemona, *Othello* is a tragedy about social and sexual politics.

TASK 12

The Roderigo subplot adds very little to the play.

- No – Roderigo is a failed suitor, whose infatuation with Desdemona serves as a counterpoint to Othello's successful wooing.
- No – Roderigo is necessary to the plot; he is Iago's first victim and is involved in key scenes, e.g. the drunken brawl and the final scene.
- No – we learn to understand Iago's motives and methods of manipulation through the villain's interactions with Roderigo.

Love defeats evil at the end of *Othello*.

- Yes – Desdemona's unselfish dying words and refusal to give up on her love for Othello prove that love has triumphed.
- Yes – Othello kills himself because he proved a faulty lover; his death affirms the importance and intensity of Othello's love for Desdemona.
- No – because the lovers are all dead, and Iago survives, evil defeats love.

MARK SCHEME

Use this page to assess your answer to the **Worked task**, provided on pages 102–3.

Aiming for an A grade? Fulfil all the criteria below and your answer should hit the mark.*

> **'Destruction and loss are the main impressions the audience are left with at the end of Othello.'** How do you respond to this idea?

ASSESMENT OBJECTIVES	MEANING
AO1 Articulate creative, informed and relevant responses to literary texts, using appropriate terminology and concepts, and coherent, accurate written expression.	• You make a range of clear, relevant points about destruction and loss • You write a balanced essay covering both themes equally. • You use a range of literary terms correctly, e.g. **tragic protagonist**, tragic outcome, villain, **foreshadowing**, **denouement**, theme, **imagery**. • You write a clear introduction, outlining your thesis and provide a clear conclusion. • You signpost and link your ideas about destruction and loss clearly.
AO2 Demonstrate detailed critical understanding in analysing the ways in which structure, form and language shape meanings in literary texts.	• You explain the techniques and methods Shakespeare uses to present destruction and loss and link them to the tragedy of the play. • You may discuss: examples of physical and verbal bullying (e.g. Othello calling Desdemona a whore and striking her); images of destruction and loss (e.g. the imagery of disease and poison associated with Iago); symbols of destruction and loss (e.g. the handkerchief, the willow song.) • You explain in detail how your examples affect meaning and audience responses to the themes of loss and destruction. • You may explore how the settings and structure of the play contribute to the presentation of destruction and loss, e.g. Cyprus is a suitable setting for a tragedy about destruction and loss because it is under siege from the Turks.
AO3 Explore connections and comparisons between different literary texts, informed by interpretations of other readers.	• You make relevant links between destruction and loss, noting how destruction leads to loss. • You make points about what is destroyed and lost in the course of the play, e.g. Desdemona's reputation, Othello's honour, the central couple's idealised love. • You incorporate and comment on critics' views of the way destruction and loss are presented in the play. • You assert your own independent view clearly. • You may take a **feminist** approach to the question, e.g. the women in the play are victims, whose reputations and lives are destroyed by men. • You may take an **historicist** approach to the question, e.g. Othello is a noble black man destroyed by an evil white man, proof that Shakespeare presents destruction and loss in ways which challenge racist views.
AO4 Demonstrate understanding of the significance and influence of the contexts in which literary texts are written and received.	• You explain how relevant aspects of social, literary and historical contexts of *Othello* are significant when interpreting themes of destruction and loss. For example, you may discuss: • Literary context – Iago is inherently destructive because he is a stage **Machiavel**, descended from the **vice** of medieval mystery plays. • Literary context – loss is a key theme of **tragedy**, usually brought about because the hero has a fatal flaw or makes a terrible decision. In Othello's case, destruction and loss are the result of excessive male pride. • Social context – Othello's masculine honour and reputation can be linked to the **patriarchal** context of the play. Desdemona is Othello's possession and when he thinks he has lost her, he seeks to destroy her in order to recover the loss of his honour.

* This mark scheme gives you a broad indication of attainment, but check the specific mark scheme for your paper/task to ensure you know what to focus on.